forbidden hearts

WHITLOCK
FARMS

Forbidden Hearts

Broken Dreams

Tempting Promises

Forgotten Desires

forbidden hearts

Forbidden Hearts

Copyright © 2023 Corinne Michaels
All rights reserved.
ISBN ebook: 978-1-957309-13-2
ISBN print: 978-1-957309-14-9

Cover Design: Sommer Stein, Perfect Pear Creative
Editing: Ashley Williams, AW Editing
Proofreading: Julia Griffis, Virginia Carey, & ReGina Kaye
Photographer: Wander Aguiar
Model: Andrew Biernat

dedication

To all the girls who trusted their hearts to some asshole who broke it.
May you find the one who cherishes you for diamond that you are.
Oh, and to the guy who broke mine—your loss.

Dear Reader,

It is always my goal to write a beautiful love story that will capture your heart and leave a lasting impression. However, I want all readers to be comfortable. Therefore, if you want to be aware of any possible CW please click the link below to take you to the book page where there is a link that will dropdown. If you do not need this, please go forth and I hope you love this book filled with all the pieces of my heart.

https://corinnemichaels.com/books/forbidden-hearts/

author's note

Thank you for purchasing Forbidden Hearts. I truly hope you enjoy this book as much as I enjoyed writing it.

Forbidden Hearts utilizes American Sign Language through the story. For better ease of reading, it is not written in proper ASL format. ASL is different from written English with it's own rules and structure. Most of the time, my characters will speak aloud at the same time as they sign. There are no clear rules on how to format sign language and I went back and forth with how to do it. In the end, I chose quote marks and italic.

As always, I do my best to write situations and characters the best possible. Any discrepancies are mine alone and based on my experiences or those who I consulted with.

On a personal note, I want to thank my sensitivity reader, Lynette. I am incredibly grateful for her help, kindness, and thoughtful understanding throughout this story. You helped make this story better in every way.

one

ASHER

"All her clothes are here, and I didn't leave anything at my place, so there should be no reason to use the key, but it's here just in case. The numbers for her pediatrician, audiologist, speech pathologist, and occupational therapist are all listed in the binder," Sara, my ex—if you can call her that since we never dated —says as I make faces at Olivia, my daughter. "You should consider moving her to the room next to yours and giving the nanny the upstairs, but I'm sure you'll ignore that suggestion. There's also a bag with her school supplies. I put some of her favorite snacks in another bag as well as some other—Asher! Are you even listening?"

I turn to Sara, making sure Olivia can still see my lips. "Yes, I'm listening. Yes, I know all of this. Yes, I will make sure Olivia goes to school, brushes her teeth, puts pants on, and eats."

"And the room?"

"I'm not moving her room. She loves her room more than the one at your house."

Sara doesn't look amused by my response. She turns to Olivia and signs while speaking the words so I can hear, which is what we do whenever having a conversation with Olivia. *"Your father is*

1

a turd. Make sure he doesn't miss your appointments and follows the schedule in the binder."

Olivia smiles. *"I love you, Mommy. I will take care of him."*

"Hey, I am a grown-up who can take care of everything," I sign and speak back.

They both laugh. "Sure you are, Ash. Now, this binder has everything. I worked hard on it, so please make sure you follow it."

She's absolutely nutty with her demands for perfection and detail. I'd much rather let things go with the flow. She's always been this way though, which is why we are much better off as friends who just happen to have a daughter.

We were a casual, fun thing. Neither of us wanted a relationship, but that's exactly what we have now—a lifelong, co-parenting friendship. It works for the most part.

"You know, I am a really good father. I've taken care of her since she was born."

Sara eyes me. "You've never had her like this. Not for months while I was out of the country."

"We'll be fine. We can't mess it up with your binder in hand," I say with a smirk.

She rolls her eyes and then moves to Olivia with tears forming. Great. This is going to be an hour-long goodbye that will make Sara late for her car and make it so the driver has to drive like an asshole to get to Philly on time for her flight. She'll probably ask me for a police escort because she's already cutting it close with her time.

Not that I blame her. I would be losing my mind if I had to leave Olivia for this long.

For the next five and a half months, Sara will be on assignment in Israel. She's filming a documentary about something she mentioned, but I tuned out. I do know that it's an amazing career opportunity for her, and that means my three nights a week are now full time. God help Livvy and me.

But we have the binder, so we'll survive according to her mother.

Sara crouches in front of her. *"I am going to miss you so much. I love you with my whole heart. Be good for Daddy."*

Olivia's eyes shimmer with tears. *"I will miss you. Can we video call?"*

She nods. *"As much as possible. I will be very busy, and there is a time difference, but I will try to call daily."*

"You're going to miss your flight," I remind Sara about that pesky thing called a plane schedule.

"It can wait."

"Yes, but it won't."

Sara rises, wiping her cheeks. "I want daily updates either by text or email. I want to know how she's doing and how you're surviving. God knows you'll only be alive thanks to the nanny."

I clutch my hand to my chest. "I'll miss you too, dear."

She laughs. "Do you have your childcare all set? You went through the agency I told you about and made sure the nanny knows ASL?"

"Was that what I was supposed to do?"

She huffs. "Of all the men . . ."

"You were lucky enough to have a child with me. I know. You're welcome."

"I could've done worse."

I take that as a compliment.

Her eyes well up with tears again as she looks at Liv.

"I can't go," she admits, tears now ready to spill over.

Time to be a dick and force her to leave. "Sara, leave now so you make your flight and you don't make this harder on Liv."

"You can't tell me you wouldn't be the same. She's not"—Sara turns so Olivia can't see what she says—"she's special. What if the agency screws up? What if you forgot to tell them she's Deaf and they send someone who can't sign? I don't want her to be stuck unable to communicate."

"I didn't forget to tell them that. I'm just as concerned as you are, and I would never go to work if they sent someone who couldn't take care of our daughter."

Olivia is completely Deaf because of complications with preeclampsia. With her hearing aids, she can hear certain sounds or pitches, but just barely, and she can't make out any words. Sara and I learned ASL as soon as we discovered her hearing loss and fought to get the best care all around, but Liv is really good with reading lips.

Sara's full-time nanny, Denise, who learned ASL as well, moved to Florida a week ago to get married. Great timing on that one.

I take Sara's shoulders in my hands and breathe deeply until she does the same. "You have a flight to catch. I am a fantastic father. Olivia will be fine. The agency said they'd get someone who could sign, all will be well."

"You're so infuriating with your constant calm attitude."

I shrug. "It's better than flipping out, especially in my job."

Cool heads always prevail. At least that's what I tell myself. I love being a small-town sheriff. There's not much trouble in town other than the kids knocking mailboxes off with a bat or someone stealing a cow and moving it to another pasture for fun. It's the same thing my brothers and I did growing up in Michigan, so I can't be too mad at them.

Although, we weren't big mailbox guys. I never saw the fun in damaging a neighbor's property, and our mom would've had our heads if she'd ever found out.

I am also the newly appointed SWAT commander, which means I have to be steady and always look at the whole picture. That is what I'm doing now.

Now that I'm thinking about it, my trying to coax Sara to leave the house on time does seem like a hostage negotiation.

"I can do this. She'll be fine. You're a good dad, and you love her." She looks down at Olivia and whimpers a little. *"I have to go, sweet girl."*

Olivia waves to her.

They both sign. *"I love you."*

Sara wipes at her cheeks and pulls me in for a hug. "I'll be back in less than six months."

"And it will be just like you left it—other than the matching tattoos we get tomorrow."

"Asher," she warns.

"Seriously, Sara, just go. I promise that I can handle this."

I have no choice because if she comes back and Olivia isn't in perfect condition, she might chop my balls off.

She grabs her bag, flings it onto her back, and heads to the front door. Sara's tears are flowing steadily as she walks out without looking back.

I stare at the heavy oak door, waiting, and she doesn't fail. She comes back into the house, scooping Livvy into her arms and kissing her cheeks. Then she punches me in the arm.

"Predictable."

She flips me off. "Be good. Don't get into trouble and don't forget to feed her!"

"It was one time!" I yell back at her as the door shuts.

Once I'm sure she's gone, I turn back to Liv. *"I'm off today and the new nanny comes tomorrow, let's make some trouble. Anyone we should invite?"*

She grins. *"Uncle Rowan!"*

I laugh because, out of any of the Whitlock brothers, Rowan is definitely the most likely to cause trouble. *"Get your sweatshirt. I'll let him know."*

Olivia runs off, and I text my brother.

> I'm heading to the creek if you want to come fish with Livvy.

> ROWAN
>
> I have to finish up on the farm, but I'll be done in about an hour. Not in the mood to see you, but since you mentioned Olivia, I'll come.

Such a dick.

See you then.

As the oldest Whitlock, it was predetermined I would take over my grandparents' farm, but they quickly realized that it was completely out of the realm of my capabilities. I hate the cows, and they hate me, so it was better for everyone that I was not in charge of anything livestock related. I gifted my brother the land and the bunk house on the back property for him to do what he wanted, and now he runs a dairy farm.

ROWAN
Don't forget to feed her before we go.

What the fuck is with everyone and feeding Olivia? I forgot one time and I'll never live it down. Unreal.

Fuck off. She's fed.

Olivia runs in with her sweatshirt, and I let her know our plan. *"Uncle Rowan has to finish work, so we can go to the farm and annoy him before we go fishing, does that sound good?"*

She squeals and, without hesitation, goes out back toward the barn where we keep all our fun toys—including the fishing gear. Liv is more like me than Sara would like. She loves the outdoors and doing pretty much anything adventurous.

Which makes her paranoid mother nuts.

I refuse to allow her inability to hear to hinder her life.

I meet her in the barn, laughing because it's really not a barn. It's more of a shack of toys. I have two ATVs and dirt bikes, which Sara does not know about. There's also hunting and fishing gear, tents . . . you name it, and it's here.

Olivia turns to me. *"Can we take your dirt bike?"*

"Not until your mother is in Israel and can't kill me."

She grins. I love that she'll cover for me.

"I forgot something," Livvy informs me and then rushes back into the house.

I watch her go through the big back door, smiling at how the house has turned out. I inherited my grandparents' house upon my mother's death. It's small, but I love it. They raised six kids in this three-bedroom house, so it's plenty big for me.

I did a bit of remodeling when my mother died.

Originally all three bedrooms were on the first level, and in order to give me, Rowan, and Brynlee more bathrooms, I gutted the attic. I put two bedrooms and a bath up there—one for Brynn and one for Rowan. Grady was never coming back, so I didn't give much thought about him.

When Olivia was born, she was in the room next to mine, but about three years ago, Brynn suggested putting her upstairs with her. I wasn't sure, but she and Brynn are thick as thieves, so I went with it. My annoying sister moved out a year later, and I converted her room into a play area. When Liv is here, I usually crash on the couch in there.

Downstairs, I just extended the house a bit to make the master bigger and then converted the other bedroom to be a suite in case I had . . . company. That way, my daughter never sees a girl coming out of my bedroom.

However, it's been a long fucking time since I've needed to worry about that.

The house phone is ringing, and it's incredibly loud because Liv can sometimes hear that noise, so I rush in to grab it because not many people call me on that line.

Yeah, I know, who the hell has a house phone anymore? Well, when you live somewhere where having reliable cell reception reminds you of being a kid holding the antenna with tin foil on the end to get a picture on the television, you do what you must.

"Hello?"

"Hi, Mr. Whitlock, this is Stephanie from the nanny agency."

Good, she's calling to confirm, and I can tell Sara to suck it. "Hi, Stephanie. I'm assuming we're all set for tomorrow?"

She pauses, and my heart sinks. "About that . . . I know it's a requirement to have a nanny who knows ASL."

"Yes . . ."

"So, she just quit, and unfortunately, I don't have another nanny with that capability. We could make it work. I'm assuming Olivia can write? She can jot down whatever she wants to say."

Not a chance in hell. "No, thank you. I'll figure something else out until you can find me someone who can use ASL."

Stephanie sighs. "I'm really sorry, Mr. Whitlock. I have searched two counties and have come up short. I'll continue to look, and if you find someone else, please let us know."

Fuck, I'm sure there's no solution for this in the binder.

"I'm sorry, Chief, I can't make it today."

"Asher, you're the SWAT commander, you have to be here. There's no one else who can take your place while Billingsly is on baby leave."

I run my hand over my face, frustrated because I know this. I can't call out, but I can't leave Olivia with someone who can't communicate with her.

I've called everyone. My sister is getting ready for finals and in the middle of a big case that she has to be in court for. Rowan said there's some big cow crisis—also, I am one thousand percent sure that Sara would have my ass if I left her with him, and my other brother is at war, so he's out.

I even went so far as to call her former nanny and ask her to leave her honeymoon and husband so she could come help me. That went over about as well as I thought it would.

My options are limited.

"I understand that, sir, but I can't leave Olivia either. She comes first."

He sighs heavily. "Yes, of course. You said the nanny quit?"

I re-explain everything about the service and Sara leaving. I have never called out. My job is not only something I love but also something I'm good at. When I was promoted to the SWAT commander, I took it very seriously. My men and women rely on me, and we're a team. Olivia is my daughter, though, and I can't leave her with someone who can't understand what she's saying. She doesn't speak.

"Well, I have a solution for the both of us."

"You do?" I ask, curious where exactly he's going to find a nanny who knows ASL on short notice.

"Yes, actually, Phoebe came home two days ago from school, and she can sign."

I laugh once. "No."

There is not a chance in hell that Phoebe Bettencourt is watching Olivia. No way. Not after the last time.

"Why not?"

While he believes his precious daughter is great, she's the worst babysitter ever. The last time I had her watch my daughter was six years ago, and I came home to find that Olivia had cut her own hair. Three-year-olds do not cut their own hair well.

"I think we both know why."

"It was a long time ago, and she's grown up since then."

Yeah, and Sara lost her damn mind when I brought Olivia

home with a new hairdo. "I'm sure she has, but I'm not trusting her with Liv."

"Listen, she's finishing her first year of grad school, she's an audiology major, and she knows ASL. I don't know what else you could want in a babysitter for Olivia. I know that Phoebe had that small mishap, but she's a great kid."

"I don't need a *kid* watching my kid, Anthony. I need a trained nanny who will not get lost in her phone while my child burns the house down." I might be a bit harsh, but it's not like Phoebe has the best track record. That girl is a flighty mess with bad decision-making abilities. Take away the hair cutting incident, I can't tell you how many times I pulled her over when she lived here. She drives like a maniac, but I couldn't even ticket her because her father is my damn boss.

"Well, then you're going to have to get another nanny who can communicate with Liv another way because you're needed here. There is no one else who can manage the team if they're called out. I gave you a solution to the issue. Give her a chance, Asher. You'll be close if anything happens, but she's not eighteen anymore."

His solution really isn't one, but I feel like I'm being torn apart. I can't let Olivia or my team down. "If I do this, I need to stay in Sugarloaf so I can be close in case of any . . . issues."

"If you're required to go to another town, I'll check in on Olivia myself. Look, you don't know when you're going to get a nanny, and Phoebe is home and not doing anything. This will give her a job, and it helps you out. I don't want to see you lose the position you worked so hard for," he says as a reminder.

I'm not sure another option is even out there. "Fine, but one screwup, and I'll step away from SWAT, consequences be damned."

And if that happens, I might lose my damn mind.

two

PHOEBE

"Are you going to tell me what happened?" Daddy asks as he sits on the edge of my bed.

"Nothing happened," I lie.

What else can I do? I can't tell him the truth about why I'm home three weeks early from my first year in grad school and not going back—at least not to that university.

My father is a strict man. A strong man who raised his daughter to be just as fierce, so I can handle the ridicule at school and the whispers, but I can't handle disappointment from him.

So, I'll lie to the only man who has never let me down.

Way to go, Phoebe. Another notch on your belt of awesomeness.

"Birdie, I may be a lot of things, but stupid isn't one of them. We both know I can smell bullshit a mile away."

I turn over to face him, knowing that if I want him to believe the lie, I have to believe it myself. That means looking him in the eyes when I say it.

His shiny badge glints in the small beam of sunlight streaming through my curtains, reminding me that he, in fact, is trained to cut through the crap. "I love you, but you're going to have to trust me. Nothing happened besides finishing my classes

13

early. All of my finals are online, so there was no need for me to sit in Iowa when I could be home with you."

His eyes narrow, but I stand my ground. There is some truth in my words.

"Then why were you crying last night?"

Shit. He heard me.

"Because Emmeline called, and we miss each other." Sounds plausible.

Emmeline MacAllister is my roommate, my best friend, and the only person who didn't call me a liar. Never once did her support waver, and if it weren't for her, I never would have survived. I know that sounds dramatic, and it probably is, but the last three months have been hell.

I've been taunted, have been talked about like I wasn't there, and have been called horrible names, but the final straw was finding out that people were taunting Emmeline as well.

That was it. I couldn't stay. No matter what happened, I couldn't let my friend deal with the blowback of my stupidity. I went to each professor, gave some excuse about a family emergency, was granted permission to take my finals online with a ten-point deduction on each one, and I left two days later.

I hadn't left fast enough to avoid yet another colossal fuckup that Emmeline had to help me clean up.

He sighs heavily. "I don't believe a word you said, but I am a smart enough man to know not to push."

I smile at him. "Thanks, Daddy."

"Don't thank me yet, Phoebe, I didn't say tomorrow I wouldn't be dumb." My father kisses my forehead. "I'm off to work. I'll be home around seven for dinner."

I guess that means I'm back on kitchen duty. "I'll be here."

Wallowing.

I flop back, wishing my mother were alive because she'd know what to do. My father is the chief of our small police department and very overprotective. Not in a bad way, but he just wants to put me in a glass case where I can't be hurt.

Really, I just want to put my past behind me and move forward. I'm not sure what that looks like because I need to find a graduate program for audiology that will accept me extremely late, take all my credits from my first year, and offer me financial aid, which won't be easy. I was at University of Iowa, which I loved. It was a great campus, and the second-best program in the country. Everything was perfect.

Until I met him.

I hear the front door close, leaving me alone in my feelings and self-hatred.

My phone rings, and Emmeline's face paints my screen.

"Why are you up so early?" I ask as a greeting.

"I never went to sleep. I'm studying, which I hope you're doing as well," her soft voice chides.

"I get to take my other final with an open book, I better pass."

I finished one last night, which was proctored over video to ensure I couldn't use a book.

Emmeline laughs. "Lucky bitch."

"Oh, yeah, I'm swimming in luck."

"You could always come back . . ."

That's not really an option, and we both know it. I can't return to the place that is going to shame me while the man who ruined my life walks around, playing the victim and still able to do it to another girl.

"We both know the answer to that."

"I feel like you should've stayed so he would have had to look at you and know that he did nothing to help you."

"We don't mention him," I warn.

Emmy sighs. "Fine, but you running away doesn't change things. You need to learn to stand your ground . . ."

"And what would that have done? Nothing. All it would've accomplished was teaching me not to cry when people called me a homewrecker. A liar. I saw all the comments, Emmy. All of them saying the same thing. 'Oh, look, another girl wanting a better grade' or 'Too bad I can't get an A for having tits' or 'Talk about desperate, he looks appalled.' None of that was true. I am not a slut or a homewrecker!"

Emmeline stops me. "I know you're not. I saw how he was with you with my own eyes."

"I know. I . . . God, I'm so stupid. Do you know how often I tell myself that? I trusted him and believed every pretty lie because he made me feel special."

"You are special, Phoebe. You're beautiful and smart, and he took advantage of you."

That may be so, but it doesn't matter. I was "that" girl. The one who sleeps with her professor. Who bought into the promises and the hopes of a future that never existed because he was already married.

"It doesn't matter. I'm back in Sugarloaf, where life is dull and I will never have to see him again. The town that reminds me of all the mistakes I've made."

"You can always come visit me at Cloverleigh Farms if you want to get away from it all."

She's offered it many times, and honestly, I may go. No one knows me there, and my father and all his keen police sleuthing will be at a distance.

"I might take you up on it." I flop back onto the pillow, letting out a long sigh. "Lord knows I could really use a freaking vacation from my life."

"What are you going to do about transferring?" she asks.

As soon as people found out about Jonathan and me, there was no other option but to leave. Someone took a photo of me with my arms around his neck, leaning in to kiss him, and posted it.

That was bad enough, but they put it right beside a photo of him holding his son and his wife. That was how I found out Jonathan was not divorced like he told me. Instead of him taking any responsibility, he told everyone that I came onto him.

The last week of my life has been hell.

"I'm going to have to apply to some schools and explain my

situation. I have the grades, but I just don't know if all my credits will transfer, so it may set me back time and money. Maybe Professor Calloway will help. She was really kind and told me to reach out if I needed anything."

"I'm sorry, Phoebs."

"It's my fault. I . . . have to accept the consequences."

"What did your dad say? Or have you not told him about why you came home?"

"I'm not telling him anything. He'll never understand, and I really can't face that kind of disappointment from him. I hate myself enough as it is."

Emmeline goes silent for a minute. "I've said it a hundred times, but you're not the only one to blame, and you're definitely not the first girl to sleep with her professor."

"*Married* professor. Married and lying professor." My heart drops because I live with this shame and regret. I don't know what to do next. Where do I go? How do I salvage this, and do I disclose any of this going forward when the questions come? "Emmy . . ."

"Yeah?"

Before I can ask her any of it, there's a knock on my door. "Shit, my dad is back. I'll call you later."

I end the call, force myself out of bed, and open the door. "Everything okay?" I ask. "I thought you left."

"I did, but I completely forgot that I need your help with something."

"Of course, with what?"

He runs his hand down his face. "I know you're home early and have things you'd rather do, but you know we're all about helping people around here."

Oh, this sounds promising.

"Right, and I have a feeling what you're about to ask me to do isn't my idea of fun."

He shakes his head. "No, but you're pretty much the only

person in the world who can help, so I need you to think before you reply."

"Okay."

"I need you to nanny for a little girl until they find a suitable replacement."

Uh, of all the things he would ask, I never would've thought it would be to nanny for someone. I have babysat a total of three times in my life. The first time, the kid ran away and I had to call my father to search for him. The second time, we ended up in the ER because when her parents said *peanut* allergy, they meant *nut* allergy. And the last time was when I was watching Asher Whitlock's daughter and she cut her own hair—and not just a trim to the bangs. No, she cut her hair to her scalp on the side. It happened so fast, and I'd felt horrible, which only just got worse when he got home and lectured me about paying attention. I hate that guy.

"Dad, we both know I am not really good with kids."

"No, but she's not little, and it has to be you. You're the only one who can handle this."

"Why?" Dread fills me because if it has to be me, then it's for a particular skill set I have, and that means it's—

"Asher's nanny quit, and I need him at work."

Yeah, about that luck I don't have, it's officially gone.

You can do this, Phoebe. You're not a little girl anymore. You are a strong, independent woman who has been through the wringer, but that's okay. It builds character. Watching a kid for the summer may not have been part of the plan, but neither was sleeping with your married professor, and you're still breathing. Asher Whitlock doesn't scare you, and you definitely are not into him. Sure, he's ridiculously hot, but you're not into hot guys. You know how that turns out. She's not three, she's nine and probably won't want to cut her hair again. You'll do this for Daddy, get some money, which you desperately need because you had to pull money from your inheritance to get home and . . . you're a mess.

As I open my eyes to exit the car, I scream when I see Asher standing there, arms crossed as he watches me through the window.

"You scared me!" I yell.

He doesn't say anything back, just looks at me and . . . dear God. This man is even better looking than I remembered. He's one of those cops you see on social media whose posts are full of comments like:

He can arrest me any day.

Excuse me, officer, I've broken the law. Come find me.

Are handcuffs included in every package?

Yeah, he's that guy. Tall, dark brown hair that has this slight wave through it, scruff along his chiseled jaw, and eyes that could do a girl in. The different shades of blue almost swirl, and one second, it's sapphire, and the next, you're sure it's aqua.

Anyway, those eyes are trained on me and not in a sexy way.

I roll the window down and try to salvage this so I don't look ridiculous. "Hey. I'm here."

"And late."

I huff. "And not late, thank you. I have five more minutes until I am required to be here, which is fantastic considering I was just told about this an hour ago."

"This is a mistake."

My brows shoot up. "Excuse me?"

"You have been sitting in your car talking to yourself for the last three minutes. Also, why are you out here?"

"Because you need someone to watch Olivia . . ." *Duh.*

"I meant the car. Why aren't you inside, meeting Olivia and preparing? I have to be at the station in ten minutes."

"You mean the one that's a whole street over?" I ask, refusing to let him push me around. "How ever will you make it on time? Listen, if you're late, I'll call Daddy and ask him to let you off with a warning. Can you scoot so I can get out please?"

He takes two whole steps back, which gives me just enough room to open the door without hitting him.

"As *soon* as the agency finds a replacement," Asher mutters.

That's a relief. I might not have to do this all summer. Thank the Lord. "You know, you could say thank you, considering I'm giving up part of my summer to help you out."

It's really hard growing up in a town like this. Every mistake you make is part of the gossip mill, and no matter how small or insignificant it is, you never get to live it down. Sometimes, you can't even live down the stuff you didn't actually do either. Like when I took the heat for the senior prank that involved putting food dye in the pool and turning half the swim team blue. Why were the fingers pointed at me? Because no one would think to upset the chief by blaming his daughter when they all want favors. All the time I took the blame and looked ridiculous, and half of it, I didn't even deserve.

I wasn't always innocent, like when Asher caught me skinny dipping in Principal Symonds's pool when she was out of town. That I totally did.

Not like the Whitlock family is without their screwups, but heaven forbid anyone holds a single one of those against them.

My big screwup hasn't even hit the gossip mill yet, and this is just me paying for being an immature teenager.

"I could, but I won't."

My eyes narrow, and I really freaking hate this guy. So, just to be petty, I drop my voice to a deep baritone. "Thank you, Phoebe. You're really saving my ass by watching my daughter." Then I go back to my voice. "You're welcome, Asher. I am so happy to help you when you're in this bind."

Not that I had a choice. My father informed me it was this, go back to Iowa, or tell him why I came home. Off to be a nanny it is.

When we head inside, the house is still quiet, but it's six thirty in the morning, so I'm not surprised. I know I would rather be asleep.

"Where are your bags?"

"What?"

"Bags, you know, clothes, toiletries . . . the essentials."

I must look ridiculous as I stare at Asher in confusion. "Why would I need a bag? I live down the road."

"Right, but sometimes my shifts go until two in the morning, and I'm always on call. Plus, we rotate days and nights. You know this."

"Right, but we live in Sugarloaf," I remind him. "Which means you never actually get called in because nothing happens. You do know I'm a cop's daughter, right?"

Asher clenches his jaw. "Did your dad not explain everything?"

He did, but I wasn't agreeing to those terms. There's no way I am staying in Asher's house. Not a chance. I live exactly eleven minutes away.

"There's no need for me to move in here, especially since this probably won't last a week. You'll get your replacement. I'll go back to my big plans." *Of sitting in bed and regretting my life choices.* "All that before I could even unpack."

"Yes, because nannies who also know ASL are so plentiful in the area. If that were the case, I would have one."

"Maybe it's because you're cheap and won't pay them what they're worth." Seriously, when Daddy told me what the pay was, impressed was not the word I would use.

"I'm not cheap. According to the agency, the pay was extremely fair and people would be lined up."

"And, yet, here I am."

"Not a nanny. Let's not forget I was there when the last kid you babysat almost died."

I knew it was coming. "Does Olivia have any allergies I should know about?" I ask, sugary sweet.

"No, which is why you're allowed here."

I let out a long sigh. "Look, you think I'm irresponsible, and I think you're a big jerk, but this is the only option you have. I am not sixteen anymore. I'm twenty-four, a college graduate, and am working toward my doctorate in audiology. Okay? I am smart, focused, driven, *and* I know ASL."

I am also the opposite of all those things at the moment, but my little speech wouldn't have been as impactful otherwise.

"Eighteen," he says.

"What?"

"You were eighteen when Olivia cut her hair."

"Okay?" I'm not really seeing the point here, but no need to fight about semantics.

"I'm pointing out that you were older than sixteen when you screwed up."

"I'm really sorry that happened. I explained it a hundred times, but you weren't hearing me. I promise that won't happen again."

He laughs once. "Yes, because she's not three."

"And I'm not eighteen. So, look at that, we both grew up some." This is really getting on my nerves. "I'm doing you a favor, Asher. No need to be a dick about it."

He sighs loudly, running his hands through his dark hair. "I'm not trying to be a dick. It's just that Olivia is my world, and I was already hesitant about this agency thing, but Sara was adamant I go through them, so I did. Then the only nanny they have who knows ASL quit, so they suggested I have Livvy write everything down instead of sign. I just . . . I tried to take leave, but your dad needs me since I'm the SWAT leader for the county. You're right, neither of you are little anymore, it's been six years, and you have managed to make it through college without any major fuckups."

I wouldn't go that far, but I'm not about to offer up my errors. "Thanks."

He smiles softly, and those damn eyes are all molten lava as they stare at me. For a second, I forget this is Asher Whitlock—my father's employee and a big jerk who hates me—and only see every woman's dream. He's a hot, older, freaking SWAT leader, who has his life together, and did I mention hot? Too bad he's also a huge grump—except with Olivia.

I shake my head, coming back to reality and my decision to never like another man for eternity. They're the worst. "I appreciate you saying it. Is Livvy awake? I haven't seen her in a while, so I would like her to be comfortable with me before you go."

"Let me grab her. My sister will probably stop by after work. Brynlee has some new clothes and other things for her that Sara will never approve of."

"Is your sister still working for Sydney?"

"Yeah, she loves it."

Sydney is one of my favorite people in Sugarloaf. I worked for her when I came home after my freshman year of undergrad because I was sure I wanted to be a lawyer. It all changed my sophomore year when I met Jenny. She was my roommate and had lost her hearing when she was nine. I learned ASL so we could talk easier, and then I found myself drawn to her story about how she lost her hearing and the things she wished were different.

The language itself isn't the same as speaking. You don't say every word with your hands and the words are signed in a different order than you'd speak them, but it makes it easier to say what you need to faster. However, I've learned how to mentally translate ASL into a full spoken sentence.

After really diving into the language and the deaf culture, it became really important to me that others have access to opportunities and high levels of care regarding their communication. So, here I am, doing exactly that.

And I'm so glad I didn't go the legal route.

"It'll be great to see her again."

Brynlee is two years older than I am. We were never friends, per se, but we liked each other well enough.

"Good. All right, let me get Olivia up. There's a binder on the table, read it, memorize it, you'll never have to ask me anything because Sara literally listed everything about Olivia in there. Her appointments, schedule, information about school, favorite colors, it's all there."

That's right, she has two and a half weeks left in school. Crap. "And what do I do when she's at school?" I ask.

"Fuck if I know . . . I'm sure it's in the binder," Asher yells as he's walking away.

Binder. Got it.

I flip open the top, and my jaw drops. He wasn't kidding. There are probably eighty pages, front and back. What in the world have I agreed to?

I read through the first page, which lists emergency information, doctors, therapist, and I stop when I see who her audiologist is. If she has any appointments, I am for sure going. I don't care what deal I have to make with Asher. Doctor King is literally the king of audiology. He is doing cutting-edge research, and I tried so hard to get an internship with him at Children's Hospital of Philadelphia—because they're seriously the best—but he had no openings.

Maybe I can beg at an appointment though . . .

Nope. Not going there. I go back to reading the information I need. I check for allergies, of which there are none listed.

That's a relief.

But, Jesus, this girl's schedule is more complex than a Rubik's cube. She has appointments practically every day after school, after school is out for the summer, her appointments are even worse. Although, Sara has allotted an hour of "fun" between sessions—I won't even go there.

I keep flipping, seriously, her mother has some major issues to write out how to make Kraft Mac and Cheese to Olivia's liking, but . . . to each their own. Immediately after that, though, I think about my own mother. How if she had a binder like this when she died, so many things would have been easier.

Someone clears their throat, and I turn, forcing myself to smile. There stands an adorable little girl with light brown hair. She signs. *"Hi."*

I lift my hand, wave, and sign back while also speaking. *"Hi, I'm Phoebe. I'm going to be your nanny, which sounds ridiculous so let's just say your older friend. Although that's not much better. Do you read lips?"*

She nods. Good, sometimes that really helps when there are others in the room as well. Not everyone signs and often the conversations move quickly.

The dread that was in her pretty blue eyes fades. *"I'm happy you're normal."*

I laugh. *"I wouldn't say that."*

Asher taps her shoulder and signs to her. *"No, she's not normal. She's more like Uncle Rowan than Aunt Brynlee."*

I step forward, Olivia's eyes going to mine. *"Don't listen to him. He has a stick up his butt."*

Asher glares at me. "Really?"

I shrug. "That's for the allergy comments."

Olivia makes a noise. *"Sign please."*

It's so easy to forget how much deaf and hard of hearing people struggle. Everyday conversations that they would normally listen to don't exist. If the people around them don't sign or face them so they can read lips, it means they're excluded completely from the conversation.

I tap Olivia's shoulder. *"I was saying that your father deserved the comment since he made fun of me."*

She nods and tilts her head at him with pursed lips.

I like this kid already.

"I wanted to ask, do you have a name sign?"

Instead of having to spell out Olivia each time I need to use her name, she would have a name sign, which is something unique about her.

"I do." Her open hand brushes down her chin and then closes.

"I love that you're sweet."

"Do you have one?" she asks, and I nod.

"My deaf student gave me it." I make the sign where I trace the sun and the sky before opening my hand like the rays are hitting my face.

Olivia smiles. *"Sunshine?"*

25

I nod. *"Apparently, I am bright and fun. Does your dad have one?"*

Olivia makes the sign which is a mix between hero and strong. Her hand almost looks like a claw as she touches her shoulder, pulls her hand back into a fist. *"Asher."*

"Did you give it to him?"

She nods. *"He's very lucky because I think he should've had something like grumpy."*

She laughs, and Asher sighs heavily. *"Go get dressed and ready for school. I'll deal with this bright light."*

I wave to her as she walks off, leaving Mr. Grumpy Cop alone with me. "Your ASL is really good," he notes.

"I'm going to school to be an audiologist, I would hope it would be."

"That was a compliment."

"Then thank you," I say with a grin and follow him into the kitchen. "You weren't kidding about the binder."

"Sara is thorough, and Olivia means the world to us, so we work hard to make sure the transitions between our homes is easy for her, which means sharing information."

Smart. "Do you have a binder she gets?"

He laughs. "Hell no. I'm not doing that crap. I tell her what I remember, and she writes it down."

I scoff. "Typical man."

"Anyway, I have to leave in a few minutes. There is a detailed page about school days and the order she's supposed to do things, ignore it. Just make sure she has what she needs. Mrs. Arrowood will be outside the school to get her from you. I already sent her an email to let her know you are authorized to drop Olivia off and pick her up."

"That was very forward thinking of you."

He winks. "It's on page twenty-two of the binder."

I laugh. "And your shift today is until?"

"It's a twelve today and tomorrow, but I am on call for the county twenty-four seven for the next month."

Yeah, this on-call thing is going to be an issue. I am all for helping, but I really don't want to live here. "Here's the deal, I'll stay here when you have a shift the next day or overnights, but on your days off, there's no reason for me to stay the night. If you get a call and need me, I'll come back over."

Asher shakes his head. "No."

"No?"

"No. If I'm on call, I have minutes. I don't have time to wait for you to get here."

I cross my arms over my chest. "I live literally eleven minutes down the road. I could run here in fifteen. That's the maximum amount of time it would take me to reach you. If you're in bed, you'll need to get up, get dressed, take a piss, probably shoo out whatever girl is in your bed . . . it'll be fine."

"Anyone ever tell you that you're still annoying?"

"Nope. Just you."

I'm not backing down on this. The last thing I need is to be living in his house. No matter how nice he is to look at, I can't stand the guy.

"I'm not going to argue this now. You can take the bedroom down the hall, and it has its own bathroom. I'll be home around eight, but I work tomorrow, so you'll need to pack a bag according to your demands. Please try not to make me regret this."

I sigh. "Go to work. We'll be just fine."

three

PHOEBE

Where the hell did Mrs. Arrowood say to pick up Olivia? I swear she said the side exit, but she should've been out of school ten minutes ago.

Shit.

I park my car and walk to the front, but there's no one here. The buses are gone, there are just a few parents left in the pickup line, and no Olivia.

I cannot lose this kid on day one.

Dropoff went great. I followed the directions and got her to school on time. Then I went back home and packed two large duffle bags, one with my personal things I'll need to bring home each time, and one with stuff I can leave at Asher's.

Laid in my bed, listened to the last voice mail Jonathan sent three days ago, and then cried until I fell asleep. When I woke up, I realized I'd slept way longer than I meant to and had to run like the devil was on my ass to get to the school. Small towns are great, until you're in a hurry. Then there's some asshole going the speed limit on a two-lane road with no passing allowed.

This was worse because the asshole in question happened to be Mr. Montvale driving a tractor, which wasn't even capable of going the speed limit. I couldn't get around Mr. Montvale no matter what hand gestures I made.

So, I was late to pick Olivia up.

My phone rings, and I accept the call without looking, hoping it's the school. "Hello?"

A man clears his throat. Shit, it's Asher, and now I'm in trouble. "Phoebe, love . . ."

No, it's not Asher. My chest goes tight and my breath catches in my throat. I can't speak, I want to rail and scream and cry as it hurts just that badly. I can't talk to him. "No," I say the word, clinging to my anger. Jonathan lost the right to talk to me.

"Just listen, I won't take long. I'm sorry this happened to you. I'm sorry you were the one who—"

I hang up. I don't want to hear his voice or his apologies. I needed those a week ago. I needed those when my life was torn apart, and he hung me out to dry, painting me as the one who came onto him, ruined his marriage, and then tried to destroy his career.

None of those were true.

I thought I loved him. I thought he was smart, funny, sweet, and we could have something real. Instead, he caused me pain and embarrassment unlike I've ever known.

I still hear his words when I begged him to tell everyone the truth.

"I can lose my job, Phoebe. I can lose everything. You're young and can survive this. I can't. Do you want me to be fired?"

Angry tears fall, and I wipe them away. I didn't want that any more than I wanted to be the laughingstock of the school, but I will not cry any more. Damn him for making me break another promise to myself.

I hope his dick falls off.

I really hate that when I cry, I look like Rudolph. Whatever, I can't think about this, I need to find Olivia. I climb back into my car and drive to the back entrance, finding them waiting just outside the double doors.

Thank God.

"Hey! Sorry, I was at the wrong exit," I call to her as I rush to them.

Mrs. Arrowood's relief is palpable as she gets Olivia's attention and points toward me. Then I sign the same thing I just said aloud.

"I get dismissed from the hallway," Olivia informs me.

Her eyes are glossy, and I feel awful. *"I know, and I'm sorry."*

"It's okay."

I smile at her. *"I'll make it up to you."*

She looks up at Mrs. A and then back to me. *"Can we go?"*

"Yes."

Mrs. Arrowood smiles and then gives me a pointed stare. "You're lucky Asher didn't answer, or he'd have lost it."

"I know. I know. I'm sorry," I repeat. This is not off to a good start.

"Don't worry, I'll make something up to cover for you."

This is why she's everyone's favorite person in this town. I had Mrs. Arrowood for sixth grade, although she wasn't Arrowood at that time, and she's the best. Seriously the best.

When we get to my car, I pull up the schedule, which I took photos of. She has an appointment with the speech pathologist two towns over in seven minutes. Yeah, that's not going to happen, but we'll do our best.

If he finds out about this, I am in so much freaking trouble. He warned me, and of course, I screwed up. It's all I ever do.

I turn to face Olivia in the backseat. *"We're going to be late, but I'm calling the therapist to let them know. Do you want a snack?"*

She nods. I grab the bag of Cheez-its out of my bag and hand them to her.

Then I make the call and find out the therapist is running behind as well, so there's no harm done, and we head that way.

Not even eight minutes into my drive, my phone rings, and this time I check the name before answering. It's just as bad as before. "Hello, Asher."

"I got a call from the school a few minutes ago."

"Oh?" I play stupid.

"Any idea why?"

I turn left onto Main Street from Front Street, hoping to shave a few minutes off by taking the dirt road that cuts out the traffic lights. "Nope. Did you talk to anyone to find out why they called?"

He sighs. "Ellie answered and said she'd call me back but that nothing was wrong."

"Sorry, I really have no idea what she could be calling for then."

"Where are you?" he asks, his voice a bit steely.

According to the binder, I should've been at her appointment three minutes ago. I've learned that lying to cops isn't always the best idea, but I'm not going to let Asher Whitlock know I fucked up on day one.

"Pulling into the building for Olivia's appointment."

"Really?"

"Yes, really."

I mean, not really, but again, lying for the greater good isn't really bad, right?

"So, then why did I just see you pass me on Front Street?"

I'm committed now. "That wasn't my car."

"No?"

"No, it couldn't be since I'm not *on* Front Street." I'm on Main Street about to turn onto the cut through.

He sighs. "Look in your rearview."

I do it, knowing exactly what I'm going to see. And sure enough, there's a police car behind me.

"Okay, I know what you're thinking. And, yes, maybe we had a slight issue, but I didn't hear which entrance to pick her up at. It's fine. I was at the school, just in the wrong place. She's safe and eating her snack. I called the therapist to explain we were running a bit late, but they are running behind as well, so all is well."

"Pull over," he says and then disconnects.

32

As much as I really didn't want this job, I do now. Not because I'm suddenly a great babysitter or anything, but because Olivia needs someone who can communicate with her. We live in a small town, and she struggles enough without having people sign to her. Okay, maybe it has a little to do with the fact that her doctors are some of the best in the country, and I could maybe learn a little from them.

Plus, what am I going to do all summer? Brood in my room? I need money, and while I'm not getting paid a lot, it's better than nothing.

Most of all, I want to prove to myself that I'm not a complete failure.

After I pull to the side of the road and park, I turn to Olivia. *"Your dad is here, so I'm just going to talk to him outside of the car."*

She gives me a thumbs-up and turns to see her dad approaching.

Here goes getting fired on my first day.

I exit the car, and Asher doesn't even give me two seconds before he starts. "Trust doesn't start with you lying to me. Especially about her safety! Damn it, Phoebe, both you and your father told me you could handle this."

"And I can. I know, I was wrong to lie," I admit. "I should've explained everything right away, but you already think I'm flakey, which I was *six years ago*, but I'm not now. I got things mixed up, and I'm sorry. More than that, I'm sorry I betrayed your trust. You have every right to fire me, Asher, and I wouldn't blame you, but I really like Olivia and can do a lot with her. I went to school for this, and if you give me another chance, I promise I'll do better and there won't be any more issues. If there are, I'll fire myself."

Laying it all out on the table is probably the best option anyway. I was wrong, I admit it. This is his kid, and he loves her. I'm sure this isn't easy for him.

Ugh, now I'm empathizing with the man.

He seems a little stunned. "Well . . . that was . . . very mature."

"I'm not the girl you remember."

He runs his hand through his thick hair, sighing at the same time. "This doesn't exactly prove that, Phoebe."

"I should've told you the truth, and for that, I am eternally sorry. Let me take her to her appointment, and I promise I'll follow all the rules in the binder to a T."

His eyes find Olivia's in the car. She waves, and he does the same. Then his radio goes off, informing him of a situation. There are very few options available, so I'm really hoping I get that second chance. "Fine. If you fuck up again, you're done."

"You should really give inspirational speeches. I mean, you missed your calling."

"Don't push your luck. I'm giving you another chance."

"Thank you. Now, I have to be at an appointment, Officer Whitlock, and since you're so kind as to let me off with a warning, I must go."

Before he changes his mind, I rush to my car.

It's almost eight, and I've done the dishes, gotten Olivia's bag together for tomorrow, and talked to Sara. That was super fun. Thankfully, I don't think she put together that I was the same babysitter who let her daughter attempt to scalp herself.

"Phoebe?" Asher calls from the front door.

"In the kitchen!"

I hear his keys hitting a bowl or something and then heavy footsteps making their way toward me. They stop, and I turn to see him.

"Hey," I say with a smile.

"Any more issues?" he asks as though he is expecting a list of them.

"Not a one." My smile is broad because I made it without any incident. "We did homework, which—super lame. You need to have a talk with the school because half of it was redundant, and

Olivia is incredibly smart and needs to be challenged. After that, she took a shower. Before you ask, yes, I checked in on her at the six-minute mark just like the binder says." He rolls his eyes, and I continue on. "Dinner was great, she ate well, and then I painted her nails because she told me mine were pretty."

"Was that in the binder?" he asks.

"Nope, but I got approval from Sara after she had her fifteen-minute video call with Olivia and then let me know all the rules—and I mean *all*."

Seriously that woman is wound so tight. I thought my mother was a taskmaster, but Sara is next level.

Asher laughs. "Good, you can deal with Sara from now on. Any time she calls, tell her I'm at work."

"I'm sure she has a tracking device on you."

"I wouldn't doubt it. She isn't normally this intense. We do the co-parenting thing really well. I think it helps we never really dated and there were no feelings."

"I thought you guys dated," I say, not really sure why.

"Not really. We had an arrangement, we ended it when it wasn't working, and then we found out she was pregnant. Now she's dating that Finnegan guy on the Ford dealership commercial."

I skip past the hooking up part and go to the interesting tidbit at the end. "Oh! I saw that one today! He is cute. Go, Sara."

Asher starts to unbutton his uniform top and lets out a chuckle. "I'm a much better catch, but I guess Finnegan from Ford isn't a bad second choice. But"—he claps his hands together—"enough about that. I'm going to shower and then eat before I have to get up in six hours."

He saunters off, going upstairs toward Olivia's room first. She's fast asleep, which seems super early to me, but Sara explained her therapy days are really hard on her and it's best to get her to bed by seven.

I lean against the doorframe, thinking about what a great kid she is. Then my mind reels a bit about Asher and Sara. I didn't know much about their arrangement, but I thought they were together. Come to think of it, I don't know that Asher has ever been linked to anyone in Sugarloaf. Weird that.

He comes back down the stairs with a soft grin.

"Everything okay?" I ask.

"She's alive and resting peacefully. Her device wasn't on, but I forgot to mention that."

"Was that the box beside her bed?"

"Yes, if she needs anything, she pushes the button, and there's a box in my room that alerts me. There's a second one that I put in your room as well."

"All right. Thank you."

He opens his shirt the rest of the way, and I really wish I hadn't looked because—sweet Lord, his body is freaking perfect.

"See you in the morning," he says as he walks toward the back hallway.

Needing to collect my wits, I go back to cleaning the kitchen, grab my large duffle bag, and make my way to where I think is my room.

The house is not big, and the floor plan is kind of in the shape of a u. You enter in the middle of the home where there is the living room, the dining area is off to the right, and the kitchen is behind it. The right hallway has a bathroom and two other doors, the left is where Asher went. It's definitely an addition of some kind, but I haven't exactly asked, and now I'm not sure.

I head to the right first, but the first door leads to a laundry area and the second opens to a room full of boxes, so that's not it.

No way is it upstairs since that entire floor is Olivia's.

So, I go to the left hallway.

There are three doors, and only one is closed. The first is a bathroom, and the other open one is definitely where he expects me to stay. There is a queen-size bed between two windows that look out to the backyard, rolling hills, and the mountain on the horizon. It's pretty much the same view most of Sugarloaf has.

I close the door and quickly change into my shorts and

camisole crop top before I start to unpack. With my earbuds in, I crank up the angry 90s girl music—because, really, there's nothing like Amy Winehouse blaring about going back to black when you're hating all of the male gender—and put my clothes in the drawers.

four

ASHER

I toss on my basketball shorts and run the towel through my damp hair. Today was a weird day. It started going down one path where I thought I might actually have to fire Phoebe and then shifted to my realizing that she's not the same girl she was six years ago. She took responsibility for her mistake and owned her error. That never would've happened before.

There was something about the way she looked at me standing in my kitchen with her big, pouty brown eyes with thick lashes framing them, that made me forget she was the nanny and my boss's daughter and not one of the most beautiful women I've ever seen. For just one second.

I open my door, heading to the kitchen for something to eat, but I stop and look around, trying to figure out what is making that noise.

Seriously, what the hell is that sound? A cat dying? No, cats don't say words or try to sing them.

I walk into the hallway, and it's much louder, which means I won't find an animal being tormented. I'm going to find the woman who is attempting to torture my eardrums. Right now, I envy Liv being Deaf because . . . this is horrible.

39

I start to walk away, needing to find earplugs, when I hear, "No more! Help!"

Moving quickly, I push open her door, expecting to find her hurt or someone in the house. Instead, Phoebe is in shorts and half a shirt that's tight to her body, singing and dancing around the room without a care in the world.

Jesus Christ. My earlier thoughts about her are smack dab in my face. She is beautiful. No, she's more than that—she looks free and happy. Something about how she stands with her mouth open, letting out the worst sounds ever while completely unconcerned about how off-key she is, has my heart racing. Her eyes are closed, her head is back, and she's just letting it out. Earlier, her hair was in a bun, and she was wearing sweatpants and a hoodie. Now that I know *this* is what is hiding under her clothes . . . I'm so fucked.

She's your boss's daughter. She's your-much-too-young-for-you boss's daughter. Again, she's younger than your sister. She's also your daughter's nanny. And she's a pain in the ass. Sunshine, my ass.

No, I do not see how perfect her ass looks in those shorts. And those curves, when the hell did she get those? It doesn't matter that she looks adorable dancing around and singing into her fake microphone.

All that matters is that she's my daughter's nanny, and the only person in the freaking county who knows ASL and will watch her. Also, she's my boss's damn daughter.

I tell myself this, but my dick doesn't seem to care.

Time to leave. I go to close her door to get away from the trainwreck that is Phoebe Bettencourt, but she gasps.

"Asher! What are you doing?" she wails and grabs her shirt.

I go to speak, but at the same time, her earbud pops out, she somehow manages to swat it into the air, and she attempts to catch it. As she does, her top rises, revealing her breasts. I am not sure what to do, so I start to go toward her, but she's too busy scrambling for the earbud while also trying to cover herself and ends up tripping on the area rug and falling on her ass.

"*Please* tell me you didn't see anything."

I lie. "I didn't see anything."

She's on the floor, trying to pull her top into the right angle as her hips move side to side. "Ugh! You saw it all!" She groans as she finally gets herself covered. "Seriously, can I just stay here until I don't want to fall through the floor anymore? It might be *forever*."

I try not to laugh—I really do—but . . . it was probably the most hilarious thing I've seen in a while.

"Let me help you . . ." I step toward her, but she raises her hand.

"Don't!" she warns as she glares at me from the floor.

"Are you okay? It looked like that hurt." I approach her, palm outstretched.

She swats at it. "Don't try to help me *now*. You saw my boobs, you big jerk!"

"How am I a jerk?"

"You laughed."

"You would've too from my vantage point."

She huffs, pushing herself up. "Why don't you recreate it, and we'll see if I laugh."

I grin. "I'm good. I wouldn't want to hurt myself. What the hell made you fall?" *And maybe we can have it happen again so I can see more clearly this time.*

Nope. No, do not even think it.

I am not attracted to Phoebe. Not even a little.

"You scared the shit out of me."

"Clearly, unless that was your attempt at dancing and flashing your boss."

Her lips move while she rolls her eyes, mimicking what I just said. Why do I find that adorable? Oh, I don't. Nope. Nothing about this is cute. Not the fact that her long brown hair flows down her back in waves or how her arms are crossed, pushing her breasts into the perfect position.

"What the hell did you just barge in here for?"

"You yelled for *help*."

41

"No, I didn't."

"Yes," I argue back. "You said, 'No more! Help!'"

She sputters. "I . . . I was singing!"

"I didn't know that! I thought someone was hurting you." I chuckle beneath my breath. "I thought maybe you were trying to deter them from attacking you with your singing."

Her jaw falls open. "You are such an ass!"

She's not wrong, but I have to distract myself from thinking about how gorgeous she looks.

"You know, for an employee, you are extremely rude. Hasn't anyone told you that you're supposed to be nice to the person who writes your check?" I push her buttons because it's better than pushing her against the bed, kissing her, and palming her breasts that I'm pretty sure will fit in my hands like they were made for me.

Doing a bang-up job at forgetting, Asher.

"Oh, and has anyone told you that as an employer, you suck? Because you're not exactly overflowing with kindness and understanding."

"I didn't fire you today when I caught you lying, that was nice."

"You don't exactly have a replacement either," she reminds me as she steps closer. "I don't know that your kindness would've extended to me if you weren't desperate."

No, I don't, but that last part isn't true either. There was something in her eyes when she was apologizing that I couldn't shake. She was so sincere, so hopeful that she'd have another chance that I knew I wouldn't have fired her.

Phoebe may not be the world's best childcare, but all I've heard for the last five years is how smart she is and how hard she works at school. She went to undergrad at Penn and then the University of Iowa for graduate school. Her father is beyond proud of her, as he should be. It would be unfair of me to think she hasn't grown up.

However, that doesn't answer the question of why would she

leave her school before the semester ended and before finishing her graduate program?

It's none of my business.

"Brynlee would've quit her job if I really needed her to."

She shrugs. "Well, I survive another day. Uh, I meant to ask, but you were in the shower. This is my room, right?"

"It actually isn't."

"No?"

She's too close. I catch a hint of the scent of lemons and sugar, tart yet sweet. The air around us charges as though an electric current has been unleashed.

I shake my head, hoping to dispel the desire I feel rising. "This is for my *other* overnight guests. You have the guest house out back."

Her eyes widen and then, as though the words just finally doused the same fire I'm fighting, she steps back and a look of disgust crosses her face. "Is that in the binder?"

I breathe and then grin. "Nope."

She turns to look at the bed and shivers. "Considering the available number of single women around here, I'll move out now. I'm not sure I want to risk cross contamination."

Phoebe starts to grab her stuff, and I laugh. "I'm kidding. Yes, this is where the nanny was going to stay."

"And the bed?"

Now it's my turn to roll my eyes. "It's clean, and it's *been* clean for . . . a while." Far too long if I'm lusting after my boss's daughter.

She throws the clothes onto the bed and grumbles. "You're infuriating."

"Again, I'm your boss."

Keep reminding yourself of that, Asher.

"Right now, I'm off the clock."

"Fine, then I'm not your boss right now, but I will be in a few hours."

She sits on the edge of the mattress and crosses her long legs. "Okay, so you're just Asher now?"

I nod.

Phoebe's eyes light up, and she clasps her hands in front of her chest. "Oh, good. Dude, I have to tell you about what happened today. So, I'm working for this grumpy old guy, and of course the most embarrassing thing happened to me right in front of him, and he *laughed*. Isn't he such an ass?"

Speaking of ass . . . nope. Stop it.

I need to get out of here.

Walking out, I toss my words back to her. "I'll be gone before you wake up tomorrow. Remember to pick up my daughter this time, okay?"

Phoebe practically growls. "I didn't forget her. I was at the wrong door—you know what, you're right. I'll do better next time, *boss*."

I smirk. "See that you do."

I kick my door shut, flop onto my bed, and make a plan to find a new nanny so I can limit my time around Phoebe Bettencourt and not imagine her completely naked.

"He's not *that* hot," I hear Phoebe whispering from inside the kitchen.

I'd hoped to avoid her before I went in for my shift. I'd gotten up early, went for my run, showered, and came to grab my coffee and go. That was the plan, but apparently, the Lord is testing me.

"No, seriously, he's not. I mean, I grew up looking at guys in uniform, so I don't have that same affliction you seem to." She laughs. "Out of uniform? Oh, I'm sure he's . . . nope. Not going there."

I shouldn't be eavesdropping, but I also can't seem to force myself to move. I'm what?

"We're not talking about how my hot boss saw my boobs,

Emmeline." A pause. "I'm done with older men—well, that's a lie, I'm done with *all* men. My plan today is to take Olivia to school and then work on my transfer applications. I decided on three schools to apply to, and hopefully, I don't lose all my credits."

Transfer? She's in her first year of grad school, why the hell is she planning on transferring?

Better question is, why do I give a shit?

I don't. All I care about is her ability to take care of Olivia until the nanny service sends a new nanny.

Just as I'm about to go back to the stairs, bang around so I don't seem like a creeper, my cell phone rings, announcing my location. I close my eyes for a second and then look at the phone.

My play is to act like I was walking into the kitchen and didn't hear a thing.

"Hello, Sara," I say as I push the door open.

"Hello, Asher. How is our daughter?"

"She's good. Where are you now?" I smile at Phoebe, who ends her call, slips her phone into her pocket, and gives a hesitant wave.

I bet I look hot now.

I'm not a vain guy, but it's not all that bad hearing you're still hot when you're inching toward forty.

Sara sighs heavily. "We're here. I miss her. I want to come home already. I don't like that the agency hasn't sent you anyone."

"We have it covered. Everything is good, and Olivia really is fine."

"If you say so . . ."

"I wouldn't lie about this, Sara. You have a huge opportunity, and I have it covered here. Phoebe is great with Liv."

And if she lets me down, then I will beg my sister to help out, but I'm hoping it doesn't come to that. She has today to prove me wrong.

"Okay. I will try my best to relax. I would just feel better if I had met her."

No, she definitely wouldn't, and since she hasn't pieced together exactly who Phoebe is, I'm not telling her. "You weren't going to meet the nanny the agency sent."

"But they're vetted."

"So is she. I have to head to work. Call Phoebe later to talk to Olivia, and be safe there."

"I am."

We hang up, and Phoebe gives me a soft smile. "It must be hard for her."

I nod. "It is. I think the longest either of us have ever gone without seeing Liv was two weeks, and that was when I went to a training program. The longest I've had her in one stretch was a week because Sara was on location. Usually, she turns down big projects, but this was one she couldn't."

"I can imagine it's not easy. Listen, I really appreciate your giving me another shot. Today will be different, there will be no mess ups. I promise." She turns and grabs two brown paper bags. "Here."

"What's this?"

"I made lunches. One for you and one for my dad. If you could give it to him . . ."

"That won't be awkward," I say with a chuckle.

"He'll know it's from me. None of you guys eat well when you're on shift. Whenever I'm home, I try to do what I can to mitigate the damage from his crap diet. There are some snacks and heart healthy sandwiches."

I don't have sandwich supplies in the house. I meant to grab them, but it's been a bit hectic since I'm the SWAT commander. It's more than just being on standby. There's paperwork, planning, and scheduling for the team that I have to do on top of my officer duties.

"When did you . . .?"

"I went this morning and grabbed some stuff for the house. I love twenty-four-hour grocery stores."

"What the hell time did you wake up?"

She shrugs. "I'm still on grad-school-kid time, which means I run on caffeine and severe sleep deprivation. I passed out last night earlier than I have in months, so when I woke up, I figured I might as well be productive."

I nod. "And why aren't you still at college?"

Phoebe's eyes widen just a touch, but I was watching for it. "Why stay when you can do your finals online?"

"So, all your friends left school early as well?"

"No, but . . . why do you care?"

"I don't," I reply.

"Then why are you asking?"

Talk about evasion. "You can just say you'd rather not tell me what happened."

Phoebe lets out a long breath. "Fine. I'd rather not talk about it."

I shake my head. "Nope. Now I want to know."

"Well, I have no intention of telling you anything. Besides, if I hadn't left, you wouldn't have childcare. So, think about that, Mr. Grumpy Cop."

While that may be true, my gut is saying something is off. "First, I'm not grumpy. Second, I didn't say I was ungrateful. I just wondered why you'd leave."

"It's none of your business."

She's right. It's not, but I'm intrigued, which is never a good thing. "Well, something clearly brought you home."

"Yes, something did." She glances at the clock. "Oh, look at the time! You're going to be late to work. I hear your boss is a real stickler about time."

If she were my sister, I would push relentlessly until I got a satisfactory answer. Brynn is notorious for running when things get rough and pretending nothing is wrong. Then the issue usually comes and smacks her in the face so Rowan and I have to pick up the pieces.

But Phoebe is not my sister.

She's my daughter's nanny.

"I'll be home late, and then I'm off tomorrow. If you could stay the night just in case . . ."

She sighs. "I would rather not."

"Okay, let me rephrase. I'll need you to stay the night with Olivia because I have a huge caseload I need to catch up on. Thank you."

"Anything you need, *boss*."

Phoebe leaves the kitchen, and I grin, imagining bossing her around in other ways.

five

PHOEBE

"Hey, Phoebs!" Brynlee says when she spots me sitting in Sugarlips Diner.

"Brynn, hey!"

"Mind if I sit?" she asks while already pulling the chair out.

I smile. "Of course not."

I've been here the last two hours, filling out applications and pulling copies of my transcripts from Penn as well as my grades and test scores from Iowa. I haven't gotten all that far because every five minutes someone comes over to tell me how good it is to see me.

"What are you up to?"

"Just waiting for Liv to be done with school and working on some college stuff."

"Oh? College stuff?"

"I'm transferring this year, so I have to fill out a ton of application stuff by the end of tomorrow."

There are really only three options to consider for schools. One in Nashville, which was my first choice the last time I went through this. The second best would be in Illinois, which I got into last time, but is way too close to Jonathan. Then the last is in Texas, which I might take just because it's the farthest from Iowa.

"Oh. Good luck. How is it going with the runtlet?"

"Good, she's amazing." I have really connected with her. This morning she got up, gave me a hug, and we got everything done per Sara's instructions.

I even sent a photo of Olivia walking into class to Asher so he knew she was delivered properly.

His text back, which read, "It's the collecting her that seems to be your issue," shouldn't have surprised me.

Well, I can't wait to prove him wrong.

"I agree, she's so special. I was going to stop by tomorrow and take her to lunch, I'm not sure if you guys have plans . . ."

I shake my head. "I'm off tomorrow, so you'll have to check with Asher."

"I'm actually going to see him in a few. I have a favor to ask him, and it's always best to bring food."

"Good to know."

She laughs. "Seriously, if you feed him, he's much more amiable. It's a Whitlock trick I learned long ago. Asher is French fries, Grady is ice cream, and Rowan is meat. Give the man a steak, and he'll do anything you ask."

"How is Grady doing? Still in the navy?"

"Yeah, he's still in and stationed in Florida for now."

"That's awesome, and he's a pilot, right?" I remember everyone talking about how he flew.

"Yup, well, I guess for now. His commission is up soon, and he's actually going to be moving back to Sugarloaf."

"Wow! Back to Sugarloaf. Not many come back after they leave. How does his wife feel about moving here?"

Brynn looks down at her hands. "Umm, I assumed you heard because of your dad, but Lisa passed away about two and a half years ago."

"Oh, I'm so sorry. I had no idea. I never would've asked." I feel awful now.

"Don't be sorry. It isn't something we talk much about around here. Grady hasn't been in Sugarloaf for so long, and they never lived here. Anyway, she had an aneurysm and just . . . it was sudden."

My heart falters for a second. "Like my mom."

"Oh, I am so sorry to—"

I rest my hand on her forearm. "It's okay. It's been a while. I was just saying that I understand." My mother's death was sudden, and it was incredibly hard. It's been ten years now, but sometimes, it feels like yesterday.

"Yeah. It was just really hard on him to lose her when their son was only a few weeks old."

I gasp. "Oh, God. He has a baby?"

Brynn nods. "He's adorable, and I hate that he'll never know his mama. I went down to help right after, but then Lisa's parents moved to Florida to watch Jett while Grady finished his commission. He's just . . . not the same."

"I'm sure he's drowning in grief. I know my father did. When it's unexpected, it just feels like you're cheated in some way. I didn't get to say goodbye to my mother or tell her all the things I wanted to. I would've apologized for the stupid fights we had or all those times I argued with her about my hair. Dad was worse, he just shut down and threw himself into the job."

"Which is what Grady's doing," Brynn says with a sad smile. "But he's coming back home. He is going to stay with me for a few months until he finds a place or builds on the land that's his, and I'll get to spend all the Auntie time with Jett. I'm hoping to throw them a welcome-home party."

"That'll be fun."

Brynlee laughs. "He'll kill me for it, but I really want him to have something to remind him that people love him and he has a family here who will support them."

Magnolia comes to the table with her shirt buttoned to the top, which is a change. Then again, she only disrobes when there are guys around. She's been here since I was a kid and is super sweet, but she's the biggest flirt I've ever met.

"Hey there, girls."

"Hi, Mags, how is business?" Brynn asks.

"You know, can't complain, other than about freaking Cooperton. He is so rude and pushy." Both Brynn and I tilt our heads to see Memphis sitting there, hat down low so you can't see his eyes as he leans back. "He hates the food, hates me, and hates the town, but he still comes in every day."

I shake my head. "He's always been that way."

He's the town mystery. Rolled into Sugarloaf years ago, bought Ellie's old farm, doesn't talk to anyone, and is perpetually grumpy. I, for one, like him. He's a man of few words, and in this world, that's rare.

"He just needs a hug or maybe a kitten," Brynn says.

"I dare you to hug him." Magnolia gestures her arm that way.

"Tomorrow."

We all chuckle, and Magnolia lifts her book. "All right. What can I get you?"

Brynn places a very large to-go order, and we catch up about the goings on in Sugarloaf. She is single, which I'm surprised by because she's smart, funny, and incredibly pretty. She has strawberry blonde hair and the most stunning green eyes that guys gush over. On top of that, she's just . . . nice.

"So, no dating?"

She shrugs. "I think you understand this better than most, but it's hard to date in this town. Put aside the fact that I am a Whitlock, my brother is a cop, my other brother is a maniac, and Grady has access to missiles, the guys here either started dating their wives when we were eleven or moved away to greener pastures."

Ain't that the truth? "The intimidation thing I totally get."

"It's so damn annoying!" Brynn complains. "I did meet a guy a few months ago, and it was going well until he met Rowan. Then, suddenly, he wasn't interested anymore."

"Then that guy wasn't worth your time!"

Brynn sighs. "I guess so, but the casualties of dating have left me battered."

Don't I know it. "Believe me, I feel you. My father ruined my prom, I ended up going alone after he threatened one of the boys who were going to ask. Jim spread the word that no one should ask the chief's daughter, or they might get shot."

She laughs softly. "So frustrating. But I've talked a lot about me, what's new with you? Did you finish this semester early?"

Always about school. I should've just stayed in Iowa until the semester was over. It would've led to fewer questions.

"No, I was able to come back early."

"Oh, well, that's good. Did you decide what school you're transferring to?"

"Not yet. I am applying to a few schools, but it kind of comes down to money."

Brynn smiles. "I know that feeling. I'm going to school at night and working full time, but Syd is great and allows me time off for classes or anything education related."

"What are you going for?"

"Philosophy."

That word makes my chest ache. Immediately, I feel the anxiety start to build as I think about that class. About *him* and his lies and the way I ate them up like Skittles, desperate for the next sugar high.

Brynlee snaps her fingers in my face. "Hello? You okay in there?"

I clear my throat and nod. "Yes, sorry. I just . . . spaced out. I woke up ridiculously early, and I guess it's catching up with me."

"I get it. I stay up studying and then fall asleep with my face in the book."

"I know that all too well." Magnolia brings a bag and places it on the table, and Brynn stands. "I should get these fries to Asher before they're cold."

I grin. "So, you're buttering him up?"

"Absolutely."

"Good luck."

She winks. "I don't need it, I have potatoes."

"I understand that, sir, but I need to apply, and they're going to request my transcripts."

I don't know why this is so hard for my academic advisor at Iowa to understand.

"I am not sure what you want me to say, Miss Bettencourt. I can't send these until the semester is over and grades have been finalized."

"Right, but most of my grades are final now."

"Most is not all, and I cannot release incomplete transcripts. This school has standards and rules, and while you have chosen multiple times not to follow them, I can't just bend to your whim. So, I suggest you wait until the end of the year and put in your official request then."

Every part of me wants to rail and fight back. Victor Waite is one of Jonathan's friends, so I'm not really sure what I expected. Maybe some professionalism?

"Thank you for your help, Mr. Waite. I'll be in touch at the end of the semester."

What else can I do at this point? I'll submit my unofficial transcripts as well as some letters from professors who aren't complete assholes and another essay. Once the year is over, I'll file the request and go from there.

The bell rings, and kids start barreling out of the doors, reminding me of just how exciting it was once you were finally done with school. I look for Olivia, but I don't see her right away. Once the larger group of kids have dispersed, she exits.

I wave, and her smile is automatic.

Mrs. Arrowood's face brightens, and she urges Olivia toward me.

"How was school?" I sign.

"Over."

I laugh. *"And now it's the weekend."*

"Will you come fishing tomorrow?" she asks.

Fishing? *"I don't think so. I have to do some schoolwork."* She makes a face. *"I agree."*

"Can we get ice cream?"

I'm pretty sure the binder had a strict no-sweets policy, which is utter crap if you ask me, but there must be a loophole. And that would be Asher.

"Let me ask your dad."

I fire off a text.

> Can we pleaaaaaaaase get ice cream?

ASHER
> Why are you asking me?

> You're the parent.

ASHER
> You're the terrible nanny.

> So, are you giving me permission to disobey the binder?

ASHER
> I didn't write it . . .

I grin at Olivia. *"Mr. Pips?"*

She nods vigorously, as any nine-year-old should. Mr. Pips is the best ice cream in the county, and it's within walking distance of the school.

The two of us walk, and she fills me in on her day. Apparently, it was very stressful. The teacher wanted her to explain something, but she was nervous to sign in front of the class.

I wish I could go in there and give her support. At her age, no one wants to be called on in class, but couple it with having issues with hearing, it's a lot. She most likely feels different already, and to have her stand up and try to answer questions probably doesn't help.

As a kid who struggled with a crippling fear of public speaking, I can empathize with her.

"I'm sorry it was a rough day," I tell her.

Livvy's smile is reserved. *"Mommy says bad days pass."*

"She's right."

Lord knows I've had enough of those in the last week.

When we get to Mr. Pips, it seems as if the whole town is here.

"Phoebe!" Devney Arrowood calls with her hand high.

"Hi, Devney, how are you?" I smile as I approach and Olivia follows. She's sitting at the table with a blonde woman I've never met.

"Good, I heard you were back. This is my friend Addison, and her peanut is Elodie. Hi, Livvy. You look very pretty. I love your nails."

I turn to Olivia and sign what she says.

Olivia holds up her hands to give Devney a better look, and she coos over them.

"It's nice to meet you," I say to Addison.

"Nice to meet you as well. Your dad is such a great guy and has been so much help with my organization. He talks about you nonstop. He's very proud."

He wouldn't be if he knew why I was home.

"Thank you. What has he been helping with?"

Olivia tugs on my arm. *"Can I color with Elodie?"*

I say the words, and Addison smiles with a small nod.

"I'm sure Elodie would love you to play," I say aloud as well as sign.

Devney winks and tilts her head to Olivia, handing her a crayon to color with. "I really thought you met Addison when you were home the last time."

I shake my head. "Nope."

Addison purses her lips. "Hmm, I think I was back in Oregon when you were home last time. I spent the summer in Oregon."

"Oh!" I say, thankful she filled me in since I was kind of lost. I've heard her name, of course, but last summer I worked in Iowa as I was preparing for grad school, so I didn't meet her. "Well, it's great to finally meet you. I feel like I've missed so much. Do you like Sugarloaf so far?"

"Yes, I love it here. The people are wonderful and your dad has offered a lot of his resources to our foundation."

"Really? That's great, what exactly do you do, though?" I ask.

Daddy mentioned something about having a runaway refuge close to here, but I hadn't realized it was something the town needed. Still, it's a great option for those in need.

Now we need to get better resources for deaf and blind children. We need more therapy options for kids with learning disabilities and physical issues. There are so many families who have to choose between hiring an agency or driving to Philadelphia for care.

Addison nods. "Right now, we provide safe harbor and rehabilitation options for runaways. We also help reunite them with their families and get them the help of psychologists. We have two chapters right now, but the other partner and I hope to open more on the East Coast."

"That's great."

Addison smiles warmly. "We are always looking for volunteers if you have time. I know you're in school, but maybe when you're home?"

While it may not be my idea of a priority for the town, it's clearly doing good for those who need it. Not only would I like to see more, but also it would be good for me to volunteer as well.

"I would love to. I hate to ask this, but would you be willing to provide volunteer hours? I'll volunteer regardless, but I've decided to transfer schools, and it would be really great to have it on my applications."

God, I hate this part. However, it's the games we play to get into school.

"Of course I can do that! I remember all too well how ridiculous schools are. My sister-in-law was a nightmare because she didn't have all the things that she thought she needed."

"Did she move here with you guys?" I ask.

Devney clears her throat. "Just Addison and Elodie are in Sugarloaf."

I feel like I'm missing something.

Addison places her hands in her lap. "After my husband was killed almost three years ago, I came here to start over. All of my family are back in Oregon still."

"I'm sorry for your loss."

Before I can say anything else, Olivia puts the crayon down and points to the counter. "I think that's my cue to get her some ice cream. It was great seeing you. If it's okay, I'll come by tomorrow since I have the day off from the nanny gig."

They both smile. "I'd love that," Addison says.

With that set, I take Olivia's hand and we head to the counter. She gets two scoops because I'm a total sucker.

"That'll be eleven dollars."

"Eleven dollars for two scoops and half a spoon of sprinkles?" I ask, eyes wide. "What, did you go out back and milk the cow and hand churn it into ice cream?"

Josiah Sandifer rolls his eyes. "Are you going to pay for your goods, or do I need to call the cops?"

I lean in. "I remember a certain story about a little boy who was on a fishing trip and thought he could catch himself so he tried to stick the hook in his own mouth. He peed his pants when they took the hook out but told everyone he fell in the water . . ." I drop my voice lower. "Do you know who that was, Josiah?"

He leans back. "Fine, five dollars. Sprinkles are free."

"Can you put it on my dad's tab?"

The little jackass laughs. "Tab? What tab? Mr. Pips says you're not allowed to put anything on a tab . . ."

Oh, yeah. During my freshman year in high school, my friends and I came in here every day and put everything on my dad's tab. After two months of it not being paid, my father got a very large bill. My dad made me work the dairy farm down the road for the whole summer with no pay. I didn't know people paid a tab. I thought it was just . . . free money.

Sometimes I sound stupid even to myself.

"Okay. Give me a second."

Unsure of how I'm going to pay for this, I dig through my purse, searching for a few dollars I always keep at the bottom, and look up when Olivia gasps.

Asher is standing next to us in his uniform with a big smile for his daughter. He signs and speaks. *"I thought I would surprise you girls."*

Olivia wraps her arms around him, and my heart thaws a little. There is something about a big grumpy asshole who melts at the sight of his daughter.

No, no, there's not.

I can't even let myself think about this. No way in hell.

"Are you getting ice cream?" he asks.

"No, I . . . wasn't going to."

"Why?"

I huff. "Because I'd forgotten that Josiah here did away with the tabs. When I was going to order for myself, he so kindly informed me of the rule change. So, I probably have enough for Olivia, and that's who matters."

Asher turns to Josiah with his head tilted to the side. "Since when did Mr. Pips do away with the tabs?"

"She didn't say it was your tab, Officer Whitlock."

Asher's eyes narrow. "You know Olivia is my daughter, right?"

He nods.

"Then . . . I'm curious why you thought it wouldn't go on my tab?"

I stand here, fighting back a smile as Asher puts him in his place.

"Sorry," Josiah says to him and then me.

Asher turns to me. "Get anything you want."

That slightly giddy feeling I had is now gone. Instead, I feel stupid and ridiculous for needing him to come in and pay for me.

"I'm okay. I don't need anything."

"Get what you want, Phoebe. I'll pay for it."

"I can pay for myself," I say, feeling slightly defiant. I don't want or need charity.

His voice drops as he leans in. "I didn't say you couldn't. Get something so you and Liv can sit and have ice cream."

Olivia watches the two of us and asks, *"Are you getting ice cream too?"*

I close my eyes for a second and then nod to her before placing my order.

Asher kisses Olivia's cheek and then grins at me. "Enjoy your ice cream. I'll see you both later."

I really want to wipe that smirk off his face.

six

ASHER

"So, how's it going with Liv living with you full time?" Rowan asks as he hands me a beer.

"It's been fine."

And it has been. I love having my daughter all the time. I just don't love it requires a nanny living with me too. It's working out with Phoebe staying at my house on the nights I work and at her place on the nights I'm off. Thankfully we haven't had to test how quickly she can get to me if a call comes in, but what's not going well is my thoughts about her.

"Liv seems happy," Rowan cuts into my thoughts.

"She is. I'm the fun parent."

Rowan snorts. "And yet, you're the least fun Whitlock out of all of us. Well, maybe Grady is less fun than you, but just marginally."

I shake my head. "And you're the least responsible." Rowan is the youngest brother. He's thirty-three, but he acts like he's eighteen most days.

"Fuck off. I run this farm, I work my damn ass off to make it profitable, and still manage to have fun. You're just pissed you never got to live like me."

He's not wrong. I am pissed, but I wouldn't change my life

either. I came home and stepped up with Brynn, which is some-thing I will never regret. Then, once I could have fun, I got Sara pregnant, so once again, I did exactly what any real man should do—step the fuck up.

"You think your life is better than mine?" I ask.

"Hell yeah it is."

I look at my daughter, who is casting her line into the creek, and shake my head. "Nah, man. See her? She's what makes my life better."

"I won't argue because Livvy is the best, but I mean, don't you wish you could come and go as you wish?"

My brother has never really had to do much. He dropped out of college because he drank too much and was failing every class. Instead of him having to rough it, he took over the farm, which suits him. His competitive nature had the farm profitable in a year, and he's looking into buying another plot of land to expand, but his nemesis, Charlotte Perry, is doing the same. God knows it'll be a bloodbath if it goes to auction.

I glance over at my brother. "I'm happy with my life."

"Well, better you than me."

It definitely is. I can't even imagine what Livvy's life would've been like had Rowan been her father.

"How are things going with the cows?"

"They're mooing and making milk."

"That's . . . good. And what about the land up for sale?"

"I'm working on it. I just need to make Charlotte think I'm not interested. That woman will do anything to piss me off."

"You really think she wants the land just to make you mad?"

He raises one brow. "Yup, but I'm two steps ahead of her."

"Sure you are."

"Hey, I meant to tell you . . . guess who I ran into yesterday?"

"No idea."

He pushes my shoulder. "Come on, guess."

"For fuck's sake, just tell me."

"You're a shitty guesser."

"You're a fucking annoying prick."

Rowan drains his beer. "I give zero fucks about that, but, since you're a dick and won't guess, I'll tell you. I saw Phoebe Bettencourt at Peakness."

Her name causes my jaw to lock. She is the only chink in my otherwise great life. She walks around in those shorts, which I swear are meant to kill me, and I have to remind myself I really don't desire her. I'm just . . . lonely. That's all.

"Good for you," I say, keeping my voice even, refusing to care she was at the same bar as he was.

"Yeah, she looks—" He blows out an exaggerated breath and shakes his head. "She's fucking hot."

"I haven't noticed." As soon as I say it, I realize my mistake. I'd have to be blind not to notice how beautiful she is, and he's going to see through that line of bullshit.

He laughs once. "Liar."

Called it.

"Okay, let me rephrase, I won't notice because she's my daughter's nanny."

Rowan leans back in his chair, lifting on the back two legs. "Maaaan, I'd like her to be my nanny. Can you see if she wants to take on a man-child?"

My brother is a fucking idiot. "No, but I'll see if our old principal, Mrs. Symonds, wants a new job since she retired."

Rowan makes a gagging noise. "That was mean."

I shrug. Olivia turns back to us, waving enthusiastically. Rowan and I return the gesture. While Rowan says he doesn't want a family, he's full of shit. I see the way he is with Olivia. He loves her with every fiber of his being. There's nothing this man won't do for his niece, and he'd be the same with his own kid. He just needs to find the right girl who he wants to have kids with.

Or one he wants more than just to sleep with.

Like I want to with . . . nope. Not finishing that thought.

Rowan leans forward, grabbing us both another beer. "So, you wouldn't care if I went after her?"

"Went after her?" I take the offered bottle.

"Yeah, you know, Brynlee said I need to grow up and need a woman, so I figure I can test it with Phoebe."

I smack the back of his head. "You deserve more than that. She's Livvy's nanny. Your niece adores her, and if you were to do that, and she decided she'd rather . . . oh, not want to be around the Whitlocks, then what?"

"From what I heard, she doesn't exactly like you anyway."

My hands tighten around the glass bottle. "I don't care if she likes me, she is great with Liv."

"Last night, she told me all about how much she adores her. She's quite chatty when Liv is brought up."

This is ridiculous. I shouldn't give two fucks about who Phoebe talks to. I shouldn't care if she talks to the whole damn town, but something about her talking to Rowan pisses me off.

"Look, do with this what you will, but I need her to continue working for me, so if you run her off, you're going to be the new nanny. Got it?"

Just then, we hear a car door slam and turn to see Brynlee walking toward us. "Hi, boys."

"Brynn . . ." I groan. She's going to start in again with her idea to have a party for Grady when he moves back to Sugarloaf, which is something Grady will not want. He isn't happy about coming back, but he's trying to figure out what his next steps are, and sometimes, you need to be around family for support.

"Hey, little sister, is that food?" Rowan asks, patting his stomach.

"It sure is. I have fries and two burgers."

Rowan stands and backs away. "Ohhh no, that's bribery food. It either means you want me to do something, or you want to adopt a Shetland pony or some shit."

"It's the first. She already tried it with me, and it didn't work."

Brynn smiles. "This time, I have a double order!" Then the other door opens and Phoebe slides from the passenger seat. "And I brought a friend who agrees."

Rowan grins. "That just sweetened the deal."

And that statement makes me want to punch my brother in the nose.

"I'm not good at this," Phoebe signs and speaks as Olivia tries to teach her how to fish. *"Please tell me there's another way to fish?"*

Olivia grins and waves me over.

Great. For the last few hours, I've done a good job ignoring Rowan flirting with her constantly and Phoebe blushing.

I've managed to keep my simmering rage buried because my brother is relentless, even with Phoebe doing a good job at brushing him off. However, I've just had to stay far away from her, but now, I don't have a choice.

"Yes, daughter?" I sign.

"Can you help?"

"Help who?" It's not like there's a group here who can't fish. Rowan and Brynlee put their waders on and have moved farther upstream to the area most of the fish are.

I don't take Liv in the water. The current is a little strong at times, and a lot of knowing when or where to go is based on the sound of the water flow.

I've almost had it take me out at the knees before.

She shakes her head. *"Phoebe."*

I turn to Phoebe. "Do you need help?"

"According to Liv, I'm doing it wrong."

I chuckle. "You grew up here and your dad fishes every weekend, so why does it look like you've never touched a pole?"

"I haven't . . ."

"What?"

Phoebe shrugs. "I don't . . . like . . . fish. I don't like to get dirty or touch guts and fish smell. So, my dad would fish, and I would read or sleep. Most of the time, I left early and went to a friend's house."

"So, you have never done this?" I ask again.

"Nope." She turns to Olivia. *"But Olivia is a great teacher."*

Liv beams at the praise. "She was taught by the best."

That earns me an eye roll. I hear Rowan hoot, which means he got something big. I turn to look and Liv notices my attention shift. She pulls my arm. *"Can I go?"*

"Be careful and stay on the bank," I reply, but she's already moving, leaving me here with Phoebe.

"You don't have to do this," she says quickly. "I was just trying to make Olivia happy."

I run my hand through my hair. "Fishing makes her happy. She'll be out of school in two days, and I guarantee she'll want you to bring her here."

"Really? I doubt it. I would bet she likes fishing so much because you like it and she wants to spend time with you."

"If that were true, wouldn't you have wanted to fish with your dad?"

Phoebe stares down the stream and then shrugs. "I guess that's true, but I still went. Especially when I was little. I would do anything to spend time with my dad. He was always working, and Mom was really insistent that he take me. Then it just became what we did. He fished, and I ... didn't."

"He never tried to teach you?" I ask.

She grins. "Oh, he tried, but I couldn't care less. I think I frustrated him that I refused to touch anything."

"Do you want to learn now?"

"Well, only if it's from the best, which you have self-proclaimed."

The Lord is testing me. For some reason, I want to help her. I want to teach her, touch her, and learn all about Phoebe, but I can't understand why. She is not the kind of woman I am attracted to—ones who are younger than my sister, clearly going through some bullshit, and completely off-limits. Yet, here I am, absolutely attracted to her but equally as determined to keep my head on straight. This will be a good test. I can teach her this, be aloof, and prove that this attraction is all in my head.

"All right, you have to hold the pole less like a lifeline and more balanced in your hand," I instruct. "Loosen your grip." I wait until her fingers aren't clutching it or trying to choke it before I nod. "Like that. Perfect."

"So, I should warn you that the last time I did this, I threw the pole into the water because I wasn't holding it tightly enough."

"Don't do that this time."

Phoebe side-eyes me. "I wasn't trying to that time either."

"Okay," I say, moving on. "We won't be casting until later."

"Casting?" she asks.

"Putting the hook in the water to catch the fish."

"That seems like a stupid way to say put the line in the water."

I look heavenward, confused how she doesn't even know what casting is. "I'll let the fishing commission know you don't like their terms."

Her eyes widen. "Is there such a thing? Because I'd like to discuss the options for gear. No one wants to wear those jumpsuit things that your brother and sister have on. They're really freaking ugly."

"They also keep you dry when you're in the middle of the stream."

"Why would someone even want to be in the water in the first place? Isn't it freaking freezing?"

This stream does warm up by the end of the winter, but it feeds off the mountain, so warm is more subjective.

"The waders help."

"And they keep you dry and warm?"

"Do you want to learn to fish or talk about waders?"

"You brought it up!" She huffs. "If the pole goes in—accidentally—you can just walk out there and get it?"

I grumble. "We're not wearing waders, and I don't have a pair with me, so let's just focus on not throwing the pole into the water."

Her shoulders square, and she nods. "Got it. No throwing the pole. Okay, so I hold it gently but firmly?"

"Yes."

"That makes no sense, you know that, right?"

The frustration in her voice makes me smile. "Sure, but it's how you do it. Then you pull the rod back so the hook is behind you and kind of toward your right."

She pulls the rod back way too fast and snags the hook on a branch. "I caught something!"

I fight back my laugh. "Yeah, the tree."

Her gaze moves to the branch. "If I were vegan, it would be a win."

"There's that. Since we're not fishing for oak trees, and you know, we're wanting *fish*. Not a win." I move to the branch and unhook her.

Phoebe sighs and goes to hand me the pole. "I'm totally helpless."

"You're not helpless, you just need to relax. Here." I move behind her, wrap my arms around her, and cover her hands with my own. "Adjust your grip. Perfect. Now, when you pull it back, take it to the side."

I tell myself to let her go, to find another way to instruct her, but I can't move.

Phoebe looks up at me from the corner of her eye. "Like this?"

"Yes, just like this."

Although what I should do is let her toss the pole in the water and cool myself off by going to get it.

No, I got this.

I am a fucking badass who can handle a fishing lesson. I focus back on the task instead of how good her body feels against mine. When I move our arms over her shoulder, she has no choice but to lean back, resting against my chest. She's tense, and a part of me is glad she doesn't seem unaffected. She fits against me perfectly. My voice drops to a soft whisper. "Breathe, Phoebe."

She lets out a slow breath. "Right. Breathe."

We inhale in tandem, and my voice is barely above a whisper when I say, "Fishing is calm and slow." And right now, my heart is anything but those.

"I . . . don't know what to do next."

I close my eyes, breathing her in, and the smell of fresh air and her citrus shampoo has my head spinning. My nose dips into the crook of her neck, and she tilts her head a little. "What do you want to do?" I ask.

This is so fucking wrong. I'm supposed to be helping her, not running my nose down the sleek column of her neck, wishing I could see if she tastes as good as she smells.

Her breathing grows faster. "Tell me what I should do."

Let me kiss your neck.

"Asher?" she asks.

"Yes?"

She shivers in my arms and then turns her head slightly, looking up at me through her lashes. "You . . . your . . . what now?"

I stare down at her and blink when I see the desire swimming in her brown eyes. Desire that shouldn't be there. Desire that is absolutely mirrored in mine.

I can't do this. I can't lust after her. She's much too young. She's my daughter's nanny and my boss's daughter.

I step back and clear my throat, hating that the loss of her feels as though ice has been dumped over my head. "Then you just swing the pole forward so the line comes with it."

A tremor runs through Phoebe, and she turns to look at me. "I . . . think I hear Brynn. I should go." She hands me the pole. "You know . . . check on Liv, too. Thanks for the lesson."

I watch her walk away, remembering how good it felt to hold her close.

seven

PHOEBE

"When are you heading back to Cloverleigh?" I ask Emmeline as her face fills my phone. I've missed her so much.

"Tomorrow. Dad and my aunt Chloe are way too excited. Apparently, there's a lot for me to help with since the wedding season is approaching."

Emmeline's family owns one of the most stunning wedding venues in Michigan. It has a five-star resort, restaurant, vineyard, and the whole family works there. She is going for her MBA so that she can help take over the front office when she graduates.

"Hey, you get to learn from your dad all your weird math stuff you geek out about."

Emmeline lifts one shoulder. "That's if I don't get stuck serving, which I'm happy to do even if it is the worst. We're sort of a do-whatever-task-you-can family."

"It's the same here, only I'm voluntold what I'm going to do." Like nannying when I never had any plans to. "I'm sure you're excited to see your sisters."

She smiles at that. "They're great and all, but I really can't wait to see my nieces and nephews. Everyone is getting big so fast."

"I'm sure your older sisters felt the same about you since there's such a big age gap," I say with a laugh. "And I'm super jealous you have this big family that you get to spend time with. It's just Daddy and me here."

"You say that, but it's also not always great having a million eyes watching your every move." Maybe not because of having a big family, but she has no idea what it was like being raised by a cop and this town. "Anyway, how is work? When are you nannying again?"

"First thing in the morning." Tomorrow is when I will not remember how it felt to be cocooned by Asher, which is something I'm still struggling with. I swear I can still feel his heart beat and the warmth of his hands as they wrapped around mine. All of it felt so good, and that is so damn bad. "He's on a three-day shift again, so I'll be there that whole time. Then I am bringing her to her appointment in Philly on Monday, another appointment on Tuesday, and then he has another three-day starting Wednesday. It's an entire week of staying at Asher's house."

Emmy leans forward, resting her head on her hand. "I know you're excited about the doctors at least."

"I am. I get to meet Dr. King, but who knows if I'll make a good impression."

"And is her dad still giving you shit all the time?"

No, he's giving me something much more complicated. "Uh, no. Not . . . exactly."

"Oh? When did that change?"

"About seventeen hours ago."

"Spill it."

There's no point in holding back. "Okay, I went down to the creek with his sister, Brynlee, to fish with Asher, Olivia, and Rowan, who is Asher's brother. You know I don't do any of that, but Brynn likes it and Olivia really wanted me to learn."

Emmeline laughs. "That sounds like a disaster waiting to happen."

"Yeah, it really was. I caught the tree and never got my line . . .

76

hook . . . whatever in the water, but—" I pause, feeling strange talking about it. Not just because I clearly make bad decisions when it comes to men, but also because I think it's all in my head. "Asher was teaching me."

"That was nice of him to put a pause on thinking you're a total dumbass." I tilt my head and raise my brow. She purses her lips. "It wasn't?"

"Sure, I guess. We can go with that. Also, he doesn't think that anymore. I've more than proven myself, and Olivia loves me."

"Good to know, but tell me what happened with Asher?"

I don't know how to phrase or explain it since I can't really wrap my head around it still. However, maybe talking about it will help?

"Ugh. He had to show me—like, touch me to show me, if that makes sense."

"Did he come onto you?" Her voice gets animated as she perks up.

"I think so . . . I don't know."

"Tell. Me. Everything."

I go over the entire encounter, explaining how I felt his nose brush along my neck and the way his voice was like sandpaper on silk. It was scratchy in all the right ways and yet smooth as well.

"I'm not normal," I say at the end.

"Why?"

"Because, seriously, what is it with me and guys who are completely off-limits? Does my mind not know any other way? My entire life was flipped upside down because I slept with my stupid professor, and now I can't stop thinking about sleeping with my boss. I think I need therapy."

Emmeline snorts. "That is true, but who cares? He's your boss, not your professor. Your life isn't going to be ruined because you want him. Also, can we just, for one second, look at the bright side to this?"

"There's a bright side?"

"Yes! You thought you loved Jonathan. You thought what you

guys had was 'life-altering,' and you'd never feel the same about anyone else, but clearly, you were wrong. If you loved him so much, you wouldn't be dreaming of being handcuffed by your hot cop boss."

I'm starting to think all my relationships are unhealthy. "As my best friend, your advice sucks."

"You're twenty-four. You're single and know for an absolute fact he is not married. Plus, you leave in, like, three months for your new school."

"*If* I get into anywhere!"

"You will," she says as though it's a fact. "I say . . . sleep with him."

I shake my head, refusing to let any of this seem like a good idea. "Emmeline, I love you, but you are truly the worst. I have made so many damn mistakes, and I don't want to make another one. He's my boss, and he works for my dad. Can you even imagine how that would go over if my *dad* ever found out? Jesus, he'd have a heart attack! Not to mention the only thing my father has ever asked me when it comes to men is that I never, ever date a cop. Which Asher is. Plus, there's Olivia, who I adore, and I . . . no. Bad idea all around, and I am really tired of making bad choices."

She lets out a long sigh. "This is the time in our life to make them. You're going to finish grad school and then have to do how many years as an intern where you'll work nonstop? If he wants you and you want him, I don't see a problem. Your dad doesn't need to know who you hook up with. If you and Asher lay out the ground rules, then Olivia isn't an issue either because, again, it's not like you have to *tell her*."

As much as I *really* don't want to think about any of this and wish I could unhear it, I can't. The way he touched me, said my name, and ugh, the heat of his body is all my mind keeps going back to.

I am supposed to dislike this man and all I can think about is him pushing me against a wall and making me scream his name.

"Thank you for the horrible advice, but I will not be doing any of that, as I need this job and don't need to complicate my life any further."

"I'm glad you have a plan."

"I do."

"And it's solid."

"It is," I say back.

"And you don't want him that way."

I hesitate and then force the words out. "I don't."

"And you're a big fat liar."

I groan. "I am, but I will not flirt or do anything stupid."

I fix my hair, fluffing it a little, apply some lip gloss, check my face in the rearview, and then groan. *What are you doing, Phoebe?*

Getting dolled up is not how I am going to keep my promise of staying away from him. I grab a tissue, wipe away the gloss, and then toss my hair up in a messy bun. There, that's better. I grab my duffle bag and head toward the house.

After pressing the four-digit code to the front door, I enter. There's noise in the kitchen, which is probably Asher getting ready to leave.

"Hello?" I call out, not wanting to startle the man with a gun.

"In here," he replies.

I head in to find him sitting at the table with a plate of eggs, bacon, and toast in front of him as he scrolls through something on his phone. "Hey," he says.

"Hey."

He doesn't look up at me. "I made a lot of eggs."

"Okay . . ."

"Grab some if that's what you want."

What I want is for him to look at me with your normal hatred so I can tell myself I was imagining whatever happened the other day.

"No thanks."

"Suit yourself."

Okay, being dismissive and barely talking is more like the asshole I know and can keep hating.

"What time does Olivia need to be up?"

"No idea."

Still not looking at me.

I purse my lips. "All right, I'll check the binder."

"Good call."

I feel a little stupid standing here, so I grab my bag and head to my room. Once there, I put some stuff in the dresser and wonder where the sweet guy from the other day went—not that I want to see him because this aloof asshole is not someone I'm attracted to, which is good.

This is all good.

I don't want him. I just wanted someone to make me feel good. Ha. Problem solved.

I do not want Asher Whitlock. I just want to be loved.

I laugh once, smiling at the fact that I figured out what the actual problem is, and head back to the kitchen, not feeling nervous at all.

He's still sitting there, head down in his phone.

"I am going to take Olivia to the nail salon today, is that okay?"

"Well, you just told me what you were doing and asked if you could do it in the same sentence, so which one am I supposed to go with?"

I groan quietly. "Both. If you say yes, I'm going to need fifty dollars."

Now his head snaps up. "Fifty bucks?"

"Yes, that's for a manicure and a pedicure."

"Is the polish made of gold?"

"Yes, Asher, they put gold flecks in the polish to keep the prices high," I say sarcastically.

He pulls out his wallet and hands me a credit card. "This is for anything Olivia related. If you need gas, use this card. If you need food, use this card."

"If we need a shopping trip in New Jersey?"

"Do not even think about it."

It was worth a try, and we are out of the two-word answer phase.

When I tuck the card in my bra, he gives me a strange look. "What?"

"What the hell did you just do?"

"Umm, nothing."

"Why is the card . . . there." He points to my chest.

"Because that's where girls put their license and credit card when we don't have anywhere else to put it. They don't exactly give us pocket options. Seriously, you've never seen Brynn do it?"

Asher pushes away from the table and grabs his plate. "No."

"Okay, well, now you know. You can't tell me you've never pulled a girl over and she had to fish her license from her bra."

He turns his back to me, putting the dish in the sink, and stays that way. "Sure. I probably have."

Not really sure where we go from here, so I change topics. "Anyway, thanks for the card."

I move toward where the eggs are still sitting on the stove, suddenly hungry, but he shifts at the same time, and our bodies brush against each other. I swear, there are sparks.

My skin tingles where we touched, and his gaze finds mine, those aqua eyes swimming with something I can't name. We are standing so close that his chest will press to mine if he takes a deep breath, and the sudden closeness sends my mind into a sea of nothingness. All I can feel and think is Asher. I inhale, and the musk, oak, and hint of spice that is his cologne overpowers my senses, but it's the way he's staring at me that makes my heart race.

How I watch the color of his irises shift from deep blue back to light as he tracks his gaze to my chest for just a moment. I wonder if he's remembering what he saw that first night when I accidentally flashed him.

I'm not imagining this. He wants me, and God, I want him too.

"I need to go to work." Only he doesn't move.

"I have to go too." The tension mounts, and my heart is pounding so hard that I might pass out.

Asher's eyes travel down my face and stop at my chest again. "We . . . are both busy."

I nod, knowing I can't speak with the tightness in my throat.

He finally steps back, running his hand over his face. "I'll be late, so don't wait up."

I manage to swallow and force the words out. "I won't."

Hell, I'll be in bed before Olivia if I have to.

He walks out, and I crumple against the counter, using my arms to hold me up. Yeah, about that problem . . .

eight

PHOEBE

"*Do you miss your mom all the time?*" Olivia asks from her seat in the pedicure chair next to mine.

She had a rough morning. Sara hasn't been able to call in two days because she's in an area where she can't get reliable reception, so she's had to rely on email. When Olivia was crying, I held her, and then she asked about my parents.

Talking about my mother is never something I like to do. Not because I don't think about her or miss her, but because it's so hard because I miss her so much.

"*I do.*"

"*I miss my mom.*"

I give her a sad smile. "*I am sure she misses you more. I know it's hard, but your mom will be home before you know it.*"

Olivia looks down at her feet, swishing them in the water before looking back at me. "*I am sorry.*"

"*For what?*" I sign.

"*Making you talk about her.*"

I reach out, resting my hand on her arm, and shake my head before signing, "*Don't be sorry. I always want to help you.*"

In such a short time, I have gotten attached to this little girl. She's so smart and vibrant. I enjoy spending time with her, and the more time that passes, the more I really hope Asher doesn't find a replacement nanny.

I want to be her friend, and being her nanny has given me this one thing that I seem to be good at.

I wish, more than anything, that I could give her the gift of sound. I asked Sara a few days ago about her hearing loss, just so I had a better grasp on it.

Technology changes so quickly, and I have to hope we will have something for her one day that will help.

"Thank you for being my friend."

"I am the one who is grateful," I tell her.

The technician starts the feet part and Olivia giggles relentlessly. I laugh because I know there's no controlling it when you're ticklish. She squirms in her seat, head back and laughter so loud that people are turning to look. She has no idea of her volume, and it's really adorable.

One of the women beside me scoffs. "Inappropriate."

I turn, my eyes narrowed. "What did you say?"

"You heard me." She looks at Liv and my blood boils.

"You need to shut your mouth, lady."

"Excuse me?"

"I said shut up. She's a kid, and she's ticklish."

The woman with her nose upturned shakes her head. "She should learn some self-control. Excuse me, little girl? Miss. Young. Lady!" Olivia clearly can't hear her. "And she's rude on top of it. If she were my daughter—"

I cut her off, unwilling to let her say another word. Not that Olivia can hear her, but I don't care. "But she's not your daughter. Thank God for that since you're a miserable hag, but put that aside, she didn't ignore you because she's rude, she ignored you because she's Deaf. She has no idea how loud she is, and I'm not going to stop or quiet her as you couldn't imagine what she probably fears in this exact situation, some bitch not understanding she can't regulate her sound."

When I turn back, Olivia is quiet as she watches me. *"What's wrong?"* she signs.

I speak so the bitch beside me can hear and sign as well. *"Nothing. The woman was saying how beautiful your laugh is."*

Olivia's entire face brightens, and she smiles at her with a wave.

I turn, glaring because if she does anything to upset Olivia, Asher is going to be taking me out of here in cuffs.

She's lucky she has the decency to wave back.

God, I hate people.

We finish up without anyone else saying a word, Olivia beaming as she looks at her nails and toes. When we get back to the house, Liv asks if she can play her video game, which I say yes to because the kid deserves some fun.

She told me about her friends on the gaming system. A few are deaf as well and they type their messages to each other while they play the game, building a world together. It's kind of cool when you think about it.

While she's up in her play area, I open my laptop and go through emails.

I delete a ton of junk mail, a reminder to pay my credit card bill, and then find a response from Professor Calloway.

Hello Phoebe,

I hope this email finds you doing well. Of course, I will help in any way that I can with your transfer. I've attached a recommendation letter as well as some contacts I think can be of help. My close friend is influential in the Dallas program, and I took the liberty of sending him a personal email on your behalf. Also, with your permission, I'd like to reach out to someone in your area who is doing a lot of great things, just in case the transfer doesn't work out. I look forward to hearing from you.

Sincerely,
    Debbie Calloway

I reply immediately.

Professor Calloway,

Thank you for your kind words and the letter of recommendation. I would appreciate you reaching out to whomever you think I would be a good fit for. Obviously, I was behind on the dates to transfer, but I have reached out to each school and asked for an exception. Luckily, two programs have already granted me the ability to submit, and surely with your letter, it will go a long way. I truly appreciate all your guidance and help with my future endeavors.

Best,
    Phoebe Bettencourt

This woman is a saint, and I am eternally grateful I was able to take her class. Professor Calloway is one of the best speech pathologists in the country, and her class was truly inspiring. I was fortunate to learn from her.

I attach the letter she wrote with the rest of my documentation and send it to both Texas and Vanderbilt. Both are amazing schools, and I pray I get into one of them. It will be a lot easier to explain to my father that I transferred instead of having to tell him I left the program in Iowa and was never going back.

The doorbell rings, and I get up to see who could be here. I smile when I see it's Mrs. Arrowood with a basket in her hand.

"Hi, Mrs. A."

She smiles. "Can I come in?"

"Of course, yes. What are you doing here?"

"I brought goodies." She extends the basket. The smell of freshly baked muffins and cookies fills the room, and my mouth waters.

Oh, I so want these. "Thank you, this was so nice."

"Well, both of my girls are gone, and I can't seem to stop baking once school is over. I tend to bring baskets around to everyone."

"I'm sure the town loves it," I say, knowing they all must. Mrs. Arrowood always had different treats in school. "How is Bethanne?"

Bethanne was four years behind me in school, and we both were cheerleaders, but I haven't seen her since I graduated.

"She's great. She's in college, doing well and studying accounting, which I never would've guessed she'd enjoy. I honestly thought she'd follow her father and join the military. Lord knows she would've enjoyed watching my hair turn gray." We both laugh. "But we all know she never would've been able to follow rules, so it's for the best. Anyway, how are you settling in now that you're back in town?"

I let out a long breath and lift one shoulder. "You know, it's Sugarloaf. I love it and hate it all at the same time."

"Home is a funny place, isn't it?"

"It is."

She takes a seat on the couch, and I take the spot next to her. "I struggled for a long time with this place. It holds both good and equally as horrible memories. Connor is the same way, but we could never bring ourselves to leave either. It's not the town that makes a home, though, it's the people and what we go through that brings us somewhere—like back home." Her smile is warm, and I swear this woman can read my mind.

I may not have a mother anymore, but Mrs. Arrowood is sort

of everyone's mom, and I find myself desperate to tell her about what happened.

"Mrs. A?"

"Please call me Ellie. You've been out of school a long time."

That's never going to happen. "Mrs. A, can I tell you something that I need to stay between us?"

"Of course, Phoebe. I would never betray your trust."

And I know she wouldn't. "I don't have my mom anymore, and I can't talk to my dad. My best friend is unhinged with her advice, and . . . I don't know."

Ellie reaches forward, her hand resting on mine. "You can tell me anything, Phoebe. I do my best not to judge others since I have my fair share of mistakes."

"You always were my favorite."

She leans in. "You were mine too."

I laugh and then exhale. "Okay, so my life is a mess. I came home early from school because I was stupid and got caught being stupid. It was just so much."

"Are you in trouble?"

"No, not like that. Nothing that I can't get out of, but I feel like I don't know who I am right now. It's like all the things the town said about how immature and stupid I was, became that in some ways."

Mrs. Arrowood scoffs. "Don't be ridiculous, Phoebe. You're not who anyone proclaims you to be. You're who you are, and no one makes the right choice every time. It's not possible. If it were, we wouldn't have that saying about hindsight. You aren't the mistakes you make—you are how you respond to those."

I let that sink in, my chest tight as I think about how I handled it. I ran, but I don't feel like it was running so much as self-preservation. The post was so bad. It was so mortifying to find out that I was *that* girl. I was holding him, leaning in to kiss him like I'd done a hundred times before, and right next to that picture, there was a picture of him and his wife and son. Oh, God, I could throw up just thinking about it.

I read every single one.

Some I've memorized.

All I wish I could forget.

"And what if I make more mistakes?" Like this feeling I have with Asher.

Her lips mash into a thin line. "Then you, my darling, are human and will find a way through it."

Then I tell her everything about Jonathan and lift a huge weight off my shoulders.

nine

ASHER

My shift is over, and I am beat. I grab my gear and start to head out, but as soon as I reach the door, Chief Bettencourt calls my name and waves me toward his office.

"Hey, Chief, what's up?"

"Nothing, just wanted to see how the call went this afternoon?" he asks as I take a seat.

"I think we handled everything well and it resolved peacefully, which was the desired outcome."

Thank God for that. Rarely do I have to assemble the SWAT team, but this was a close call. It was a domestic call that escalated when we were informed of possible weapons and that the suspect had priors.

Thankfully, there was only a short standoff before we were able to get him to comply.

"He surrendered without provocation?"

"He did after some convincing. We were able to take him in, but she wasn't willing to talk or press charges, so he'll most likely be released. The bruises on her face were enough for us to remove him from the home at least."

He huffs once. "I wish the laws were different and victims were more willing to come forward. We've had a few instances, and I'll never forget responding to Ellie's call. Still haunts me to this day."

"Thankfully, that ended well," I say, not sure what else to say at this point. Ellie Arrowood's ex-husband was a horrible bastard. Kevin caught Ellie trying to leave him and lost his mind. Hadley ran to the neighbor for help, called the cops, and then went to her house to try to stop him. She and Connor have been married for a few years now.

Still, it was one of those cautionary tales about falling in love with the wrong guy.

"Hopefully, the laws will change so more people are willing to press charges. I know Sydney has been working hard at a reform bill."

He nods. "She's a good egg that one."

Everyone loves Sydney Arrowood. She handled my mother's estate. Mom moved back here when Brynlee was in middle school. After her fourth divorce, she decided maybe she should stay single, return home, and take care of my grandparents. We all agreed that was a wise choice, especially after being married to the douchebag that is Brynn's father.

"She was a big help when my mother passed away."

He gives me a sad smile. While my mother was a disaster in the love department, always finding the rotten apples, she excelled in every other part of her life. Her kindness was unparalleled, which made her loved by this community.

"No one in this town was sweeter than your mother, and I miss her. She was a good friend."

"I do too."

Her cancer diagnosis rocked our family. Brynlee was only fifteen, and I immediately moved back to take care of them both. Mom was gone two months after I got here. Rowan came once he quit school to help, and Grady, well, he marches to the beat of his own drum. His navy career was just starting, and there was no way he could do anything but wish me luck.

"You boys have done a good job with Brynlee," he praises.

I think we have too.

She gave me the chance to screw her up so when I had my own kid, I wasn't a total shit parent. When Sara told me she was pregnant, I didn't freak out or wonder what I was going to do—okay, maybe I had a little. Neither of us were exactly happy, but it was the hand we were dealt, and I stepped up immediately.

"She would probably disagree, but she's alive and has all her appendages."

Chief Bettencourt laughs. "I felt the same way about Phoebe." Ahh, Phoebe, the one who is currently watching my entire world and who I can't seem to stop remembering seeing half naked on the floor. "When her mother passed, I wasn't sure what I would do. I had this fourteen-year-old kid, no clue about anything to do with her school, activities, or day-to-day life. Of course, no one expects tragedy."

It's funny how the mind works, considering what we do. How many times have we walked to someone's door after a car crash to give them bad news? Too many to count. We just never think it'll happen to us.

"No, we don't, but thankfully, Sara is organized and has a living life bible for that kid. If something were to happen, I wouldn't even miss a beat. I'd just need to find long-term childcare."

I'd probably have to quit my job.

"I'm glad Phoebe came home early and could help you out with Olivia."

I would be glad too if I didn't think about fucking her six ways till Sunday. However, the one thing no one seems to be asking is why, exactly, Phoebe came back home a month before school ended, but you know what? I don't give a shit. All I want is for Liv to have childcare who can sign.

Which is Phoebe.

"Me too. I'm glad you were able to get her to agree."

He laughs once. "I think that girl would've agreed to carry

95

cows by hand if it meant she could avoid telling me what's going on."

So, he thinks there's something too. I remind myself that it's not my problem. "I'm sure she'll tell you when she's ready."

"Not if she's anything like her mother." He sighs. "Anyway, I just wanted to see how today went and let you know that I am going out of town for a few days next month. You'll be acting chief during that time."

"Me?" I ask, confused. The last time he went away, he had someone brought in.

"You're the most competent officer I have, and I need someone who I trust and knows this office. You've done well with commanding the SWAT team, so it isn't as if you can't handle an office of four. Unless you're not sure you can manage?"

"Of course I can do it."

I'm just surprised he went this route. Not because I don't think I'm competent or can do the job but because, last year, an assistant chief position opened, and I thought he would consider me, but he didn't. Instead, he went with someone from another town, which didn't last. He moved here, hated the fact he couldn't get groceries or fast food delivered, and was gone within six months.

Since then, the position has been vacant.

"Listen, I know I pissed you off when I hired Bentley last year, but I didn't think you were fully ready or that you'd like the position."

"You didn't even give me a chance."

"No, I didn't, but I am now for a few days, to see how it goes."

Good. I can more than do the job, and it would mean being off the patrol. I'd be able to have a more stable schedule, which in turn makes figuring out childcare less of a nightmare. It would mean giving up the SWAT team, but in the long run, it would be much better.

"I appreciate that, Chief."

He stands, extending his hand to me. "If you can handle Phoebe for the next few months, you can handle anything."

And with that ringing endorsement, I head home.

I drive the eight minutes—I grin because Phoebe was wrong about the time—back to my house.

When I get there, Olivia is sitting on the couch with her laptop. I flicker the lights so Olivia will look up. Her smile makes the whole shit day disappear.

"Hi, Dad."

I smile. *"Hi, Olivia. It's late,"* I tell her.

She shrugs. *"I couldn't sleep until I saw you."*

It's definitely past what Sara would demand be her bedtime, but the kid is almost ten and it's summer vacation.

"I'm home now, why couldn't you sleep?"

"Someone at the store said you could be hurt."

I jerk my head back at that. *"Not at all."*

"You were with someone with a gun?"

I sigh heavily and pull her to my chest. I know I shouldn't think of this as a blessing, but one of the things I've never really worried about is Olivia hearing about the dangers of my job. I'm able to shield her from worrying about a lot of nothing.

Sugarloaf is really pretty uneventful, and the SWAT team has only been called out twice this year. It's not something that's utilized a lot, but we need to have one.

I release her and wait until her eyes meet mine and sign. *"It was not a gun, and I was completely safe."*

Olivia doesn't say anything, she just wraps her arms around me again. I hold my daughter, hating that she was scared or worried.

Phoebe comes out of the left hallway and sighs heavily when she sees me. Jesus fucking Lord, does this woman own clothes that aren't designed to try to kill me? She's in those damn shorts again and a cut-up sweatshirt that just lets the littlest bit of her stomach show.

She smiles. "Hey, you're home." Her hand goes up to stop me

from speaking. "I know it's past Olivia's bedtime, but I thought it was best she saw you in the flesh. I've been that kid, worried about her dad because she heard about something happening while he was at work. She was worried no matter what I told her."

"It's fine," I assure her.

Olivia sits up as I speak and looks to Phoebe, who smiles down at her. *"See, totally fine."*

"You could've had her call me," I tell Phoebe.

"I could've, but we watched a movie and just waited. Sometimes you need to actually see your dad and hug him."

"You speak from experience?"

She shrugs, her coffee mug in her hand. "I am a police officer's daughter. It comes with the territory."

I lift Olivia's chin so she can read my lips. "Go to bed, I'll come up in a minute."

My daughter nods, walks over to Phoebe, and the two of them sign back and forth, but I don't catch all of it. Phoebe winks at her, nods twice, then Liv runs up the stairs to her room.

"What did she say?"

"She asked if I would come up to say good night and if we could watch the next *High School Musical* tomorrow."

"She likes you a lot. It seems she's forgiven you for letting her chop off her hair."

She huffs. "Yes, imagine that . . . maybe you should try working on that too."

"I have forgiven you. I just haven't forgotten."

"In your old age? Must be taking your Gingko Biloba daily," she teases.

"I'm far from old."

"You're much closer than I am, buddy. You're what? Forty? I can't remember how old all you Whitlocks are."

I'm much too old for her. "I'm thirty-eight."

"See? You're pushing forty while I'm still in my prime."

She absolutely is.

I clear my throat. "Go on up, I'm going to change, and then I'll come say good night to her." Maybe I'll get my head out of my ass while I'm at it.

Phoebe walks away, and I head to my room. I really don't know why I'm so attracted to that woman. She's every damn thing I hate—flighty, young, flighty, irresponsible, young. I say those words over and over hoping to drill it into my head. She's fucking younger than my sister.

But there's something about her sarcastic mouth and how she pushes back that is incredibly sexy.

I put my gun in the safe, hang up my uniform, and change into gym shorts and a T-shirt. When I make it upstairs, Phoebe is still there, sitting on the edge of Olivia's bed, grinning as they sign back and forth. There are no words coming out of Phoebe's mouth, but her lips are moving so Liv can read them.

She's really good with her. For all my hesitation, it's clear Livvy really likes her.

They laugh, and then Phoebe pulls the blanket up, tucking her in.

Olivia looks over, waving. *"How did you know I was here?"* I ask her, already knowing the answer.

"I smelled your cologne."

While she may not be able to hear, her other senses are not dull at all. She feels vibrations, smells, and feels shifts sooner than anyone else in the room.

As I move closer, Phoebe stands and then leaves us alone.

"I like Phoebe."

"I can tell."

"She's fun, and she doesn't treat me like a little kid," she tells me.

"You are a little kid."

Olivia scoffs. *"I'm almost ten."*

I eye her. *"You just turned nine."*

"Ten is next."

I smile and then kiss the top of her head. *"It's late. Get some sleep. I love you."*

She lifts her hand, making the I love you sign, and I do the same so we can touch each finger together. I've done this with her for so long that it's become our version of a secret handshake.

I head down the stairs to find Phoebe in the kitchen, singing to herself—much quieter this time—as she washes the dishes. The desire to go behind her, wrap my arms around her, and kiss the crook of her neck is . . . ridiculous. It's fucking ridiculous.

I do the only thing I can do, which is to walk away and lock myself in my damn room until she falls asleep.

ten

PHOEBE

Last final finished.

I smile and close my laptop. Nothing like burning the midnight oil. I worked really hard on this sixteen-page paper about the evolution of hearing aids and what needs to be done going forward.

The research part was mind numbing. But I kept imagining how I would've felt if it were Olivia going through the different treatments, and I started to really get into it. Especially once I hit my stride about the future.

However, my future requires sustenance right now. I am freaking starving.

I head to the kitchen for a bag of chips but stop when I get to the living room and see the television on.

Hopefully Olivia didn't come down when she should be asleep. When I reach the recliner, I find Asher there, remote in his hand, snoring.

God, he's so cute. His dark brown hair is pushed to the left and the scruff on his face makes him look rugged. He shifts a little, still fast asleep, so I grab the blanket off the back of the couch and drape it over him.

The urge to run my fingers through his thick hair is so great that I can't stop myself. Asher lets out a soft sigh as I do it a second time.

Then his eyes fly open as his hand wraps around my wrist.

Shit.

He stares at me, breath coming fast.

"I just put a blanket on you. I didn't mean to wake you."

He closes his eyes for a second and then opens them. "Sorry."

"I'm sorry too. You were asleep, and I just thought you might be cold."

He releases my wrist and then stands. "I wasn't."

"Right. Sorry."

I rush into the kitchen to grab the food because I don't want to look like a total idiot. Gah. The last thing I should've done was touch him. What the hell was I thinking? I am so stupid.

Exiting the kitchen, I see him standing in the hall between our rooms.

"Thank you for putting the blanket on me. That's what I meant to say."

I nod. "Sure." There's this thick, uncomfortable energy between us, and I speak to try to eliminate it. "I yelled at someone today because she was being a bitch to Olivia."

Asher's face shifts, and his jaw grows tight. "What happened?"

"This lady didn't know she was Deaf, and I got pissed. I don't know if you'll hear about it, but people have big mouths and like to gossip. It wasn't a huge deal. I just wouldn't let anyone be rude to her."

He steps closer. "Who was she?"

"I don't know her," I admit.

He takes another step. "What did she say?"

Asher is so close I have to tilt my head back to look at him. "She thought her laughter was obnoxious and that Olivia was ignoring her when she tried to get her attention."

"And what did you do?"

"I told her to shut up."

He grins. "Good."

My heart is racing so hard that I can't focus. I want to kiss him. Oh God, I want to kiss him so much.

Asher's hand rests on the wall beside my head as he leans in so that there's practically no room between us.

I force both hands to stay at my sides, both clenching the items there.

"This is bad," he admits, his voice barely a whisper. "I shouldn't . . . want this."

"Want what?" I breathe the words, not wanting to break the spell.

"You."

I don't know where my courage comes from, but that word snaps my control. I drop the food and reach for him as he slides his arms behind my back, pulling me up. My legs wrap around his middle, and Asher pushes me against the wall.

Then his lips are on mine.

My hands hold his face, loving the way the scruff pricks at my skin. He moans into my mouth, and then his tongue slides against mine.

He anchors me with his hips, kissing me deeper as his one hand moves to my breast. "I've thought about you, your mouth, your body, these perfect tits and how much I want to lick them."

My head falls back, breath escaping like a hiss. "I have too."

"Do you want that, Phoebe? Do you want me to taste your perfect skin?"

No. God, maybe. Yes, yes, yes.

I nod.

He chuckles, his tongue running down my neck where his nose traced the other day. "I want to hear you tell me. I want the words, beautiful, sinful girl."

"Yes. Kiss me."

Asher's mouth finds mine again, and I sink into the delicious heat of it. I want him so much, and even though I know how wrong this is, I just can't stop it.

His hand finds the bottom of my sweatshirt, pushing up along my bare skin until his palm cups my breast, and he groans.

I removed my bra when I was taking my test. Now I'm grateful because he has unfettered access.

"You are trying to kill me, aren't you?"

"Definitely not."

"That's what you're doing, walking around here in those shorts and no bra, looking far too fucking perfect. You're sin, Phoebe, and I am going to hell."

"Take me with you."

That earns me a grin, and then his mouth is on my breast. He runs his tongue around my nipple, sucking and flicking it quickly. I grip his hair, holding him there. Never have I felt this good. I whimper as he pulls back and blows cool air on my taut nipple before taking it deeper into his mouth.

"Asher," I say, feeling so much.

The heat of desire, the fear of regret, the need for more of this —of him.

All of it wars within me, knowing we shouldn't do this and not caring enough to stop.

And then, like cold water on a burning fire, a noise stops us both—Olivia's bedside alarm blares.

He drops me, my feet slamming to the ground, and he pulls back, staring at me like he can't believe I'm here and wishes I weren't.

eleven

ASHER

F uck.

Fuck, I wasn't thinking.

I never should've touched her. I fucking swore I wouldn't, but then she told me about the salon and how she stood up for Olivia, and I've never wanted to kiss anyone that much.

So, I did.

Now my throat is tight, and I'm struggling to gain control of the situation.

And . . . I'm a fucking piece of shit.

"I'll go," I say.

Phoebe's hand is covering her mouth, and she looks at me, her gaze watery.

"No, I should go to her." Phoebe tries to walk away, but I step in front of her.

"I will go to Olivia, please go to your room and lock the fucking door."

"But?"

I stare at her, wanting more even when every part of me knows I shouldn't. "Lock it."

I push past her, needing not to see her lips, her eyes, or her perfect body. There is no way to unsee, untaste, or unfeel her skin and mouth.

She is every goddamn fantasy I ever wanted.

Taking the stairs two at a time, I put Phoebe and what just happened behind me. I walk into Liv's room and find her sitting up in bed with tears streaming down her face. Her bedside light is dimly lit, and I reset the alarm button.

"What's wrong?" I ask, sitting on her bed.

"Bad dream," she signs before launching herself at me. I hold her, feeling the tremors run through her body.

Slowly, her breathing calms down, and my rioting emotions do as well. She sniffs a few more times and then pulls back.

I brush her hair off her cheek. *"What was the dream?"*

She looks away and then back to me. *"I was alone and running. I couldn't see anything, but I knew I was scared. Someone was after me, and I couldn't get help."*

My heart breaks at the haunted look in her eyes. *"You're not alone."*

"I know."

"I'm always here."

She nods. *"It was a dream."*

Yes, but sometimes dreams feel so real that, when you wake, you aren't sure if it really happened. I kiss her forehead and tap her nose. *"I love you, and nothing is chasing you. You did the right thing calling for me."*

Her eyes go to the door, and I half expect to see Phoebe there, but she's not.

Olivia turns to me, and I wonder if she wanted her and is wondering why she didn't come. I turn her face to me. *"I told Phoebe I would come and she should stay."*

Liv gives me a sad smile. *"I wanted you, anyway."*

I grin. *"I'm glad."* She hugs me again, and I squeeze her tightly before pulling back. *"Are you okay?"*

"Yes." She yawns. *"Thank you."*

I wink. *"Anything for you."*

Once she's all tucked in, I head to her doorway. She rolls over, back to me, and I stand here watching. In Olivia's life, she's dealt with a lot of shit. Doctors, exams, nonstop running around, and then being tossed back and forth between my and Sara's places. Losing her long-time nanny wasn't easy either. Yet, she's proved her resilience time and time again.

I don't know how many times a kid can feel this kind of struggle and come out on top.

I close her door and head down the stairs, tensing as I near my hallway. Like a coward, I peek toward Phoebe's door before walking into the hall, making sure it's closed, and for both our sakes, I hope she locked it.

As soon as I reach my door, hers opens. "Asher?"

My head thuds against the heavy oak as her voice washes over me. "I told you to lock the door."

"And I did. However, you didn't say for how long."

I swear to Christ. "Until we both aren't idiots, that's for how long."

"Well, then it seems we're never leaving our rooms, are we?"

I turn to look at her, keeping my back against the door. "What happened . . . it was wrong."

"It wasn't wrong, but it shouldn't have happened."

"You're damn right it shouldn't have. Your father is my boss, and you're Olivia's nanny, for fuck's sake!"

She shrugs. "All of that is true."

"Right, so it was wrong. If that alarm didn't . . ." I run my hand through my hair. "It won't happen again."

If I say it enough, maybe I'll believe it.

"That's what I wanted to say. I don't know what happened, but it's clear we weren't thinking. I like hanging out with Olivia and helping her with things. I don't want to screw this up."

"So, we agree that was a mistake?"

Her pouty lips form into a fake smile. "It was a mistake. Good night, Asher."

I turn the handle, opening my door. "Good night, Phoebe." I step inside and close the door on her and any feelings I had.

"Why the hell are you so grumpy?" Brynn asks as she sits across from me at Sugarlips. "Is it because Magnolia keeps giving you come-fuck-me eyes?"

I hadn't even noticed she'd come to the table. All I keep thinking about is how bad I fucked up by touching Phoebe.

We managed to avoid each other this morning, which probably had a lot to do with my leaving at four in the morning. Not a chance in hell I was going to try for small talk. I worked out for three hours at the gym, sweating and pushing myself to the limit.

All was going well on shift until my sister showed up, reminding me we had a lunch date before her trial this afternoon.

"I'm not grumpy."

"And what, my darling brother, do we call this . . . attitude?"

"Tired."

Which is true. I didn't sleep for shit last night, and if I am grumpy, it's from lack of sleep.

Brynn swirls her spoon in her coffee. "If you say so."

She doesn't deserve my attitude. "I'm sorry."

"It's fine. I'm used to you and the other two being assholes."

No lies there. "Let's start over. You wanted to have lunch because?"

She leans back, her hands go to her lap, and she sighs deeply. It's basically her go-to posture when she's being evasive, or she's uncomfortable.

This is going to piss me off, I know it.

"I heard from my biological father three days ago."

Yup. Right over the edge.

"What did he want?"

Money if history proves correct. Rowan, Grady, and I all have the same father, who was our mom's first husband. She had us pretty much back-to-back, but he decided that life was too short for kids and left. Brynlee's dad was her fourth husband, who was the worst of all of them.

"He said he's clean now and wanted to talk."

My sister doesn't need my attitude, but I am struggling to keep my mouth shut. "Howie doesn't usually just want to talk."

She places her clasped hands on the table. "He needs a liver transplant."

And there it is. "Why didn't you lead with that?"

"Oh, I don't know, Ash, maybe because it's no secret you hate him."

"Of course I hate him. He's a fucking piece of shit who hasn't called you in how long? Years? And now he needs something so he picks up the phone? Where was he when Mom died? Where was he when you . . ." I release a calming breath. Brynn is a grown-up now, she doesn't need me to flip out. "I'm sorry, Brynn. It's just that every time he comes around, you end up hurt."

"I knew you wouldn't approve, but I'd hoped you'd understand."

Her face falls, making me feel like the worst possible human. My sister's heart is a hundred times too good for this world. No matter what she's going through, she's loving, forgiving, and understanding.

It's easy for me to hate Howie, but . . . that's her father.

It doesn't matter that he walked away when she needed him, she still wants to know she's loved by him.

"I understand, Brynn. I just wish he wasn't the man he is. I wish he'd been here to see you graduate, to go to prom, to do all the things that I was so privileged to watch, but he couldn't be bothered."

Brynn's eyes meet mine. "He was drunk and strung out, Asher. He is a raging alcoholic. He has been the worst father, but he's the only one I have. I'm not stupid or blind to what he is. I'm fully aware of his level of selfishness. You, Grady, and Rowan made sure I saw what *good* men are capable of. You three stepped in and became the best father figures I could've ever asked for. Rowan was the fun dad, always in trouble and being an idiot." She laughs. "Grady was the one who helped me see the whole picture when I was confused. And you ... you are the most protective and wonderful man I know. I have the best brothers in the whole world, and that is enough for me. However, I am not the kind of girl who can sit back and let someone die. He's sober, and he needs me to at least see if I'm a match."

"He needs?" I ask.

She shakes her head. "No, *I* need."

I reach my hand out, and she places hers in it. "Then I'll hold your hand and be by your side."

Brynn squeezes my hand once. "Because you're a good man."

I'm really lucky she still believes that of me because, right now, I'm not so sure.

twelve

PHOEBE

"**D**on't be nervous," I tell Olivia as we park the car in the underground lot at Children's Hospital of Philadelphia.

As soon as we got about six miles away, her entire mood shifted. Gone was the girl reading her book, smiling at the words, and texting someone. Instead, it was closed on her lap as she tapped her foot nonstop.

"I'm not."

I tilt my head with a smile. "*No?*"

"*I just wish my dad were here.*"

I wish I *didn't* wish your dad were here.

It had been two days since that incredible kiss. Two days of him leaving before I woke up, working later than before, and heading to his room as soon as he's done checking on Olivia.

Such a fucking chickenshit.

"*I know you do, and I know I'm not a parent, but I'm on your side.*"

"*They always hurt my ears,*" she tells me.

That's not okay. "*If something hurts, squeeze my hand, and I'll stop them.*"

Relief washes across her face, and she nods.

We exit the car and walk up to the audiology department. The hospital is bright with blues and greens on the walls and paint-

117

ings of sea animals moving between the colors. It's whimsical, and yet, it still feels very much like a hospital.

I sign her in, handing the nurse hardcopies of the authorization forms that allow me to be present during Olivia's appointment, which Sara and Asher had already signed and emailed to them.

Liv and I take a seat in the teal chairs that face a television that has closed caption scrolling across the bottom.

She crosses her arms and leans back.

Minutes go by, all with her kind of moping while I take it all in. This is where I want to be. In this hospital, helping children just like Olivia. I want to make a difference for families and provide options when it feels like there are none.

A nurse calls Olivia's name, and I tap her arm.

She signs. *"Hi, Liv, pretty shirt."*

Liv shrugs, and I fight back a laugh. She's never this moody, but it's kind of adorable.

"I'm Phoebe, her nanny."

The nurse extends her hand. "I'm Lila, I'll be taking her back for some testing, and then Dr. King will be in to see you." She turns to her. *"Come on, Liv, we'll see Phoebe later."*

Olivia looks up at me, gripping my arm with both hands, her eyes pleading, and I step forward. "If you don't mind, I'd like to come with her. Olivia expressed some anxiety regarding the testing. She said it hurt the last time, and I promised her I'd be here. I know you probably don't care, but I'll be starting my second year of school for audiology. I'm aware of the rules, and I'd like to be in the room to support Liv."

Lila shifts her weight, pulls her lower lip between her teeth, and then sighs. "Well, I . . . you're acting as a guardian or parent, right?"

"Yes."

"We can let one parent or guardian in the room, but it's important the testing remains absolutely silent. Otherwise, the results might not be accurate."

"I understand," I assure Lila. "I will just be there to support her. I won't say a word, and if she lets me know something hurts, I'll raise my hand."

Lila nods.

I pat Olivia's arms and then sign what Lila just said about my going back with her. Her lip wobbles just a little before she pulls me in for a hug.

We're just turning to follow Lila back to the exam room when a deep voice calls my name. "Phoebe! Wait!"

I turn to see Asher rushing toward us, wearing his uniform. Today is his day off, but he's on call, so he isn't really supposed to leave the area.

Something must be wrong.

"What are you doing here? Is everything okay?"

Olivia makes a noise and then goes to her father. He holds her tight to his chest and glances at me. "Everything is fine." His eyes find mine. "I knew she needed me. She started texting me when you left, talking about how scared she was, and I just got in the car."

Oh, my ovaries have officially exploded. "You left the area . . ."

"Of course I did." His matter-of-fact tone leaves no room for anything else. His daughter needs him, so here he is. That simple. He stands, coming to his full height, which is an impressive six-foot-three, and smiles that ridiculously sexy grin at Lila. *"I'm her father. Sorry I'm late."*

Lila drops her head to the side. "So glad you could make it, Officer Whitlock. It's great to see a father who is just . . . so concerned for his child. You must care about her very much."

"Well, Olivia is my world."

"She's a very lucky little girl to have *you* as a father." She bats her long lashes, fluttering them at the end.

For the love of God. This woman has no shame, and I want to rip her eyes out.

Why? Why do I want to do that?

That's right, I'm a damn mess who wants to hump her boss and hates any woman who looks at him.

I really need to get my shit together.

"I think I'm the lucky one," Asher says back.

Her giggle is like knives on a chalkboard. "I do hope you won't get in trouble for leaving work. I can see you must be very important."

Uh, no, he's not. I mean, sure, he's a SWAT commander, a great cop, and everyone loves him, but that's probably because they don't know what an asshole he can be. All of that is great, but he's not like *very* important. More like mildly important.

This chick is ridiculous.

I sigh heavily, causing them both to look at me.

"Sorry, I was just concerned about Olivia and her anxiety," I try to cover up the fact that I hope Lila falls on her face.

"Of course. Let's take her back, you can go back to the waiting room since a parent is here."

Now I really hate this bitch.

I want to argue because there goes my chance to meet Dr. King. He's the best freaking doctor ever, and I had a plan on how to bring up a possible internship, and . . . ugh. Now it's all ruined. Stupid Asher and caring about his daughter.

As much as I want to be a brat, this isn't about me. I turn to Liv and sign. *"Your dad is here, so I am going to wait. You be brave and tell him if anything hurts."*

She shakes her head so hard I worry she's going to give herself a concussion.

Even though I know she can't hear me, I say her name, squatting down and grabbing her shoulders. *"Stop. Stop. Stop."* Taking her face in my hands, I force her to look at me. I speak slowly so she can read my lips. *"Talk to me."*

Her eyes are full of unshed tears. *"I want you."*

Asher is on his haunches beside me. *"You want Phoebe?"*

"And you," Olivia says.

He looks up to Lila. *"Phoebe will go in as well."*

"But . . ."

Asher doesn't hesitate. "Like I said, she will have both of us with her."

And just like that, I freaking want to maul him. Throw him on this floor and kiss him until we can't breathe.

Since that would be really inappropriate, I just smile.

He grunts in return.

And the kissing desire is gone.

The nurse nods and then escorts us into the room. It's a soundproof chamber, which feels strange when we first enter it, and there are three booths along the back wall. The table in the middle has cubes to stack, headsets, and other items they use during hearing exams. "Is the room soundproof for a reason?" I ask.

"Yes, we have a lot of children who can't go in the booths, so we have both options. The booths are preferred, though." She turns to Olivia. *"You guys can sit here, and Daniel will be out soon to get you."*

The hospital in Iowa didn't have that option, and it's pretty smart if you ask me. Which no one did, but whatever.

One of the audiologists exits the booth with a smile, and I instantly relax since it's a guy who will not be hitting on Asher. *"I'm Daniel, and I'll be doing Olivia's hearing tests."* He turns to Liv. *"Are you ready?"*

Olivia nods and turns to me. *"This part doesn't hurt."*

I grin. *"Good."*

Nothing in that booth should hurt. It's all sounds and tests to see if she hears anything.

Once she's gone, Asher and I return to our seats. "Thank you for before."

"For what?"

"You made sure that I could be back here."

"Olivia wanted you to come back with her, Phoebe, and I need for Liv to be comfortable. It's why I came here when she said she needed me."

About that . . .

"What if you get a call?"

"Then your dad is going to have to handle it. I called him, let him know I had to leave, and that I was going to be unavailable for a few hours. I'm not always proud of the things I do, but I will always put her first." He jerks his chin to the booth. "It's why we . . . the other night."

My stomach drops as I think about his hands on me, his rough voice, and his lips. Oh, I thought his eyes were sinful, but then I had his kiss. "We already discussed that."

I don't need this to be any more awkward than it already is. "It deserves a second discussion. What happened just now, her clinging to you, needing you with her? If I took that away, what kind of father would I be?"

"Why would you take that from her?" I loathe the desperation in my voice as much as the desire that courses through the words.

I do not want to want him.

Yet, I do.

"Because you already can't stand me half the time, and *when* this goes bad, it'll be Olivia who suffers. It doesn't matter if I want to touch you, kiss you, or relive that goddamn night over and over because I won't. I am not going to give in to you, not again."

I cross my arms over my chest. "When did you hear me ask for anything from you? We kissed. Once. I don't see what you're so spun up about."

I'm pretty proud of myself for the way I held that false bravado together.

He leans forward. "Your mouth said one thing, sweetheart, but your body says something else."

My jaw falls open, and I glare at him. "I think you're confused."

"Your nipples are hard, and you squirmed in your chair. It can't happen."

I hate him. I hold on to that because it's so much easier to dislike him than it is to see all the good things I'm not allowed to have.

"You're ridiculous. I don't want it to happen. The other night, I clearly was not thinking."

"Neither of us were."

"Right, so that's that."

He laughs once. "That has to be that."

Does he want more of that?

It doesn't matter because we both know it's stupid. I'm leaving in a few months if I get accepted into another program. I sure as hell won't be staying around here. I need to put my past behind me, move on, and be the woman I know I am.

This, right here? Administering tests and coming up with innovative ways to treat hearing loss, is what I want to do. I want to help provide families with better, more affordable options.

"Which is why I said it was a mistake."

Asher looks away. "Be her nanny and her friend."

"What do you think I'm doing? Look, I have proven myself with Olivia. I may have sucked as a babysitter years ago, but I don't right now. I'm juggling college applications, nannying, bouncing from house to house, and dealing with the most horrible, mortifying, and humiliating experience of my damn life, and the last thing I need is to complicate that any further, so shut up. I've already agreed that the other night was a bad idea. Let's move on already."

He moves in. "What experience did you have that was humiliating?"

I jerk back, hating that I spilled that little tidbit. "Nothing."

"Bullshit. You just said it. Is that why you left school?"

"No. Nothing happened, I was confused."

"Why did you leave school then?"

"No reason."

There's no way I'm telling him about Jonathan. I don't need him thinking I'm a homewrecker, even though I had no idea.

His hand moves to my chin, tilting my head so I can't look away. "Who humiliated you?"

My gut clenches, and I want to cry. Not because of what happened, the horrible shit people said, or because I ran away with my tail tucked between my legs. No, because the way he's looking at me—as if he'd destroy the person who hurt me if it meant I wouldn't feel this way for another second—makes me ache.

This is stupid. I shouldn't want him. I shouldn't care that Asher Whitlock seems angry that someone hurt me. All of that is irrelevant because we will never be.

We can't.

I'm not good enough, and he'll figure that out.

"It doesn't matter," I say, pulling my face away.

"It matters to me."

Oh, fucking crap. Why does he say these things? Doesn't he know the whole mistake thing and the we-can't-do-this excuse just vanished?

"Please don't . . ."

"Don't what?"

I close my eyes for a second. "Don't care. Don't ask me this. Don't want to protect me like a knight in shining armor. Don't be so damn perfect when I am trying really hard to dislike you so I don't kiss—"

"All right, Olivia did great!" Daniel says as he exits the booth.

I stand and put a smile on my face as Olivia comes rushing out. *Did it hurt?* I ask her.

She shakes her head.

Good. I'm glad at least one of us is making it out of this appointment without any pain.

thirteen

PHOEBE

"And you're going to help with the dance-off in a few weeks?"

"Yes, Daddy."

"Because it's important. We need to help raise money for Run to Me. The police department is sponsoring it," he says as he stirs his coffee.

"No more of this." I reach forward, taking it from his hand. "You've had six cups today, you need water."

"Where do you think coffee comes from?"

I roll my eyes and grab him a green smoothie from the fridge. "Water or this."

"What the hell is this crap?" He reads the ingredients on the back. "Spinach? You want me to drink spinach?"

"It's better than the garbage you eat and drink all day. It's good, I promise it doesn't taste like spinach. Just drink it."

He opens the top, sniffs it, and exhales dramatically.

"Oh my God, Daddy! You have been pepper sprayed, tased, and who knows what else, and you're going to scoff at drinking something healthy? Please, drink it for me."

That gets him. He takes a sip and mutters, "Daughters and their guilt."

"Yes, because you don't dish it out. I'm doing the dance-a-thon again for you."

"You're young and win every year. Plus, it helps both the police department and Addison."

It's the only reason I agreed to do it this year. Run to Me is doing a lot of great things, so if I can help Addison out by spending twenty-four hours dancing with someone, then I will.

Sure, I win every year.

Sure, I'm sort of a badass when it comes to this competition, and while there might be a war between Connor Arrowood and me because he tried to sabotage me last year, that doesn't mean I'll lose my medal.

I just need to find a partner.

"I'm happy to, once again, be crowned as queen."

"It's a four-dollar medal made from the scrap metal of a cruiser."

"Doesn't matter, it's for winners only."

Dad sighs dramatically. "You're so much like your mother some days."

"Since you loved her so much, I take that as a compliment."

"It was, just don't be like her and fall for a small-town man. You have bigger dreams than this town, kid."

I'm trying my best not to do just that, but I keep that to myself.

"I don't plan to stay here."

"Good, but maybe don't date anyone because no one is good enough for you."

He's so wrong there. It's me who is a damn mess and shouldn't be allowed near anyone, but my father never sees my faults. When he goes to open his mouth, I finish it for him. "Especially a cop. I know. You are aware that you're a cop and a really good man, right?"

"Yes, which is why I want to prevent you from making the same mistake your mother made when she settled."

My mother never once felt as though she settled, but it's cute he thinks that.

"Fine, I promise. Now, I'm going to my room where I plan to veg."

My father kisses my temple. "You're a good girl, Birdie."

I'm something. I head into my room, get in my comfy sports bra and shorts, climb into bed, and pop on *Friends*. One episode later, the doorbell rings, and then my father is yelling for me. "Phoebe, someone is here to see you."

I sigh, pull on my sweatshirt, and head out to see who this mystery guest could be. Since Olivia is camping with Rowan, and I have the next two days off, I really have no idea who it could be.

When I get to the front door, my eyes go wide because Melinda, a friend from high school who I haven't seen since the day we graduated, is standing there.

"Melinda, hi."

"Hey, Phoebe! I heard you were home, and I wanted to stop by."

Melinda was a friend, but like, not really a friend. She was always nice to me, but I got this vibe about her that always caused me to pull back. I think it had to do with her not being able to have more than one friend at a time, and when she moved on from one to the next, she didn't do it amicably. It was uncomfortable to watch.

"It's been a really long time. How are you?"

"I'm good. I just moved back to Sugarloaf about a month ago. My ex-husband got the condo, and I got shipped back here."

"I didn't know you got married." Because I really didn't care . . .

"Really? It was a big deal around here, but I guess you left right after we graduated. Anyway, I met Shane my freshman year of college, and we got married that year. It was a whirlwind. His parents own Temple Construction, do you know them?"

I nod. Everyone knows the owners of Temple Construction,

but I don't really care that she married their son. "Sorry things didn't work out with your husband."

"It's fine. Sometimes it just isn't meant to be. Thankfully, my settlement was very generous. Anyway, I came by because a few girls from high school are heading to Peakness tonight, and I wanted to see if you'd like to go."

"Oh, I don't know . . ."

I really don't feel like it. I have a full night of binging mindless television and not thinking about the current state of my life.

"Come on, for old times' sake."

I look down at myself and sigh. "I'm really not in any state to go out."

"You look amazing, and I can head home, change, and pick you up in an hour. What do you say? We'd love to catch up, and who knows, you might meet someone."

"In Sugarloaf?" I challenge. There are really only two guys in this town who I would ever date. One is my boss, the other is his brother, and they are both off-limits.

"You never know."

Dad walks into the living room, clearly having heard the conversation. "You should go. You've been working nonstop. It would be good to get out for some fun."

I force myself to smile. "Sure, I'll go. I'll be ready in an hour."

After the most extensive pep talk of my life, I showered, did my hair and makeup, and found the most flattering outfit I could.

These pants make my ass look fabulous, and the deep v-cut of my top crisscrosses in the back. If I'm going to go out with these people, I might as well look good doing it. Plus, Emmeline gave me some shit that I am vitamin-D deficient, and not in the pill form. Might as well go out there and fake it so she'll back off.

"Ready to head in?" Melinda asks as we pull up to Peakness.

"Ready as ever."

"And you're sure you're fine being the DD?"

"Totally fine." I really don't need to mix alcohol with my bad decision-making skills.

Inside, the music is loud, the bar smells eerily like my misguided youth, and my favorite bartender is slinging drinks.

I smile and head over to her. "Carmen!"

"Whoa! Hello, sexy thing!" She pushes up onto the bar, and I do the same so she can kiss my cheek. "You look . . . wow."

I laugh as I do a slow spin. "Thank you. I'm young and ready for some fun."

She looks over at Melinda. "And with . . . new friends?"

"Well, I wouldn't go that far, but it's slim pickings in this town and I'm bored."

"Good. You should have some fun instead of spending all your time nannying for the stick-in-the-mud cop."

I push my lips up into a smile. So much for my Asher-free night.

"Tonight is about having a good time. Any prospects?" I ask, scanning the bar.

Carmen tilts her head toward one guy at the end. "He's a good guy. Matt or Mike, I can't remember, he comes in every Friday, doesn't drink too much, and is in construction or something. Not overly talkative, sticks to beer, and typically leaves alone."

"Typically?"

She grins. "Well, when one of the vipers doesn't try to convince him. I'm not quite sure he's ever hooked up with them, or they follow him out to look like it."

I lean on the bar, chin in my hands. "Tell me more. Who are the vipers?"

Carmen laughs. "Melinda and her friend group. So, I guess that includes you tonight as well."

I stand up, feeling a mix of emotions. "A snake is scary and venomous."

"Yes, and do I take it you're on the prowl?"

I nod once. "I am tonight."

The funny thing about being on the prowl is that there has to be prospects to look for. Right now, the only guy here is Matt or Mike or whatever his name is, and as long as he hasn't touched any of them, it could work. Time to be sexy and alluring.

Whatever that looks like.

"Hey there," I say as I come to a stop at the chair beside his.

Matt-Mike looks me up and down and then lifts his chin. "Hey."

Okay, this is going swell. "Is this seat taken?"

"Nope."

I move around the chair and take a seat. What the hell do I do now? I am the worst viper ever. "So, are you from Sugarloaf?"

Oh, Phoebe, you are so not good at this.

"No. I just work on a farm here, but I live a few towns over."

That was at least a whole sentence, so we're making progress. "Which farm?"

"Arrowood."

"I know them well. The whole town does. I'm Phoebe." I extend my hand to Mike-Matt—or was it Matt-Mike?—and he returns the gesture.

"I'm Micah."

Carmen was off on that name. "It's nice to meet you."

"Same." He lifts his hand toward Carmen. "What can I get you?"

"The check."

I could die. Right now. I could just . . . drop dead on the floor because I just got shut down after two seconds. In my sexiest outfit with my tits basically on display.

She walks off, and Micah gets to his feet. "Look, it was great meeting you, but I know who your daddy is, and there's no way I'm going to get mixed up with the chief."

"I'm not sixteen," I say, no longer trying to be cute. "It's not like my father monitors my dating life."

"That's what you think, sweetheart."

The way he says sweetheart makes my skin prickle. It's not

132

warming or cute. It's condescending, and his voice is too high. Not that low gravelly sound that he . . .

No.

No, it's Micah's voice, and there's nothing wrong with it . . . other than the word he used and his tone and maybe his pitch too. But that's all.

Not wanting to be brushed off, I get to my feet and walk around. "Well, it was great talking to you. I have to get back to my friends."

I turn before he can say anything else and head over to Melinda and the two other girls who I cheered with. "Ahhh!" Rebecca yells as I walk over. "It's you! You look freaking hot. Trying to pick up some guys, I see."

"No, just needed to feel pretty," I say, pulling her into a hug. "You look amazing."

"Thanks, marriage suits me."

"And me!" Tara says as she thrusts her incredibly large rock in my face.

What is it with all these girls and getting married?

Also, how are they the vipers if all but one of them has a husband at home? Oh, my head hurts.

"Wow, congrats to all of you! Seems like I missed a lot of weddings."

Tara pulls me into the chair beside her. "Tell us everything. Why are you back? How is it working with Asher freaking Whitlock? He's so hot. Every girl here has a huge crush on him."

"I'm sure your husbands all love that," I joke, but not really.

Once again, that thread of jealousy starts to wrap its way around my throat.

"Oh, please," Melinda says with a laugh. "Tara's husband is a developer, and he's never around. He couldn't care less what she does as long as she's discreet."

"Melinda!" she hisses.

"Becca is a different story. Her husband is overly jealous,

which is why she flirts so damn much. She likes reminding him how lucky he is," Melinda finishes.

At least Becca doesn't seem bothered by what she said. "It works for us."

"Then that's great." I have no room to judge any of them. "As long as you're all happy."

Tara takes my hands in hers. "In about an hour, this place will be packed. The ranchers all need to clean up, and then they'll come down, needing a tall drink of woman."

"I can't wait."

We spend the next hour catching up. They seem equally excited and confused by my career choice to be an audiologist. Melinda is actually the most supportive one since her niece is hard of hearing, and she asks me a million questions.

As we talk, eat some appetizers, and they pound drinks, the bar fills up a lot. There are definitely more guys than girls, which works perfectly for me.

"All right, it's showtime."

"Showtime?" I ask as Melinda and Tara rise.

"It's time to get free drinks."

I lift my Diet Coke and shrug. "I'm good."

Now I understand why they needed me to be the designated driver, they have a system. Not that it bothers me to be the sober one. My grandpa was a raging alcoholic, so I tend to avoid drinking when possible.

Melinda and Tara head to the bar, leaving Becca and me at the table. "You're not going?" I ask.

She shrugs. "I actually think I might head home. I'm going to get a ride."

"Okay," I say, not sure what else to say. "I can take you."

"No need. I have a meeting in the morning, and I can get a ride. Can you tell the girls I said I'll call them tomorrow?"

"Sure . . ."

She ducks out, leaving me alone. Well, I came here to flirt and be young and stupid, so I might as well.

Before I can rise, the chair beside me slides away from the table. "Seat taken?"

I look up to see a tall man, maybe thirty, with dark brown hair and brown eyes. Potential, although the eyes are meh.

I really prefer blue.

No, I don't. Jonathan had brown eyes, and I liked them just fine. Not that I want to think of him either.

Ugh. Focus, man here. Fresh bait.

I lean back in my seat, letting him get a better glimpse of my assets. "Nope, by all means."

"Thanks. Haven't seen you here before, are you new in town?"

I fight back a smile. "You could say that."

"I could?"

"I lived here for a while and just returned."

"Ahhh," the man says. "You're one of the prodigal children of Sugarloaf."

"Now, that is probably the best descriptor I've heard."

"Name?" he asks, leaning his arm on the table and shifting just a bit closer to me.

"Phoebe. You?"

"John."

Nope. Way too close. Not even going to touch that one. I give him a smile. "It was great talking to you, John, but my friend is waving me over."

He looks around, trying to see my fictitious friend, but I'm already walking away. I head to the bar, get a refill of my Diet Coke, and Carmen laughs. "Stay away from that one. He's a player and leaves with a different girl every weekend."

"I don't care about that. It was his name that had me coming over here."

"His name?" she asks, grabbing beer from the cooler behind her.

"Long story."

"I'll buy the lady a drink," a new guy offers from my right.

He's a little shorter than the last guy, but his eyes are beautiful blue, not aqua, but more denim.

"Thank you. I'm Phoebe."

He clinks my glass with his beer. "Leo. Can I buy you a drink?"

"I'm the DD tonight, but I appreciate the offer."

"Ahhh that sucks." He chugs the remainder of his beer, and I size him up. He's really good looking—not hot but doable, and he seems nice.

"So, Leo, what do you do?"

"This and that."

"Wow, sounds mysterious." The sarcasm drips, so I tack on a smile.

He laughs, the sound deep and a little awkward. "Right now, I'm working for a friend, his name is Rowan."

Of course it is.

Well, this night just keeps going down the Whitlock path, and I want off.

"Rowan is a great guy," I say, starting to stand, and Leo follows.

"Are you leaving?"

"You know I just—" I start to say, but a loud bang has me turning toward where two guys are getting in each other's faces. I must have heard the barstool being knocked over.

One of the fighters is Austin Arrowood, and there's no way I'm going to let him be a fool and end up in the papers for this.

"Excuse me," I say quickly and start to walk toward them. My three-inch heels suddenly do not feel like such a great idea, but here we are. I step closer and slide my arm between them. "Hi, honey, there you are," I say to Austin, my hand on his chest.

"Phoebe?" His eyes widen, and then his gaze goes back to the hulking guy in front of him. "Step back."

"I would, but I was searching everywhere for you, love. Why don't we leave now? I'm tired and want to go."

"Need your girlfriend to protect you, Arrowood?" the big— and I mean huge—guy taunts.

This is so going to be bad.

"I'll fucking kick your ass any day of the week."

Oh, Austin, you so won't, but that's cute thinking.

I turn to face the monster, my back against Austin's chest. "Why don't I buy you a drink, and you can just go back to your fun night."

"Get out of my way, bitch."

"That was rude," I say, inhaling and trying to remember what Daddy says about these situations—smile and get out of the way.

Too bad I've never been one to listen.

I spin back to Austin, place both hands on his chest, and shove him back. Only, he doesn't move. "Let's go. You can't get into a bar fight."

He tries to move me to the side, but I lean into him so he can't. "Move, Phoebe."

"You move. Come on, let's go."

"Yeah, go with your girlfriend, maybe you can hit that since you can't find the ball."

Jesus, this guy is a prick.

The guy grabs me from behind, and this time I can't hold on to anything as he moves me to the side. Austin decks the guy, and I scream because, when the guy throws me to the side, I lose my footing, twisting my ankle, and fall. I land on the gross floor of the bar, my ankle throbbing, and before anyone can move, there's a deep voice from above me and shiny black shoes right by my face.

"Step back, or you're all going to be in the back of a cruiser."

Great. Asher is here.

fourteen

ASHER

"A bar fight? You got in the middle of a goddamn bar fight?" I ask, trying to help her up.

When she stands, I see what she's wearing and realize my mistake. I should've left her on the floor. I scan her from head to toe, taking in her perfect skin, the way her breasts push against the fabric, and shoes that I want digging into my shoulders.

Jesus fucking Christ.

"Well, it wouldn't have been a fight if I got . . ." She steps toward the chair and winces. "Ouch!"

"Sir, do you want to take them both in?" Deputy McNair asks as he stands between Austin Arrowood and Brit Murphy, who I've had to take to the station multiple times.

Phoebe takes another step, sucking in a breath. I need to deal with this and then her.

"Sit," I instruct her and then turn to McNair. "Take Murphy over there and get his statement."

Austin has his hands raised. "I didn't start it."

"I didn't ask that. What happened?"

He relays the story of how Brit was taunting him and how he couldn't look like a pussy in front of his friends.

"Where does Phoebe come in?"

139

Austin sighs. "She tried to break it up by getting between us and pretending she was my girl. She had her hands on my chest, trying to get me to let it go, but then Brit grabbed her."

My vision goes red. First, she thought it was a good idea to step between two testosterone fueled idiots. Second, that meathead actually had the balls to put hands on her?

"I need to check with McNair to see if Brit wants to press charges since you're the one who threw a punch."

Austin looks down. "I just got so pissed."

"I know the feeling," I say under my breath.

Brit doesn't want to press charges, said it was barely a feather's touch. I swear that guy just likes to piss people off.

"Go home, both of you," I say, frustrated with the waste of my damn time. "If I hear of any more issues, it's not going to matter who wants to press charges, I'll haul you both to jail, and you can deal with the consequences."

Now to handle my second issue.

Phoebe is sitting on the bar with her leg propped up on the counter, and McNair is there, holding ice to her ankle.

Once again, I feel this surge of anger toward another man touching her. I don't know what the hell my issue is. Oh, I remember, I'm lusting after my daughter's nanny. Tonight has made it a hundred times worse.

Seeing her around my house is difficult, but that is a controlled environment. Having to see her around other men who are staring at her long legs and the fabric clinging to every rise and fall of her chest is infuriating. The low cut of that top reveals the perfect amount of skin to leave me desperate to see more. Jesus it's enough to bring a man to his knees.

Here she shines.

Here she's desire and promise of all the things that could be, and I don't want her anywhere near these people.

I walk over before I have enough sense to stop. "It should be fine. The swelling isn't bad, just ice it."

"Thank you, I didn't know you were an EMT before this."

McNair smiles and rubs his thumb along her ankle. "I was. I've seen my share of sprains, and this shouldn't be too bad."

Her warm eyes are on him, and I feel the very thin string keeping me in line grow taut. "That's enough, McNair."

The kid looks up at me, confusion in his gaze. "Sir?"

Great, now I'm barking at the rookie. "I'll take it from here. Why don't you get back on the road in case a call comes in."

Phoebe eyes me and then smiles softly at McNair. "Thanks, Joey. You were a real hero coming over here and helping."

"Of course, Phoebs. I just wanted to check on you."

Phoebs? Does everyone call her that now? "And you did your job, now go back on patrol," I snap, not giving a damn that I'm acting like a prick.

As soon as he's gone, Phoebe leans back on her hands. "Any specific reason you tried to rip Joey's head off?"

"Any specific reason you thought trying to stop a fight was a good idea?"

She shrugs. "I was trying to diffuse the situation."

"That's what the cops are for."

"I'm basically a cop," she says, pushing herself upright and placing the ice back on her ankle.

My brows lower, and when she doesn't elaborate, I ask, "I'm sorry, what?"

"I'm like a cop by proxy. I've heard all the stories, been given all the tips, and have listened to my father drone on for days about how he does things. So, I do the same."

"Cop by . . . proxy? Are you insane?"

Phoebe shakes her head. "Listen, Austin was going to end up in trouble, he was a good friend when we were kids, so I wasn't about to let some guy screw up his career."

I rub my temple, trying to calm myself before I say something I'll regret. "I'm not even going to dignify that with a response. So, you came here alone, did whatever you were doing before the fight, and then put yourself in a dangerous situation. Really smart, Phoebe."

She huffs a laugh. "I'm not alone. I came with friends." She looks around, scanning the crowd that has all gone back to normal. I'm still fuming, thinking about the men who were near her, touched her, or tried to flirt with her. Then I can't release the frustration about her getting hurt. Her grunt brings me back to the conversation. "Unreal. I'm the DD, and they left me."

"Who?"

"The people I didn't even want to come out with."

"So, how are you getting home?"

"I'll walk."

Phoebe hops down off the bar and then winces. That's it.

I scoop her into my arms, and her eyes widen. "Put me down!"

"You can't walk, I'm taking you home." I turn to Carmen. "Give us a call if there are any further issues."

Carmen's brows raise. "Sure thing, Asher." Then she turns to Phoebe. "Well, you came here looking for a man to take you home. Guess you got that, just not the way you planned."

Phoebe groans. "Shut up." As I carry her out of the bar, a few people clap, and she raises her heels up in the air. "And that's how you do it!"

I swear that this woman is going to drive me to drink.

We aren't two steps from the door when she starts to squirm. "You made your point, put me down."

"No."

"No?"

I don't want to. Holding her like this feels too good, and I refuse. "You can't walk, you hurt your ankle, and you don't have a ride."

"I can hobble."

"You're going in the car, and you're going to stop fighting me."

"I would rather crawl!"

I'd love nothing more than to see her on all fours, but that's definitely not what she's talking about. "Not today, sweetheart."

She sighs. "You're being ridiculous."

"I think the word is chivalrous."

"Oh, that's rich." She scoffs.

The cruiser is only a few feet away, so I slow, taking advantage of the last few steps. "I thought this was the dream. A guy coming in and literally carrying you out after you're hurt."

"Yeah, that only works if that guy actually is available."

I am . . . not. I am not.

"I see." We reach the car door, and I carefully put her down. "Climb in."

She groans. "Great, now I am riding in the back of the cop car. I should've stayed home."

"Why didn't you?"

"Melinda."

I let out a deep laugh. "Melinda is doing her best to screw her ex out of her system."

Phoebe's gaze meets mine. "How would you know that?"

"She's not exactly shy about it."

Her lips purse. "Have you been one of her conquests?"

The tightness in her voice causes a ripple of pleasure through me. "Would it bother you if I was?"

"No." She answers way too quickly.

"I think it does," I challenge.

We stand here—her back against the door and me way too close to her, and I lean closer, inhaling the trace of citrus and sugar that lingers on her skin. "It doesn't. You and I can't happen, remember?"

"I remember."

And I do, so I step back. "Get in."

She climbs in the back, and I mentally prepare myself for the drive.

"How is your ankle?"

"It's fine. I just twisted it, so I'll probably be completely normal tomorrow."

I hate that she's hurt. I could pummel Austin for letting her get in the middle and Brit for actually hurting her.

"I'm taking you back to my house," I tell her.

"What? Why?"

"Do you want to explain to your father why I'm dropping you off in a cop car—injured? No."

"You asked me this and answered for me, so thanks for that."

"You're welcome." I pause a moment, then say, "Besides, it'll keep you out of trouble if you're there." *Because I want you there.*

"Doubtful."

We drive in silence, mostly because I'm not sure what other asinine bullshit is going to come out of my mouth. There is no good reason that she can't go home. She's a fucking grown woman and can take care of herself. I just want her in my house. I want her close and not with any other man.

After a few minutes, Phoebe is unable to keep quiet. "So, did you sleep with Melinda?"

I grin. I knew it bothered her. "Nope."

"Good."

"Why is that?"

I turn down Main Street, taking the long way back home. "Because I would hate to see her take advantage of you."

"I'm not attracted to her."

"Right. I mean, she's like fourteen years younger."

So is she, but I am fucking burning for her. I don't reply to that, and then turn down my street.

I park, open her door, and find her glaring at me. "I could've gone home."

"Well, I brought you here. Grab my neck."

She does, and I lift her out of the car before carrying her to the door. Once I get it open, I bring her to her room and set her on the bed.

"Now what?"

"Stay here."

I stomp off to the kitchen, fill a bag with ice, and grab a towel. When I get back to Phoebe's room, her legs are stretched out in front of her and her arms are crossed, swelling those perfect breasts.

I grab a pillow from the floor, lift her leg, and prop her ankle on it. Once she's settled with her ice, I give her two Tylenol. She takes them, still scowling at me.

"Take me home, Asher."

"No."

I'd rather take her here. She sits up, softening her gaze for the first time. There is tension between us, growing more and more the longer we spend in each other's space, and I hate her for it. I hate myself for not being strong enough to shut it down.

"This isn't a good idea. Take me home, please."

"I'm off in twenty minutes. Just stay here, ice your ankle, and try to stay out of trouble. When I get back, we're going to settle this."

I leave, cursing myself the entire way, and debate pulling a double just to avoid the mess I left in my home.

Olivia is gone. Phoebe is there. And I want her, fuck the consequences.

fifteen

PHOEBE

Ugh that man!

That ridiculous, irritating, overbearing man brought me here because I can't walk and left me. At first, I brooded, but then, I was angry. Now? Now, I'm furious. I am going to kill him when he gets here.

If I can make it to the living room.

I'm hopping my way down the hallway, which has never seemed as long as it does right now. I will make it there and sit smugly until he walks in and finds me *not* where he ordered I stay.

Ordered. Like I'm a damn child.

I'm not a kid, and I go where I want, thank you very much.

Well, I would if I had my car, a ride, or Uber actually existed here.

I see headlights flash through the window, and my heart accelerates.

I'm out of time.

I jump faster, putting a little weight on my bad ankle, noting it doesn't hurt as much as it did before. I must win.

Damn him and his thinking he could tell me what to do.

As soon as I round the corner, the door flies open, and my chest heaves as I stare at Asher.

He looks regretful, angry, and filled with unabashed desire, and I am sure he sees the same in my eyes.

His bag falls to the floor, and then he's in front of me in two heartbeats. He doesn't say a word, and I don't need him to because there is nothing either of us need to say, this is beyond that.

My mouth opens to say something—I have no idea what—and then his lips are on mine, robbing the air from my lungs. Strong arms hold me to him, and I cling to his shoulders as his tongue swipes against mine. There is nothing tonight that will stop this, and no alarms are going to go off other than the one inside me that's telling me not to do this.

It's telling me not to blur another line, make another mistake by wanting a man I shouldn't, and I hit snooze on the feelings I refuse to acknowledge.

His hand moves down my back, grabbing my ass and molding our bodies together.

"Fuck, Phoebe," he moans as his mouth is moving down my neck. "I can't resist you. Just . . . one . . . taste," he says between kisses to my shoulder.

This top was not made for sexy times. It's the cutest crop top that makes my boobs look freaking phenomenal in the front, but it crisscrosses in the back and has this weird zipper thing on the side. He tries to pull it down, but it doesn't budge.

"Take it off," he orders.

I need control. I can't just give in to him. "You want it off, you take it off," I toss back, and then he turns me, forcing my chest to the wall, hands splayed there.

Well, there goes control.

He slides the zipper down so slowly it feels like it takes a year. He presses me closer to the wall, and his erection is hard against my ass.

"When I saw you in that bar today, I almost lost my fucking mind," he admits, his hands moving to the straps that are really

148

going to give him a hard time. "I saw you on the floor, and I wanted to lift you in my arms and haul you out of there."

"You did exactly that."

"No, I had to go talk to people, pretend that you weren't there, and ignore the way every man in that bar was staring at you."

My stomach flips. "Asher," I say his name on a sigh when his hands snake around my front, kneading my breasts beneath the shirt.

"This isn't happening, Phoebe. This, right now? Me touching you and kissing your perfect skin? We aren't doing it, do you understand?"

Yes, this is a dream anyway, one that I hope I won't wake from. "What is happening then?"

"I'm not sure because I am trying not to name it, but I can't make myself stop."

Thank God for that. I might combust.

His fingers drift down my stomach to the button of my pants, snapping it free before sliding the zipper down as his teeth nip at the base of my neck. "How is your ankle?"

Do I have those? I can't seem to remember. I put my weight down and then flex it. "It's much better."

"Good." He moves my hands up the wall. "Keep your hands like this." Then he's moving to the waist of my jeans and sliding them down. "Step out."

What am I doing? What am I doing? I ask myself this over and over, but then I lift my foot and let him remove my pants. "Asher . . ." I fight for some freaking control because I'm losing it. If we do this, then what? Will he hate me? Will I hate myself?

The last one is definitely not going to be how I feel, but I know his rules and how he feels about me. I know how I feel, but God, when he's near, every excuse disappears. Right now, I don't care about his reasons or mine.

His fingers move up my legs, around to the front of me, and he rubs my clit. I moan, my cheek against the wall.

"Stay like this," he orders then drops to his knees. "I'm going to lift your leg, so balance."

Oh. My. God. I can barely breathe. Asher puts my back to the wall and then lifts my injured leg, putting it over his shoulder, then the other leg, and I drop, all my weight there as he holds me up, but before I can say anything he's kissing the inside of my thigh.

"Asher, stop," I say quickly, stopping him from moving to do exactly what he plans to do. "I need to explain that, I don't . . . it doesn't . . . happen for me like this. Please don't take it personally. It isn't you, it's me."

He laughs and pushes my legs farther apart as my heart races, afraid that this is going to go down a very bad path. "No, baby, it's not you, it's whoever did it before. I'll stay here for hours if that's how long it takes. You're going to come this way. You're going to let me lap every drop from this pretty pussy until you fall apart."

"Oh God." My head rests against the wall as he takes one long lick. "Asher."

He moans and shifts us again, giving him a better angle. His tongue moves up and down, over and over, flicking my clit and causing me to pant. I can't move. I'm completely at his mercy, and it feels so good and so incredibly frustrating.

"Asher, please," I plead. "Please, more."

His fingers move to right under my thigh, pushing me higher, and his tongue plunges deep inside of me. I want to writhe as he fucks me with his mouth. I want to force him where I want him, but I can't do anything because I'm against the wall.

"Do you like this? Do you like my face between your legs, tasting your sweetness?"

Oh, do I ever. "Stop talking," I say with frustration.

"Would you rather I do something else?" His voice is teasing. "Would you rather I lick this pussy until you come?"

"Yes!" I moan, slapping the wall.

"Yeah, I bet you would. You taste so good, beautiful. I could stay here for hours."

"I want to come," I tell him.

"Then I better get to work."

Asher's tongue presses against my clit, flicking it, and then he moves his hand so his thumb is just lightly penetrating me. I have never felt this good, this free, while being unable to move. He is actually going to make me orgasm like this. "Oh!" I gasp. "Oh, shit! Asher!"

I'm so close. He penetrates a little deeper, and my orgasm rips through me so hard that I feel as though I'm falling, and I don't dare try to stop the ripples of pleasure that are rioting through me. When I open my eyes, I'm on my back, looking up at the ceiling. I push onto my elbows, and Asher is still against the wall, but gone is the lust-crazed man. He has been replaced by someone far too serious and very much unwelcome.

"What the fuck are we doing?" he asks, his blue eyes filled with regret.

"I think we both know what we were doing."

"Phoebe." His voice cracks, and I will not let him say it. I refuse.

I will not let him say how we can't do this. How this is wrong. How I am wrong for him. I've done this dance, and I left with more than a twisted ankle. Were either of us thinking? No. Clearly, this wasn't planned, but it happened, and I need to keep my dignity.

"Hand me that blanket."

He grabs it off the back of the couch, and I wrap it around myself like a protective shield. I will not let him give me all his bullshit reasons.

"I am not asking for anything, so you can relax. We both had a long night, and we're clearly not thinking right."

"I owe you—"

I lift my hand. "If you say an apology, I swear to God, I'll punch you."

He smiles. "Glad you stopped me."

"Look, we're both consenting adults. No, this is not a great idea, but we didn't do anything we can't move on from." I push up to my feet, my legs a little wobbly, but I stand tall. Asher rises as well. "I love Olivia. I love spending time with her. I will be leaving in a few months for whatever grad program I get into. And, like we said, this didn't happen."

He nods slowly. "Right."

Time to get out of here before I say something really stupid. "I'm going to sleep. You'll drive me home tomorrow?"

"Of course."

I try for a joke. "Well, you abducted me tonight, so I wasn't sure."

Asher doesn't smile. "Phoebe." His voice has an edge to it. "I'm not going to apologize. I'm just going to say that I have never wanted someone as much as I want you. I have never been completely out of my mind to the point that I couldn't walk away."

My heart is beating so hard that I get a little dizzy. "It doesn't change a thing."

"No, it doesn't change the fact that you work for me, my daughter adores you, and you're my boss's daughter."

"Cards are stacked against us. Good night, Asher."

"Good night, Phoebe."

I lie in bed for hours, staring at the clock, wondering how I keep managing to get myself in these predicaments. My eyes are closed, almost at the brink of sleep, when I hear the creak of my door. I keep my breathing even and feign sleep.

Asher's fingers brush the hair back on my face, his thumb grazing my cheekbone. "I shouldn't be here. Why am I unable to stop myself with you?" His voice is soft, almost dreamlike. "You are going to wreck my world, and I'm going to let you."

Then his lips press against my forehead, and he leaves, taking all the restraint I had left with him.

"Hey, Phoebe!" Brynlee grabs my attention as I'm in the cereal aisle at the corner store.

"Hey!" I smile, walking over and giving her a big hug.

"How are you? I heard you got hurt the other night."

"Hurt?"

She looks down at my ankle. "Maybe I was wrong . . . but I heard you tripped and twisted your ankle."

"Oh! Yeah, but today, it's much better. I rested and iced like I was instructed to do."

By her bossy brother as he drove me home.

That was about all we said to each other the whole time. When I woke in the morning, he was in the kitchen, drinking his coffee, and as soon as I entered, the awkwardness of pretending the previous night never happened was in full effect.

"I'm so glad. I was going to call, but it turns out the rooster I found the other night is a bit randy, and he was trying to enforce his will on my hens. I have sixteen now and Rowan is building me a new coop, but anyway, between that and my court case today . . ." She looks down at her watch, and my head is spinning with her rooster story that makes no sense, but it's Brynn and she's always kind, so I let it go. "Which is in twenty minutes, I'm going to be late, but I need sugar."

"Mine is chocolate."

"When you're stressed?"

I nod. "Before any big exams, I eat so much chocolate it almost makes me sick."

"I need anything chewy. Gummy Bears, Twizzlers, or Sour Patch Kids are my jam." She tosses them into her basket.

"All of those will rot your teeth." This man is everywhere. Brynlee turns to see her brother strolling toward her.

"Thank you for the concern, brother of mine." She grabs two more bags of candy off the shelf. "However, today is not the day for reformation."

"Can't say I didn't try."

She smiles and then kisses his cheek. "Gotta run. I'm glad

your ankle is well, Phoebs, and next time you want to go out drinking, let me know. Melinda and her crew are . . . well, assholes."

"Consider myself reformed on that."

She heads to the front, leaving me alone with Asher.

"Hey," he says quietly, giving me a smile.

"Hey."

"Is your ankle doing okay?" Asher asks with concern.

"Yeah, it's actually totally fine. Don't worry, I won't need to miss work."

He looks down at his feet. "I'm glad it's better. Liv comes home tomorrow, and I know she'd be devastated if she didn't get to see you."

And what about him? Would he be sad or relieved?

Get it together, Phoebe. He would feel nothing because you are nothing. So what if he gave you an orgasm? You do that all on your own.

Sure, they aren't as good as the one I had two nights ago, but that's not the point.

"Yeah, she sent me a text this morning with a photo of the fish she caught."

Asher lets out a deep, throaty chuckle. "Hopefully, she didn't send Sara the photos of her on the dirt bike."

God, she'd come home to kill Asher and Rowan. "That's definitely not authorized in the binder."

He grins. "No, it's not."

Asher looks at the basket and then my hands. "Cereal?"

I'd forgotten I was holding a box of healthy grain cereal that I will never eat. My current mood is not for healthy options, it's for high sugar and processed garbage that I'll regret later. I slide that one back on the shelf. "Cereal is the breakfast of champions."

"Liv loves it."

"I know," I say, reminding him that I do, in fact, know about his daughter's likes. I also know that, every morning, he eats the same thing—three eggs, two slices of bacon, and one slice of toast. He calls it his three-two-one plan. "Are you switching your breakfast-food team?"

"Nah, I was just going to surprise Liv with one of her favorites."

I go to grab the box at the same time Asher does. Our fingers touch for just the briefest of moments, but I feel the contact all the way down to my toes. I pull my hand back, and his eyes find mine.

The two of us are still and then he shifts back. "Sorry, go ahead."

I could do that whole, no, you have it game, but I'm tired of games. I'm tired of wanting him, of wishing there weren't so many reasons we can't give in fully.

I take the box and smile. "Thanks. Have a great day."

I turn to walk away, head high, feeling like we just had a semi-normal interaction that didn't end with me looking like an asshole. Take that for a grand exit. Only, I don't actually have that. No, instead, I trip on nothing in the middle of the aisle, and my arms and legs go flying as I fall straight into a display of cans.

The display, which Mr. Cooke probably spent six hours setting up, is completely destroyed, and the cans spread out like marbles on the linoleum floor. "Jesus! Are you okay?" Asher asks. I'm sprawled out on the floor, limbs outstretched, hair in my face, and pride left in aisle two.

"I'm fine."

"Let me help you." He gets low, extending his hand, and I steel myself for when we touch. Thankfully, I'm prepared for it, but when he pulls, it's a bit too hard, and this time, we both go flying back, and I land on top of him.

"That didn't go as planned."

He smiles. "No, definitely not."

"One day, I'll stop embarrassing myself in front of you."

"I truly hope you never stop."

The connection changes, and I realize I am still lying on top of him. I go to move, but his hand is on my back.

"Oh my heavens!" Mrs. Cooke says louder than anyone would ever need to be inside. "Are you two all right? Jimmy! Your cans are everywhere, and Phoebe is lying on top of Sheriff Whitlock!"

I drop my head to his chest as she announces that bit of gossip. "Kill me now."

"Huh? She fell?" Jimmy yells.

"Yes!"

This time, Asher doesn't stop me from rolling off to the side. "It's all right, Mrs. Cooke, we'll clean it up," Asher says as he sits up. "I just fell back and—"

Mr. Cooke calls again from the front register. "Where did she fall?"

She turns her head, yelling even louder this time. "I said she was on *top* of him!"

Mr. Cooke yells back equally as loud. "Why was she on top of him?"

"I don't know! Maybe she tried to save him and fell!"

I can do nothing at this point but laugh, which I do, hysterically. My eyes begin to water, and Asher is laughing as well. It's just too ridiculous that the two of us are on the floor with cans of olives rolling around us while Mr. and Mrs. Cooke have a screaming conversation about how we got here.

"Are you all right, dear? Did you hit your head?" Mrs. Cooke asks. "Maybe Asher was too hard for you?"

I force myself to stop for a second, but then I laugh so hard I make a choking sound, which causes me to snort, and that sets off another round of hysterics.

"Jim! I think Asher was too big and hard for Phoebe!"

"Oh, stop. I can't breathe!" I say between my fit of giggles.

Asher stands and turns his back to me, but his shoulders are still bouncing. Finally, he stops and rests his hand on Mrs. Cooke's shoulder. "Thank you for checking on us. I am going to help Phoebe clean up this mess. You and Jim just take care of the other customers."

"Okay!" she says quickly before walking off.

My laughter finally stops. The two of us start picking up the cans, and he chuckles. "Well, now the town knows you were on top of me."

"And you were hard," I say, giggling again.

"You know this will go around."

I nod. "It's fine, most people think I'm ridiculous anyway, so I'll be able to explain it."

"I don't think you're ridiculous, Phoebe. Anyone who believes that, doesn't know you."

"Thank you for saying that."

"I mean it."

I tuck my hair behind my ear and focus on stacking so I don't fall on top of him again.

sixteen

ASHER

"Y ou're really sure you want to move back here, Grady?" I look out the back window, watching Olivia, Rowan, and Brynn. They're playing some sort of dodgeball, but it looks more like peg Rowan in the head.

Hopefully, the game is still going when I am done with this call. That looks like fun.

"Sure? No. But my commission is over, my in-laws want to move back to Arizona, and it would be good for Jett to meet our family."

We've all met him, but we haven't seen him much since he lives so far away. Even when Grady is not deployed or flying, he hasn't been back to Sugarloaf since Jett was born.

"We're all happy about it, don't get me wrong, what are your plans for work?"

"I'm finishing up my pilot instructor class here, so I figure I'll do that."

"Solid plan."

He laughs once. "It's something."

"Well, it'll be nice having the band back together. I know Brynn gets all sentimental about us all being on the same land again." Little does he know that most of Brynlee's land is the land for misfit animals.

"I'm not sure how I'm going to handle staying with Brynn for long. Hopefully the builder moves fast."

I offered up my place, but he thought it was better if he stayed with Brynlee. They have always been close, and she'll help with Jett where . . . that ain't happening here. I work too much, and according to him, I am not as happy as she is.

"You had options."

"The frat house with Rowan or prison with you? No thanks, I have lived with drill sergeants before, and I'd rather not do that again. Brynn will dote on Jett and doesn't come with contingencies."

"You could have lied and said Brynn needed it since she collects broken things, but hey, you always were a jackass."

He chuckles. "She's like a bad version of Snow White."

She really is. "Instead of just singing to the animals, she keeps them all."

It's like a fucking menagerie over there. "Well, Jett will love it."

"Probably." Brynn screeches my name, and I glance outside to see her waving for me to hurry up. "Hey, as much as I'd love to continue this convo, I have to go peg Rowan in the head with a ball."

Grady goes silent for a second. "I'm not sure where to go with that one."

"When you get home, we'll play this new game. See you in a few months."

"Can't wait."

We hang up, and I head out back where Brynn is carrying Olivia on her back and trying to keep away from Rowan, who has possession of the ball.

"What are the rules?" I ask and sign at the same time.

"Hit Rowan!" Brynn yells as she ducks.

Sounds easy enough.

Rowan, Brynn, and I take off after the ball. Brynn has no shot since she's carrying Liv on her back, and Rowan is a good five feet behind me. I move quick, but he leaps on my back, reaching for the ball over my head.

I toss him off, grab the ball, and grin. "Now what?"

He looks over to the door. "Hey, Phoebe!" I turn, and he swipes the ball from my hand, laughing as he tucks it under his shirt. "Made you look."

I'm going to kill him. Rowan is running across the lawn and I am standing here, wondering if fratricide carries the death penalty or if a jury would think this was justified.

"Asher!" Brynn scolds, snapping me out of it.

Liv is no longer on her back and is signing at me. *"Now he is going to win!"*

The hell he is.

I move toward him, he dodges to the left, but I anticipate his move. "Nice try with the Phoebe thing," I taunt as I step to the right when he does.

"I thought so."

"You're a dick."

"And the rumors are true." Rowan chuckles.

I'm going to kill him. I step forward, but my brother steps back, glancing toward Brynn.

"Your niece is going to be devastated if you hit her."

He snorts. "Please, she has the meaner throw of the two of them."

We circle each other, and Brynn yells, "Go for the ankles, Ash!"

Rowan moves his eyes away from me just long enough not to see me lunge, and I wrap my arms around him, tackling him to the ground. We roll around, each of us taking turns smashing the other into the ground, but eventually, I get control of the ball. He moves me onto my back, trying to grab it back from me, but there is no way I'm not giving up. I'm tired of losing.

I'm losing my mind, my head, my goddamn willpower. I will not lose this ball.

I push my hips to the side, tossing him over, and jump to my feet with the ball raised in victory.

When I turn to Brynn and Liv, they're both staring at us. Olivia has her arms crossed over her chest, wide-eyed and confused. Brynlee, on the other hand, has her lips pursed, hand on her hip, and is tapping her foot. *"Are you two done?"*

"I got the ball," I say slowly so Olivia can read my lips since I can't use my hands.

"You also lost your minds. Idiots," she sighs and turns to Olivia. *"Let's go inside and have some cake, leave these two to clean up."*

As soon as they walk off, Rowan sweeps my legs out from under me, and I fall on the ground with a loud thud. "Fuck! That hurt, you stupid bastard." I turn my head to look at where he's sprawled out on the grass next to me.

"Maybe you'll remember that next time you dig your thumbs into my elbow."

"You deserved it for the bullshit earlier."

"What? When I made you think Phoebe was here?" His voice has way too much glee in it.

"I didn't care if she was here, it just caught me by surprise."

He sits up, and I do the same, now that I'm sure my tailbone is still connected. We both groan. My hand moves to my shoulder, and I try to rub the pain away while Rowan pushes on his back, stretching and wincing. "We're fucking old."

"Speak for yourself."

"Well, since I'm the youngest and I'm saying that I'm old, that makes you decrepit."

I flip him off.

"So, what's up with you and the nanny known as Phoebe?"

"Nothing." It maybe would have worked if I'd said it less forcefully and not as quick.

Rowan lifts one side of his mouth. "The rumors are true then?"

"I have no idea what the rumors are, but I'm sure they're not true."

He manages to get to his feet and extends his hand to help me up. I grip his forearm and take the aid. "They're saying you fell on each other, or for each other. I didn't pay attention until I heard your name."

"It was on. She fell, I fell, it was an awkward situation, and that was that."

Rowan's demeanor shifts to being a bit more serious. "I see the way you look at her."

"I don't look at her any way."

"Sure, Ash. Continue to play the role of the Boy Scout, but I'm not stupid. You two keep dancing around each other, and it's cute to watch. I'm not saying that you shouldn't do whatever it is that you want to do. Hell, if anything, I'm telling you to break out of this monkhood you've entered and enter another realm with lots of debauchery."

And the seriousness is over, not that I expected it to last that long. "You need help."

"I don't deny that, but you need to fuck the nanny out of your system."

"I don't need that," I clarify.

In fact, the absolute last thing in the world I need is to do anything with the nanny. Phoebe is beautiful, smart, and funny. She is also not going to stay in Sugarloaf and has the potential to screw up my job and life.

"Mind if I do it then?"

I don't take the bait. He wants me to react like every part of me is screaming to, and I won't.

So, instead, I shrug. "If you want to, by all means."

Then I turn and walk away, clenching my fists because the idea of anyone touching her causes rage to course through every fiber of my body.

seventeen

PHOEBE

I lean my head against the car door as I drive. It's late, almost one in the morning, and I'm exhausted. There's no food in my father's house, so I am on my way back from the twenty-four-hour grocery store two towns over. I don't understand how my father thinks his diet of coffee and ginger ale is adequate, but it isn't.

I pull up Emmeline's number and dial, the girl is nocturnal like myself.

"Hey!" she answers happily, far too awake than any person should be.

"Ehh."

"Wow, you sound excited to talk to me."

"It's not you." My voice is clipped.

"Oh? Well, you're in a swell mood."

I am. "I'm irritated, sad, and ready for bed."

She laughs once. "Did something happen when you were volunteering?" I was at Run to Me for about four hours, helping Addison inventory supplies and create kits to give out to the runaways who come in for help. They were packed with necessary hygiene products along with resources and information that could help. Each runaway is asked to give basic information along with what the shelter can do for them, whether it's help from law enforcement, rehabilitation clinics, or reuniting them with their family.

"This girl came in today," I explain. "She was about seventeen and ran away because she was in love with her teacher. He promised her that he'd protect her, that he loved her, and they could be together, but they had to leave in order to be together."

Emmy sucks in a breath. "Wow."

"She was so young, you know? She believed everything he said."

"And you saw yourself," she finishes.

I saw this girl who thought she had something real that was really a work of fiction. It was so hard to listen to her and not feel like I was just as naïve as she was, and I have, like, seven years on her. I should've known better.

"She was so hopeless by the end. These guys of power who prey on women like that make me sick. I wanted to wrap her in my arms and tell her it would be okay, but that's a lie."

"Why is it a lie, Phoebs? You got played, same as she did, and you came out the other side of it okay."

I roll my eyes. "Yeah, look at me, the winner who is now lusting after her boss, who keeps trying to convince herself it's totally okay to have feelings for a man I definitely shouldn't have feelings for."

She groans. "Whatever is brewing with Asher is nothing like what happened with Jonathan! Nothing. Asher isn't promising you the world. He's not married, lying, or trying to get you to drop your panties so he can get what he wants. If anything, it sounds like the man is trying to put a chastity belt on you to avoid it."

I laugh, imagining him with a medieval metal plate. "That's probably the only way we're going to avoid it at this point."

"Sooooo, you like him?"

"You know I do, but I also am tired of making the wrong choices. I just . . . Paige, the girl from tonight, had this bright future, and now she's alone and worried her parents are going to go after the teacher."

"They should!" Emmeline says with anger lacing each word.

"I agree. Men like him shouldn't get away with these things."

Her story broke my heart. Paige was sixteen when they started their affair, and she was so emphatic that he loves her even though he abandoned her. She ran away three weeks ago, and each time he was supposed to meet her, he came up with some other excuse for why he couldn't. For the last week and a half, she's been living in the treehouse on the Arrowood farm, waiting for him to contact her and tell her it was clear so they could run away together.

He never showed.

"What ended up happening with her?" Emmy asks.

"She asked us to call her dad but then gave us the teacher's number instead, which was a whole other issue."

"Oh God."

"Yeah," I say around a sigh. "Addison wanted me to make the call so I could learn the procedure. Em, I was beyond disgusted. He pretended as though he didn't even know her. Said she was a student, but that he wasn't sure why she was reaching out to him. Never mind the fact she had his freaking personal cell phone number. But then, I heard a woman talking to him in the background."

I feel physically ill thinking about her. The woman who called him babe and asked who was on the phone. The woman who he clearly is either married to or living with. The woman who that teenager will never replace because he wasn't going to leave her.

"No wonder you're so upset."

"It's like the universe wanted to punch me in the face."

"You definitely got a right hook," she jokes.

I turn onto the backroad, taking the shortcut to my father's house, and the lights on my car start flashing.

"Shit! Em, I gotta go, something's wrong with my car," I say as the car sputters, jerks, sputters again, and then rolls to a stop.

"Are . . . you"—her voice is breaking up—"call?"

My phone beeps twice, letting me know I've completely lost signal, and I toss it onto my passenger seat and get out of my car. I look toward the hood, thankful nothing is smoking, and then I glance up and down the road I've broken down on. There is nothing within miles of this stupid dirt road, and the half moon really isn't giving me enough light to see. I try to remember what my dad said about tires and all that, and I walk around, kicking each wheel. They all feel fine—I think.

Okay, next step, pop the hood. I open the driver's side door, pull the lever, and release the lock to open it up. For a solid minute, I stare blankly at the engine, and then I decide it was a stupid idea to look because I don't know shit about cars.

I close it, go back to the driver's seat, and turn the key again, hoping maybe it just needed a break. We all do sometimes, right?

Nothing.

The lights come on, which means it's not the battery, and that's when I see that the gas gauge is on empty.

Fuck my life.

I left Run to Me, and the light came on, but I told myself ten times that I'd get gas after grocery shopping. Clearly, I forgot.

All I could think about was Paige and her piece-of-shit teacher.

It's now one twenty-five in the morning, my father is definitely asleep, and I have no fucking service.

"Curse you Sugarloaf!" I scream up at the sky.

I have two options. I can hunker down in my car and wait for someone to find me, or I can start to walk until I get service on my phone. Considering I had some about twenty feet back, I pull my coat on and start to walk.

I must look ridiculous, holding my phone up and walking around in circles like that commercial where the guy keeps asking, "Can you hear me now?"

No, no one can hear me because I still don't have a single bar.

"I swear, this is the worst week of my life!" I scream. "I

knocked over all the cans in the store and fell on top of Asher. Then I thought, *hey, Phoebe, volunteering will feed your soul*, only to find a girl who is just like me. But, this? Ohh, this is really the icing on my crap cake," I mutter, still walking and hoping for just one damn bar to call my dad. "Now you run out of gas."

I move farther down the road. My car is no longer visible, but I keep twisting left and right until, finally, the bar appears. I stop moving and dial my father's number. He doesn't answer. Figures.

I call again, still nothing.

I swear, that man can sleep through a war in the living room.

Then the battery on my phone turns red.

"And now my phone is about to die!"

Of course it is.

I could call the station, but then there would be record of this. Brynlee is another option, but it's the middle of the night. That leaves . . . Asher.

He's the last person I want to ask for help, but . . . I don't know who else to call, and I am so fucking tired.

So, here it goes.

He answers on the second ring.

"Phoebe?"

"Hey, uh, I'm stranded on Old Mill Road."

"What the hell are you doing out there?"

"I'm stuck here. I have almost no battery on my phone, so I can't explain more, but could you . . . come get me or maybe just bring a can of gas . . ."

This is mortifying. Seriously, I just want to crawl into a hole and never come out.

"You ran out of gas?"

"If you can't come, that's fine. I'll call the station and see if Joey is working," I say, frustration flowing through my voice. "I don't want you to have to wake Olivia to come."

"No. I'll be there. Brynn and Rowan were here playing cards two minutes ago, so I can grab Brynn to stay here."

"Thank you."

It will take him about fifteen minutes to get here, so I go through all the ways that I can explain this so he doesn't give me hell for it. I come up with a whole lot of nothing. I was stupid, that's that, and I feel stupid, so there's that too.

More than anything, I really don't want to listen to it from him.

He'll never understand why this upset me. Why some girl, I don't know, had me so distracted I forgot to get gas.

I've worked so hard to get him to see me as a smart, responsible, and mature woman who manages her life, and then I have this shit happen.

My stomach is in knots thinking about the loads of bullshit that are coming my way. I really don't think I can take it. Not tonight. Not when I'm this raw.

What feels like an eternity later, headlights illuminate the field, and a second later, Asher's pickup pulls up next to me. He has an old truck that doesn't have a radio or power anything, but it's well built and could withstand a war. Sort of reminds me of the man behind the wheel.

He gets out and looks to where I'm leaning against my closed driver's door. "I don't have any gas other than diesel, so why don't we leave your car here, you can stay at my place, and we'll take care of it in the morning before I leave for my shift?"

Sounds like a terrible plan, but I'm not going to argue with the guy who just drove all the way out here to help.

I grab my groceries from the back, and because I'm having the worst day, when I lift the last bag, it rips open, spilling the contents on the dirt road.

"Fuck!" I yell and tears threaten to spill over. I'm so angry, so upset, and I can't control my fucking emotions. "Like one thing? I can't have just one goddamn thing go right?" Asher is already crouching to pick up the contents, so I shake my head, wiping the traitorous tear that fell, and grab one of the cartons of ice cream that is already oozing out the sides. "Of course."

"Ice cream melts, Phoebe, it's not bad luck."

"I'm aware that it does, however, it wouldn't have melted if I'd gotten home."

He scoffs. "If you put gas in your car, you would've gotten home."

I throw the carton on the ground and straighten. "I know this. I'm not stupid. I forgot, okay? In the midst of my already shitty fucking night, I forgot."

"And if Olivia was in the car?"

"Then I wouldn't be having this shitty of a night, would I? I would be at your house with her," I snap back.

Asher runs his hand through his hair. "You go from fucking brilliant to a headcase in two seconds."

"And you go from the hero who drove out here in the middle of the night to judgmental prick in the same time span!"

He takes two steps toward me. "Get in the truck."

"Here we are again. You trying to order me into a vehicle!"

Fighting with him feels so much better than bursting into tears. This is the first time in hours that I'm not thinking of that girl or horrible men. Asher is not a horrible man, he's kind, considerate, hot as hell, and when he's angry, the fire burns hotter.

I am stoking it and living for the sparks.

"You called me!"

"Oops, my bad," I say and move to the other side of the car to pull the rest of my groceries out.

He grabs my arm, spinning me around. "What is your issue?"

"Men. Men are my issue. You all think you can boss us around. You think you're so smart and smug. Take what you want, and then what? What about what I want? Why is it all about what you want? Huh?"

"You don't want to know what I want right now, Phoebe. Now, get in the truck so we can get out of the cold and you can get some sleep!"

"I'm not cold."

Asher lets out a deep breath, which fogs between us like some

171

silent punctuation to him proving his point. "You want to stay out here? Fine. I need to get back to my daughter. Brynn needs to work in the morning, and I can't stand out here and fight with you about whatever has you pissed and has nothing to do with me."

He's right. My anger has nothing to do with Asher, and it isn't fair of me to take it out on him. I also don't want him to leave me here—not that I really think he would, but I don't want to call him on his unspoken threat. As though nature can suddenly hear me, a coyote wails from somewhere that is way too close for comfort.

"Fine, I'll get in the truck," I say, as though it was my idea.

He huffs. "Great."

I grab my purse from the front seat while he gets the rest of the groceries—without a bag ripping on him—and then gets into the truck.

I plug my phone in and then shoot a text off to Emmeline to let her know I'm okay and my dark knight has arrived to scold me all the way home.

He heads down Old Mill Road, and five turns later, we're at the entrance of his farm. The road twists a little and then the sign comes into view. I sit with my arms crossed, my pouting at an all-time high of absurdity, but I am overtired, sexually frustrated, and pissed at myself, so there's no pulling back.

When we pull up, Asher sighs. "Go on in and get to bed, I'll bring your groceries up."

My initial reaction is to cry, but I don't speak. I've reached the stage of self-loathing where I'm so upset that I am about to break.

So, I nod, not wanting to lose it in front of him, and head inside.

"You're here!" Brynn says when she sees me. "Is everything okay?"

"Everything is fine," Asher explains as he comes in, carrying all eight bags as if they weigh nothing. "Car broke down, and it's been a long night."

Brynlee looks to me. "Are you okay?"

No, I'm totally not okay.

"I'm just a bit emotional," I confess, knowing that there's no way I can lie as my lower lip trembles.

"Do you want me to stay? We can talk . . ."

"No, I just want to sleep, if that's okay."

"Of course. I'm sorry, Phoebe, for whatever has you upset. Just know that if you ever need me, I'm here."

I appreciate that. Brynlee has always been nice to me, but since I started nannying for Olivia, she's truly become a great friend.

"Do you need me to bring you home?" Asher asks his sister. "I know you have court in the morning."

"Absolutely not. I am fine driving the mile to my house." She gives her brother a hug and taps his nose. "I love you. Get some sleep." Then she turns to me. "You too."

"I will."

Then the house feels too quiet, and I have the deepest urge to see Olivia. To know she's safe and not talking to some random asshole who might be telling her all the things she'll want to hear just so she'll believe the lies.

So many lies.

So many men who will do or say anything to gain what they want.

As I start to move toward the stairs, Asher calls my name. "Phoebe? Where are you going?"

"I just . . . I need to see Olivia for a second."

He nods once. "I'll go with you."

We head upstairs, and he opens her door, allowing me to walk in first. As soon as I see Liv, my emotions get the better of me, and tears drop from my lashes before I can stop them.

"Why are you crying?" he asks.

"I wish I could protect her from the horrors of the world. How do you do this? How do you love someone so much and know that, someday, something will break her heart?"

Asher looks down at Olivia. "I just hope that I've loved her enough that she'll know she can get through it. People prey on the innocent, so it's my job to protect her the best way I can."

They prey on the foolish too. On people like Paige and me who are too naïve or too stupid to see the truth that is right in front of us.

"And what about those who aren't innocent? What about the ones who just trust the wrong people? How do we protect against that? How do we help those people who need it?" A sob leaves my throat, and I hate myself.

I hate that I can't control my feelings. I hate that I am falling apart in front of this man because I am better than this. I have worked for weeks to prove that, and now, I'm losing all that ground in one day.

Before I can do anything, I'm lifted into Asher's arms, and he's carrying me back downstairs. I bury my face in his neck, unwilling to look at him.

"Easy, sweetheart," Asher says softly, his lips brushing the top of my head. "Easy. Breathe."

He pushes my bedroom door open and then sits on the bed with me in his lap.

"Why are you truly crying?"

The soothing tone he uses has me so close to telling him, to unloading all the shit that has been weighing me down.

I wouldn't be able to handle the censure in his eyes or withstand the disappointment in his voice, though.

It's stupid, really, because Asher means nothing to me. I'm supposed to tell myself that he's the grumpy asshole who works for my father or the untouchable father of the girl I look after.

But he's more than that.

At some point in the last few weeks, he's started to be more. The single father who loves his daughter with his whole heart. The protective brother who will do anything for his siblings. The sheriff who leaves his house in the middle of the night without

174

question to help a woman stranded on the side of the road. More than that, he's become the man I want more than air.

The thing is . . . he can't be mine. Not ever.

Instead of embarrassing myself even more, I suck in a breath, sit up straight, and move off his lap. "I think I'm just exhausted."

"Don't," he warns.

"Don't what?"

"Don't pull away from me or tell me this is just exhaustion. I saw you when I pulled up, and it's not about being tired. I saw your face as you talked about someone hurting Olivia. I know there's something hurting you and can see it play across your face when you don't think anyone is watching." He shifts closer, and his hand moves to my cheek, rubbing away the trail of tears. "I see everything, even when I wish I didn't. So, don't lie to me."

My throat is tight as I look at him. "You see me?"

"Everywhere I look."

A riot of emotions moves through me, and I wonder if anyone ever has really seen *me*. After my mother died, my father only sees her when he looks at me, and I'm a constant reminder of the woman he loved and lost. Jonathan made me think he saw me, but he never did. He only saw what he wanted and then took it, leaving me the fool in the end.

But Asher . . . he's different.

"And what do you see?" I ask, afraid of the answer but unwilling to let this moment go.

His eyes close, and he brings our foreheads together. "I see a selfless girl. I see a smart woman who is going to change the world. I see a woman who is so fiercely protective of the people she loves that she'll do battle for them. I see the most beautiful and desirable woman in the world. What I can't have. What I want. What keeps me up at night. What has my entire belief system at war, trying to convince myself that I can't give you what you want, even if I wish I could."

Each word is like a balm over my battered soul. I want him. I want us and this and him, consequences be damned. "What if I wasn't asking for anything?" I say, my heart pounding.

"I don't know what you mean."

I bring my lips closer, just a breath apart. "What if you can have it? What if it's just ours until I leave? We have a limited time, and I don't know that I can keep resisting this. Not after the last time. Not when you make me feel like this. We can have this, even if only for a little while."

His nose moves against mine, causing a shiver to run through me. "No one can know."

"I won't tell if you won't."

All the things I told myself, all the reasons this is a bad idea, seem inconsequential. All that seems to matter is him and the bone-deep desire I have for this man.

We can be temporary. Sure, he's my boss, but only until I leave to go back to school. Yes, he works for my dad, but if we keep this between us, then my father will never know. Asher isn't married, and he isn't one of my professors. We wouldn't be breaking any rules unless they are ones we set for ourselves. So, why can't we do this?

His hands move up my arms and then cradle my neck. "Our secret."

eighteen

ASHER

ine. That word vibrates through me like a tuning fork. I need to make her mine. She offers me what I want, what I need, and I am going to take it.

My mouth finds hers, and she opens to me, so trusting, so sweet. I revel in the taste of her, knowing I could drown in it.

Despite all the reasons this is wrong, this feels so right. This is an agreement between adults, and she wasn't wrong when she said that no one else needs to know.

For the next few months, though, she'll be mine, and then she'll go back to school while I go back to my life. It's as simple as that.

Phoebe's hands fist in my hair as I shift her so she's straddling me. The heat of her is almost too much, but then she leans back, her eyes finding mine in the haze of lust, and she rips her top off, leaving her in her sports bra.

My dominant side kicks in, needing control. "Take the bra off," I order.

Phoebe doesn't like to be told what to do, and I want nothing more than for her to learn that I'm in charge here and now.

Her brown eyes flash with indignation, and I smirk, rocking

back onto my elbows. I push her again. "I want to see your tits, sweetheart, take it off for me."

"Or what?"

My cock swells at the defiance in her voice. "Do you want to push me and find out?"

Phoebe grins. "Maybe I do. Maybe I want to see what you'll do when you meet a girl who doesn't just bend to your will."

I push her off my lap, and she glares as I stand, looming over her. "I'm not some college boy who wants to play grown-up." I pull my shirt off and toss it to the floor.

Her eyes drink me in, and I let her get her fill. "No, you're definitely not."

"We can play games, or you can be a good girl and do as you're told."

"I'm not very good at following directions," Phoebe replies.

I grab her ankles, pulling her to me, and she squeaks. "Take off your fucking bra and let me see your perfect tits. Then I promise you'll like what I do next."

I step back and help her to her feet, wanting to keep the upper hand with her. I love that she doesn't back down to me—or anyone, really—but right now, I want to strip her of all of that.

Slowly, she hooks her fingers under the band around her ribs and pulls it up. Her breasts fall from their confines, and I move in before she can get it over her head. My tongue laps at the perfect nipple, and her head falls back as she tugs her bra the rest of the way off and tosses it away.

"Asher."

I moan as I suck her nipple into my mouth. Her fingers thread into my hair, holding me there.

Moving to the other side, I give it the same attention, and as much as I want to drive her crazy, I want to taste her. I want to lick her and make her come with my head between her legs.

I push her back onto the bed. "I have fought every urge when it comes to you," I tell her, angry at her for making me break my own rules. "I've told myself this would never happen again. That I wouldn't let you tempt me to hell." I lean over her so our mouths are a breath apart. "But since I can't seem to resist, I'm going to make sure you never forget what we share. This time, I'm going to give and give and give until you ache everywhere for me. You'll never forget how good I make you feel."

Phoebe lets out a long sigh. "I don't think that's even possible."

I'll replay this over and over once she's gone.

"I want to see you bare, Phoebe. I want every inch of you on display. Take off your pants, sweet girl."

I want to take my time and memorize her body. I'm greedy for her. She obeys this time without comment, and I fight back the grin. She's even more goddamn beautiful than my dreams conjured. Her body is lean and curvy in all the best places. I run my hand from her breast to her pussy. "Because you listened so well, I think you deserve something."

"Oh?"

I pull her hips to the edge of the bed and fall to my knees. "I think I should lick you until you scream. Make you come on my tongue before you take my cock. Did you like how you came with me between your legs before?"

"Yes."

"Good, after I taste you again, you're going to come on my cock."

She moans, falling back on the bed as I adjust her legs over each of my shoulders. I kiss the inside of her thigh, moving up to where I want her most, and smile against her skin as she trembles. When I arrive at her center, I run my tongue along her seam, groaning as I taste her sweetness.

Phoebe shifts, and I move my hands to her hips, holding her down as I do it again. Over and over, I push my tongue against her clit, listening to every moan and paying attention to each move she makes. She whimpers when I flick it harder, and I bury my head even deeper, making shapes and circles against the nerves there.

"Asher, oh God—" she pants, and I adjust again.

I push higher on my knees, coming at a different angle, and lift her hips. I stroke over and over that same spot, and her head starts to thrash back and forth.

"I'm . . . oh, so close. Jesus, you're a God."

I cup her breast, squeezing and plucking her nipple, then I take her hand and place it there.

She understands what I want her to do, and she pleasures herself. I am fucking hard as a rock watching her watch me.

My tongue pushes into her, keeping my gaze locked with hers, the moment feeling too intimate, but I won't look away.

I'm going to enjoy watching her fall apart as the waves of pleasure take her under. I suck on her clit and adjust so I can finger her at the same time. Phoebe lets out a low moan, and then she bows up off the bed, twisting and making me have to hold her in place because I want every drop of her pleasure.

Tremors wrack her body as she goes limp, and I ease the pressure of my mouth before kissing my way up her body. When we're face to face, she smiles and laughs softly.

"Well, you've definitely proven that it's not a me problem."

I grin, pushing her dark brown hair back. "No, definitely not." I look at the clock and laugh. "Not even five minutes."

Her eyes widen. "What? No way."

I kiss up her neck to her ear and nip the lobe. "And I'm not done with you yet, sweetheart. You're going to come again."

Phoebe's hand moves down my spine slowly, her legs wrapping around my waist. "You're very confident of this." She slides around to my front, going to my waist.

"Do you doubt me?" I ask, licking the shell of her ear. "Do I need to prove it again?"

"I like when you prove me wrong."

Maybe in this only because most of the time she enjoys challenging me. Every time I think she'll fail, she doesn't. Phoebe not only likes to challenge, but she wants the same in return.

I hover over her. "You continue to do that."

"I know."

"And I do the same to you."

Phoebe blushes. "Yes, you most certainly have." She twists her hand down into my pants, rubbing my cock. "I want you, Asher."

"You have no idea how much I want to be inside you right now."

"Then do it, please." I shift back enough to push my pants down, freeing my cock. "Holy shit."

I grin because every man likes it when a woman sees him naked and says that. I move my hand to my dick, stroking it as she watches. "How should I fuck you? On our knees so I can slap your pretty ass? On your back with your legs on my shoulders as I take you deep? Or do you want to ride me, bounce on my cock while I lie here and watch your perfect tits?"

Her lips part, breathing growing heavier. "I . . ."

"You what? You want all of it?" I ask, inching toward her. "Or do you want me to pick?"

Phoebe shakes her head, and I love that I've scrambled her brain. "All of the above."

I lean down, taking her bottom lip between my teeth. "Good choice."

Then I'm flipping her onto her stomach and pulling her hips up. Phoebe gasps as I push a finger into her.

"I am never going to recover from this," she says as she lifts onto her hands.

Neither am I.

I push another finger into her, pumping and twisting as she moans. Her muscles clench around me, and I want to fill her, feel her contract around my dick.

"Phoebe, I wanted to make you come again like this, but I am losing my mind."

She's so perfect, her body bending to my will.

"Take me. God, just take me."

I go to line up and then remember I don't have a condom. "Shit. Do you have a condom?"

183

"In my bag!" She points to her purse. "I'm on the pill, too, so we're covered either way."

Yeah, not taking any chances. I dump everything out of the bag and find the condom. I get it on while walking back to her, watching as her ass sways invitingly, and I can't help but slap it.

"You just spanked me!"

"That's for not listening earlier." I do it again, and this time, I slide the fingers of my other hand into her. "You like that."

She bites on her lip and nods. Yeah, I thought she might. "Asher, please."

I push down on her back, forcing her ass to rise higher, and then I slide deep. The feeling is unlike anything I've ever felt before. Her heat is almost too much, her tightness is perfect, and I am so fucked.

She keeps pace with me, letting me hold her hips, and I love the sound of her skin slapping against mine. I pull her up so her back is to my chest and move slowly while I hold her face where I can kiss her.

The two of us are sweating, and the sounds of sex fill the air. We move in tandem, each of us finding a way to go deeper than before, her hands are wrapped around my neck, putting her breasts on full display, and I fondle her.

"I can't take much more," she says, but I am going to prove her wrong.

"You haven't given me what I want," I tell her, and she falls forward, resting on her hands as I pull out of her. "Get on your back."

She does, and I push her legs apart before sliding back in, moaning as I do. "You feel so fucking good, sweetheart. You're so hot and tight. You're perfect."

"It's too much. I can't . . ."

"You can. Feel us. Feel me deep inside you. Feel how good it is." I take her hand, moving it to where my cock is pushing in and out of her. "Look at us, Phoebe."

She lifts her head, watching as I fuck her. "So fucking hot."

"Damn right it is. You're mine right now. You're mine, and I'm so deep inside you. Do you feel it?"

"Yes!" she cries out.

I entwine our fingers and move them to her clit, playing with the nerves that are already overstimulated.

"That's it, baby, feel how wet you are, stop thinking and feel. Feel all of it." She's barely able to catch her breath, and I can feel her growing closer. "You're going to make me come, Phoebe. You're going to make me lose my fucking mind because you feel too good. Does it feel good for you?"

"Asher!" She screams my name as she falls apart again, and I don't even get to watch because I can't stop myself. I follow her into one of the most incredible orgasms of my life.

It's all I can do not to collapse on top of her, and my arms shake as I hold myself up. What I don't know is whether they are shaking from endorphins or because I've just made the biggest mistake of my life. Does the reason even matter if the result of both is the knowledge that I'll never be able to let her go now that I've had her?

That question scares the fuck out of me.

nineteen

PHOEBE

I can't help but giggle. I'm like a stupid little girl, and I can't stop.

I thought I knew what great sex was, but . . . yeah, I'd had no idea. He spanked me, and I really fucking liked it. Who knew? He made me orgasm twice, which I have never done before.

The entire night is just kind of . . . surreal.

Asher Whitlock, my employer, the police officer I can't stand, and the bossy asshole, is still buried deep inside me. I must be dreaming.

I giggle again, and Asher pushes onto his elbows, staring down at me. "Are you laughing at me?"

"No. Definitely not at you."

"Then at what?"

It's probably not the best reaction to laugh after earth-shattering sex, but I honestly just can't believe it.

"The kind of . . . unbelievability of this whole night." I run my fingers through his hair. "First, the whole runaway thing, then my car running out of gas, and then us ending up here—together —naked."

"I like you naked."

"That makes two of us."

Yeah, he is fucking perfect, and seeing him with his shirt open was absolutely nothing compared to seeing him naked. His chest all muscles and dips and valleys. He has that perfect V-shape at his hips, and don't even get me started on his arms. Those are totally my thing, and Asher has arms that I want to stay wrapped up in. They come with an added bonus of having a half sleeve hidden under all those clothes. I run my fingers along the lines, tracing the outline of a dove with its wings open. It's holding a vintage lock in its feet and there is a flower below it.

I can feel his eyes on me, and for some reason, I'm much too vulnerable to look at him. Instead, I focus on the black-and-white ink on his arm and shoulder. "Why a dove?"

He pushes my hair back and tilts my face to meet his eyes, which are currently light blue with a dark rim around the edge. "For my mother."

"And the lock?"

"Because of my last name."

"And where is the key?"

He moves his arm a little and it's inside the flower.

I smile. "It's beautiful. I need to clean up."

"Hey, are you okay?"

I nod. "I'm fine. It's been a long night, and it is"—I glance at the clock and my eyes widen—"four in the morning."

Asher kisses my nose and then pushes up. There is a sense of emptiness as soon as he's gone. Not going to unpack that right now, I'll find another time to dwell on it. I grab my blanket, wrapping it around myself, and he heads into the bathroom.

I hear a click of the lock and flop back down. Well, that was unexpected. I didn't think I would ever actually go through with it—or that he would either. Yet, we both did.

I force myself back up, my legs wobbly as though I'm a newborn giraffe taking its first steps. The contents of my purse are scattered across the floor, but the one case there reminds me to take my pill. Especially since I'm back on the sex train again. I swallow it without water, and I try to get dressed before he comes out, throwing my sweatshirt on and grabbing my shorts. However, my leg gets caught in my shorts, causing me to hop around in a bid not to fall.

Of course, he comes out right as I'm mid jump and gets to watch as I fail to stick the landing.

I land on my ass, one pant leg twisted and looking like an idiot.

He laughs. "I swear, you and your clothes."

This time, I don't swat his offered hand away. He picks me up, tosses my shorts to the floor, and carries me to the bed.

"Asher!"

"Stop complaining."

"I need my shorts."

He climbs into the bed beside me, tucking me against his chest. "Uh, what are you doing?" I ask once the shock wears off.

"We have a few minutes."

As happy as I am to lie in his big, strong arms, we can't do this. What if Olivia finds us? Or, the more possible outcome, what if I start to want more than just this agreement of sex until I leave?

I can't do that. I can't get my heart tangled up in our very noncommittal relationship.

"Asher, we can't . . ."

"Why not?"

"Because!" I say as though that reason is valid in every way.

He shifts, tightening his hold. "Just close your eyes."

I huff because I can and then do as he says. I listen to the steady beat of his heart and let the rhythmic motion of his hand going up and down my back lull me into a hazy calm. Asher moves, draping my leg over his and resting his hand on my bare ass.

I am in that pre-sleep state where I am not fully there but not really awake either. The deep timbre of his voice rumbles against my ear. "I am in so much trouble with you." His lips press against my forehead. "So much trouble."

I wake, and it isn't one of those peaceful, eyes fluttering slowly mornings. No, it's a sit straight up in a panic as I pat myself to make sure I'm alive kind of awakening.

My breathing is labored as I look around, noting the subtle differences from when I passed out.

One, Asher is gone.

Two, my lights are off.

Three, it's freaking eleven in the morning, and I needed to be up at six.

And four, everything is back in my purse, which is now hanging from the hook on the door.

Well, that was sweet.

I get up and throw on a pair of leggings. There is sound coming from the living room, and I rush out, pissed that I am clearly an asshole and horrible nanny. It hasn't even been twenty-four hours since I screwed my boss, and I'm already messing up on the job.

Olivia is sitting on the couch watching a show and eating popcorn, which I am sure is not in the binder.

I walk around her, throwing my hair up, and she smiles at me. *"Morning."*

"Good morning, why didn't you wake me?" I ask her.

"Daddy said to let you sleep," she explains.

Right, well, that's great. *"I'm sorry."*

She shakes her head. *"I'm not a baby anymore. I can watch television."*

This is true, but still, as her nanny, it's my responsibility to make sure she doesn't burn the house down. I look at the coffee table where there is evidence of her breakfast choices. KitKats and a bag of Doritos.

Not that I wouldn't eat that, but I know for a fact that Olivia isn't allowed.

I crouch down, hand extended. *"Popcorn."*

She grumbles and hands it over.

I sign for her to go brush her teeth so we can get stuff done today. First thing I need is my car so we can go food shopping again, buy more condoms because I only had one, and stop by my house to grab my bag.

My phone pings, and I nearly jump at the vibration.

ASHER
Are you awake yet?

> I am. Why did you let me sleep?

ASHER
You were exhausted. Olivia can handle herself for a few hours.

> She shouldn't have to.

ASHER
You could just say: thank you for letting me sleep, Asher. I really appreciate it and all the orgasms you gave me last night.

> I could, but that's not really my style. However, those were much appreciated. I need my car. Is there any way you can come get me today?

ASHER
Look out front.

I walk over, and sure enough, it's sitting in the driveway.

> That was sweet of you.

ASHER
Do I get my thank you now?

191

Thank you, Asher. I appreciate my vehicle and the orgasms.

ASHER

Trouble. All right, I need to work. Behave, and I'll see you later. Are you staying the night?

I gnaw on my thumbnail. Technically, I don't really have to. He's off tomorrow . . . well, he's on call, but that kind of counts as off. I would normally stay at my house because I hadn't wanted to be here. After last night, though, I really want to be here. I want to be in his arms and come apart again.

God, I'm a mess.

I'm not sure yet. I'll let you know.

ASHER

Stay the night, Phoebe.

His command causes my stomach to flip, and I slip my phone into my bra before I text him something ridiculous and head to my room. Once there, I shower quickly, not washing my hair. I grab my best friend—dry shampoo—and put my hair in a fishtail.

I know it's not actually possible to look different after mind-blowing sex, but I swear the girl in the mirror isn't the same. My lips look plumper, face brighter, and the bags under my eyes are gone.

Or I'm insane. Either is possible.

My fingers rub against my lips, and it's as if I can feel his touch.

I roll my eyes, groan, shake myself out of my sex-stupor, and grab my phone.

When I check my email, my stomach drops when I see one from University of Texas.

Instead of opening it, I text Emmeline.

> I got my decision from Texas.

Maybe six seconds pass, but it feels like hours.

EMMELINE
And????????????

> I don't know.

EMMELINE
Huh?

> I didn't open it. I'm afraid.

EMMELINE
Don't be a chickenshit. Just open it! No matter what, you have other options.

She's right. I should look.

I exhale deeply, pull my emails back up, and open it.

Dear Ms. Bettencourt,

Thank you for your interest in University of Texas.

Blah, blah, blah.

· · ·

We would like to invite you to come to pursue your AuD at University of Texas.

I scream and dance around the room, my legs going up and down quickly as I spin in a chaotic circle. I got in! I got into one of my top schools. I could cry, and I know this is one hundred percent thanks to Professor Calloway.

She must've pulled some very big strings.

Needing to tell someone, I rush out into the living room and then take the stairs two at a time. When I get to Olivia's room, I press the doorbell on the wall that will flash a light to let her know someone is outside.

She opens her door with a sour face, but I don't care because I am overflowing with joy. I sign quickly. *"I got in!"*

"Where?"

"University of Texas! I got a spot for next semester."

I told Olivia about how I left Iowa and wasn't going back as well as how nervous I was about it. Normally, I wouldn't have said anything to her about it, but I used it as a way to be relatable and to let her know that it's okay to be afraid of things but push through them. She does it with her appointments and therapy, and now, she sees me doing it with school.

She jumps up, her frown now a bright, wide smile. We hug and jump around in circles. My relief is so unreal. If I hadn't gotten in, I would have had to push a year back, which wouldn't have been the end of the world, but it wouldn't have been great either.

Liv leans back. *"Texas is far."*

I nod. *"It is, but so was Iowa."*

"I didn't know you before." She sighs heavily. *"I'll miss you."*

I am going to miss her so damn much. In only a few weeks, Olivia has become very important to me. She's wonderful, smart, beautiful, and has the potential to do anything she desires.

"I will email all the time."

"*Promise?*"

"*Yes. I will visit too. We should celebrate.*"

Her blue eyes, the ones that are just like her father's, brighten. "*Ice cream?*"

I laugh. "*Perfect.*"

twenty

ASHER

"Late night?" Chief Bettencourt asks as he slaps my shoulder. "You look exhausted."

Yeah, I was doing rude things to your daughter until four AM. Fuck my life.

"Just busy, that's all."

"How's my baby girl? Is she behaving?"

I look up. "Phoebe is great with Olivia."

"I mean with you. Are you guys getting on okay?"

What the fuck is happening? I swear I'm making up these words in my head. He can't possibly be asking this.

"I'm not understanding," I say for clarification.

"You and Phoebe don't exactly get along. I had to basically threaten your job to get you to hire her. Did the two of you come to some kind of understanding and put the past behind you?" The way he says that makes it clear he thinks I'm an idiot.

"Yes, we definitely have an understanding now."

One that includes naked time and secrets.

"Good. Has she said anything about school?"

Even if she had, I wouldn't tell him. Whatever happened in Iowa, she isn't talking about it. "Nope."

He nods. "That girl can keep a secret just like her mother could, and she lets it eat at her."

A text comes through, and speak of the devil . . .

PHOEBE
We are coming to the station now.

Is everything okay?

PHOEBE
Worrywart.

I glance up at her father. "Phoebe and Olivia are actually on their way here now."

His chest puffs up, and the usually dour man actually seems excited. "Really? Wonderful."

About two minutes later, Olivia rushes through the door with Phoebe right behind her. Our desk officer buzzes them through. Then Olivia runs to me and wraps her arms around my middle. I hug her tightly, and when I look over at Phoebe, I have to remind myself to breathe.

She really is bright like the sun, and looking at her for too long might cause me to go blind.

Her hair is pulled to the side and twisted into some braid thing. The same lightness I saw in her eyes last night is still there. Her cheeks redden when she looks at me, and then she turns her gaze to her father.

"Hi, Daddy." Her voice cracks a little.

"Pleasant surprise," Chief says, pulling her into his arms. "I feel like I haven't seen you in ages."

Olivia releases me, signing quickly. I shake my head. *"Slow. I missed what you said."*

She rolls her eyes and starts again. *"Phoebe has news."*

"Phoebe has news?" I say aloud and sign so everyone knows what we were saying.

Phoebe turns to Olivia with pursed lips, but there isn't a single trace of anger. *"You weren't supposed to say anything."*

"Sorry." Olivia grins.

Phoebe rests her hand on Liv's head. "So, I have big news."

"What is the news?" I ask.

"I got into Texas!"

"Texas?" Both Chief and I say at the same time.

"Yes, I'm still waiting on Vanderbilt, but at least I got into Texas! I'll only lose about two credits, which isn't ideal but not terrible either. The program starts in August, and I'll need to get an apartment. Shit. I should do that sooner, I'm sure they're already full. All of this is . . ."

I do my best to sign all of what she said, but I lose track and basically summarize. *"Phoebe got into schools. She's happy. Has a lot to do."*

Olivia taps my hand. *"I know. We celebrated."*

"You did?" I ask her.

"Ice cream."

Of course my daughter convinced Phoebe to get her ice cream. Sara is going to kill me if she finds out how many sweets Olivia's been eating. Whatever.

This . . . thing we're doing has an official expiration date, which is a good thing. Knowing that she isn't going to somehow convince herself that we should keep going is exactly what she needs. There is a buzzer at the end of this ticking clock, and when it goes off, she's gone and we go our separate ways.

When she comes home from school, she'll probably want to visit Liv, and we can fuck again then. All of this is kind of the perfect arrangement, honestly.

"When would you leave?" I ask Phoebe.

She pulls her lower lip into her mouth. "Not sure, but don't worry, I'll help make sure you have childcare set by then, and I'll stay on even if you get a new nanny before I leave so that she's all set with Liv."

That's what I should've been worried about, but it was more about how much time she and I have.

"Well, congratulations."

She smiles. "Thank you. I . . . hope to celebrate more—soon."

Chief laughs loudly. "Congrats, Phoebs! I am glad you found a better school. You're off tonight, right? We should do dinner and maybe we can watch some of our old shows?"

Phoebe looks to me, and I shake my head just slightly. We're going to celebrate tonight, but it won't be dinner and a show—well, not *that* kind of show.

She runs her teeth across her lip and then looks back to her dad. "I think dinner sounds great, but I have plans tonight and will probably crash at my friend's house."

"Dinner it is then." He kisses her cheek and then winks at Olivia.

"Can I play a game?" Olivia asks after he leaves.

I point to my phone on my desk, and she grabs it before opening some app.

Phoebe moves close to me. "You're sleeping at a friend's?"

Her warm brown eyes find mine. "I thought you wanted me to stay the night."

"I do."

She looks around the room, moving closer when she sees it's safe. "Are you my friend, Asher?"

"I'd like to think so."

"Then, do you have plans for our sleepover?" Her voice is sultry, and I wish we weren't here so I could give her a preview of my plans.

I drop my voice, even knowing my daughter can't hear. "I plan to show you how I celebrate, and you're going to enjoy every bit of pleasure I pull from your body. I'm going to make you light up the sky."

She grins. "I can't wait."

Neither fucking can I.

Phoebe's hot mouth is wrapped around my cock, taking me deep. "That's it, sweetheart, take me deeper," I instruct.

Not that she needs much instruction when her just being near me is enough to set me off. I don't know what it is about this girl, but I am unable to stop myself.

The second I knew for sure that Olivia was asleep, I scooped Phoebe off the couch and tossed her onto my bed.

We tumbled together, kissing, tearing each other's clothes off, both of us desperate for the other. She came once already as I proved to her that the last two times I'd eaten her out weren't flukes. Then she stood, pulled me to my feet, and dropped to her knees.

I nearly came when she looked up through those long lashes and asked me to tell her how I liked it.

Like this. I like it just like this.

"You are so good," I praise her. "You feel so good, look so perfect on your knees with my cock in your mouth. Do you like it?"

She moans around my dick, and my head falls back. "Fuck, Phoebe."

I'm losing control. I want to be inside her again, to make her orgasm harder than she did last night.

My hand is tangled in her hair as I pump my hips, and it becomes too much, so I move quickly, missing the feel of her mouth already.

Then I'm pulling her to her feet and chuckling at the pout she gives me. "I was enjoying that."

"Oh, so was I," I say before I take her mouth with mine.

She is more than I ever dreamed. She's warm and willing but also cold and defiant. It's a mixture blending together into something that is just so her.

Phoebe places her hand on my chest, trying to push me back onto the bed. I allow it, but she looks a bit too smug as she stands at the end of the bed. "It's my night." She tilts her head to the side. "I want to celebrate."

"Isn't that what we're doing?" If I'm being honest, I'm definitely winning tonight as well.

"Oh, we are, but . . . I really want to celebrate."

"And what do you have in mind?" I ask, lacing my fingers behind my head.

She climbs up on the bed and braces herself over me, letting her hair hang in a curtain around us. "You."

"I'm all yours, sweetheart. Use me to celebrate your victory."

Her lips press against mine, and I can feel her heat. I grab her hips, dimpling her flesh as I squeeze.

"I want"—she kisses me softly—"to have"—another kiss—"my way."

I bite her lip. "Fuck me, Phoebe, and have whatever you want."

She sinks down, and I could die. Her body is so tight, and while last night I was deep inside her, this angle feels even better.

I push her up, angling her hips forward and her chest back. She's so beautiful, so perfect, so much better than I deserve.

Her hips move, and I hold on to her, letting her control the movements. She tightens around me even more, and God, it feels so damn good.

"Yes, it does," she says, and I realize I said it aloud.

"I'm close, Phoebe." Her hands fall to my chest as she breathes harder. She's close too. I slip my hand between us and start to rub her clit.

"Oh, oh God, Asher. I can't."

"I'm not going to be able to hold back, sweetheart," I warn.

This is too good. Too fucking much.

She moans, and I increase the pressure.

Come on, Phoebe. I need you to come.

Her nails score my chest, and I feel her come apart. I hold on, wanting to savor this one, to feel every pulse of her around me.

When she falls to my chest, I push my hips up, and the sound that comes from me is almost angry.

We fight to catch our breath, and it's a handful of seconds later that I realize what we've just done.

The wet feeling drips down my leg and panic sets in. "Phoebe," I say, angry that I didn't think. How the fuck did I not think about it?

I am always careful.

I have a nine-year-old reason to be extremely careful.

She lifts her head. "Hmm?"

"I . . . forgot. Damn it!"

Dawning seems to hit her, and she moves quickly. "Towel?"

"Bathroom."

She rushes in there, tosses a towel at me, and then grabs my zip-up, closing it around her.

"I'm sorry." Phoebe walks over, her face ashen.

"You're sorry? For what?"

"I didn't think. I just *wanted*—"

No way am I going to let her shoulder this. I know better. "This is on me. Look, whatever happens . . ."

"Asher, chill." Phoebe takes two steps to me. "I'm on the pill. I take it every night before I go to bed. I never miss. We're fine. It was one time, and I just had my . . . you know, like six . . . days ago. We're fine."

I let out a deep breath and nod. "Well, if it isn't fine, just know that I would never hang you out to dry."

She smiles and then wraps her arms around my middle. "I know that. Look at how you are with Olivia. You're a wonderful father and co-parent. Truly, we have nothing to worry about. I know that feels like famous last words and all that, but . . ."

I laugh and kiss her nose. "It does, but from now on, we leave nothing to chance."

"Deal. No more insane lusting after you and impaling myself on your dick."

"I wouldn't go that far," I say with a laugh, grateful for the levity, even though I still have a pit in my stomach.

"Do I go back to my room, or do we . . ." She looks at the bed.

I may be rattled, but I don't want to send her back to her room. "We cuddle, Sunshine."

We climb into bed, and she rests her head on my chest. "Sunshine, huh?"

"I see why your student chose it now."

She grins. "Because I'm bright and sunny."

"Sure."

Phoebe tucks her head in the crook of my arm. "I like this."

I kiss the top of her head. "Good. So, tell me about Texas."

Her head pops up, resting her chin on my chest. "It's a great program, even if it isn't quite as good as the one at Vanderbilt, they're going to take all but two classes, so it won't set me back all that much. The money I make this summer will cover it."

"Why transfer? I don't get it."

She shrugs. "Change is good."

I'm not buying that. "Yes, but I remember your dad talking about the hell you went through to get into Iowa."

Phoebe looks down at her hand. "Iowa wasn't for me, okay?"

"I'm going to assume this has to do with whatever that humiliating experience was?" I push carefully.

When her brown eyes meet mine, there is pain lurking in them. "Today has been a really good day. I've racked up four orgasms in eighteen hours, got into my audiology program, and feel pretty damn good, so let's not ruin it."

"Okay. Subject dropped." I lift three fingers, giving her the Scout's honor.

She grabs my hand, pulling it to her and lacing our fingers. "Thank you."

"For?"

"Being sweet."

"Did you think I wasn't?" I ask.

Her laugh is short, and she tries to cover her mouth. "You were so mean to me! You basically called me ridiculous at every turn and didn't want me to watch Liv because you thought I was inept. So, yeah, you were not what I would call sweet."

I shift, forcing her to sit up. "And you were what?"

"I am the freaking ray of sunshine to your cloudy overcast flowing around."

I scoff. "Bullshit. I'm fun."

"I didn't say you weren't. I said you weren't sweet, but I was wrong. You are sweet, like a melted marshmallow under all that charred outside."

"Oh, fuck that." I dive at her, tossing her down, and I cage her in. "I'm not a melted anything."

She giggles before blowing the hair away from her face. "Total mush."

"Do I feel like mush?" I ask, already growing hard again.

Seriously, what the hell kind of magic does this girl possess? I am like a teenager again.

"No, definitely not mush there." Her eyes sparkle with amusement.

"Say it again, and I'll find something else you can do with that mouth."

She grins, the mischief dancing across her face. "Is that a challenge?"

"No, baby, it's a promise, and I look forward to keeping this one."

Phoebe can't help herself, and I am not even a little upset about it as I lean in and kiss her.

twenty-one

PHOEBE

"**Y**ou had sex!" Emmeline yells, and I want to die.

"Emmy! I did not!" I quickly grab for my earbuds in my purse. "I was calling because I got into Texas!"

Thankfully, the only person close to me is Mr. Hubenak, who is almost a hundred and can barely hear, and his daughter, Daisy, who is banging her married neighbor, so she'll never repeat what she heard.

However, Magnolia is a concern. She does her best to appear as though she didn't hear, but I know she did, so I just keep acting as if my friend is insane and has no idea what she's talking about.

Once my earbuds are in, I glare at her. "I'm so happy!" I drop my voice. "Seriously, I'm going to kill you."

Emmy laughs. "Please, Phoebs, you totally had sex. I can see it."

"Yes, I got my acceptance a few days ago."

"Oh, are we talking in code?" Her eyes widen, and she smirks.

"I can't talk long," I say loudly and then drop my voice. "Because I am going to need to commit a crime against my best friend if she keeps this up."

"Ha! Bring your ass to Cloverleigh, I dare you."

"You are seriously such a pain in the ass."

She shrugs. "I hear this daily. My father is ready to talk about making me be a waitress because he says I'm testing his nerves and my sisters have already worn him down, so I'm at a disadvantage."

"And you are quite the trying one."

"Yeah, it's true. So . . ." She leans in with her brows almost up to her hairline. "Was it good?"

"Umm, beyond good."

She drops the phone and screeches. "I knew it! I knew it! Ha!" A second later, she's back on screen. "Good for you! All of this is great because he's not married, he's totally not looking for a relationship, and . . . you are leaving for college soon. See, perfect situation, and apparently, the sex is fantastic."

I hate that she's right. "I'm going next week to tour the school and look for an apartment. I feel like I can't make a choice without at least visiting it."

"That's smart. And what is a dance-a-thon thing?"

"My father had the brilliant idea to host a twenty-four-hour dance-off as a fundraiser. You have to dance the entire time and only get two breaks. Picture hell, but with dance shoes."

"Do you have a partner?"

"One of the cops who works for my father."

Emmy's brows raise. "Interesting."

"Joey is a good friend, and it's totally not interesting."

She laughs. "Please, sounds like Asher is pretty possessive, so I doubt he's going to like another man's hands all over you for twenty-four hours."

"Well, too bad. It's for charity."

"Fine, fine, but don't say I didn't warn you. Hey, you know what? Maybe I could meet you in Texas. I'm sure my dad would be cool with me taking a long weekend and giving him a reprieve."

I grin. "You're driving him that crazy?"

"I ask a lot of questions because he does things ass backwards in my opinion. Plus, when I'm home, he's just strict. Mom is pretty laid-back and understands I'm twenty-four and a grown adult. Dad sometimes still sees me as little. I stayed at my sister's last night, but she and her husband are still all touchy feely, so I left Millie's. I tried to go to Felicity's, but she's really busy and had the kids in every activity. I'd hoped that, when we got older, it would be more even, but they're just in a different place." There's a layer of sadness in my friend's voice that hurts my heart.

"What about Audrey?"

Her face brightens at the mention of her twin sister. "Audrey is doing amazing in Paris and studying all the ways to make pastries."

"I sort of envy that."

"Me too. Especially because she met a guy and is all . . . in love."

My heart flutters at that statement, but I lock it down. Hell no. I don't want love. I don't want to think about love. I want to dream of nothing but orgasms and walking away unscathed, thank you very much.

"Love is dumb," I say, needing the reminder.

"I want love."

That is sort of shocking. Emmeline is the opposite of me in so many ways. She's strong, funny, smart, and hasn't done any of the dumb shit I have when it comes to men. She's careful and really deliberate about who she goes out with. The last guy chewed too aggressively, and she ended things over it. The guy before that, when he held her hand, he sweat too much. The one before that talked about his favorite show too much.

It's a one strike and you're out with her.

"You want love?" I ask.

"Everyone around me is in love. Everyone. My sisters are obsessed with their husbands, who are equally obsessed with them. My parents are—" She makes a gagging noise. "I can't even. My whole family is happy with these people who complete them.

Even my traitorous twin is all ga-ga over some guy, and I can't find one I want to date for longer than a month."

I smile at my friend, who is a juxtaposition of wants and reality. "Love is flawed, Emmy. It tricks you into seeing the bad in a person and somehow making it tolerable. When you meet the right guy, that will happen. None of the toads you've kissed have been your prince."

"And is this new guy your prince?"

I shake my head. "No, he can't be."

"Good, remember that because you, my soft-hearted friend, tend to forget that love can also make it hard to see the jaded edges until you're already wounded."

"I haven't forgotten." I don't know that I ever can.

Olivia and I are in the kitchen because she wanted me to teach her how to cook my mom's famous potato pickle soup. I don't know that it's actually famous, but she made it for me any time I was sad or just needed some comfort.

Liv had a rough day today. She was supposed to meet up with a friend from school, but when I brought her to the meeting place, we waited, waited more, and no one showed. So, I called the parent, asking where they were, to which we were informed she was already out with her friends and Liv was never included in the plans.

I did my best to shield her, stating the girl got pulled away, but she could see. I'm guessing this isn't the first time something like this has happened.

"*Pickles?*" Liv asks as I use the grater, making them as fine as I can. A lot of recipes have you dice them, but Mom shredded the pickles down to an almost paste.

"*It's good. Trust me.*"

She continues to cut up the potatoes like I showed her, and we work in the kitchen together. While it simmers, we sit at the table as she talks to Sara on video. This call couldn't have come at a better time, she needs her mom.

Sara says hi to me, I wave and go back to looking at apartments in Texas. Everything close to campus is crazy expensive, but I don't really want to have to drive, and I don't want some random roommate.

I got super lucky with Emmeline, and I doubt I'll have that again.

The front door opens, and I hear the telltale sign that Asher is home. His keys clank in the bowl that sits by the door, there's a thud of his duffle bag hitting the floor, and then the click of the shelf drop-down that holds his gun. If you walked by it, you'd never know it was a gun safe, but there's a fingerprint lock at the top that releases a hatch on the bottom of the shelf, allowing you to lock up your firearm close to where you might need it.

Dad has, like, six of them in our house, and he loves them so much that he started buying them for the guys at the station.

When he enters the kitchen, I have to remember to breathe. I don't know how I ever thought he wasn't all that hot. He's more than that, and in the week since we've started this thing we're doing, I have gotten to see and feel just how perfect his body is.

That's it, Phoebe, think only of the body, not the man beneath it all.

I cannot go down that road. I'm leaving for college, preparing to live my very structured and planned future.

Olivia jumps up, dropping the phone on the table, and I laugh. I lift Sara into view. "Sorry, Asher came home."

"Of course she ditches me for him," Sara says, seemingly fine with being cast aside. "How is she doing after the incident?"

"She's okay."

"What incident?" Asher's deep voice sends a shiver down my spine.

Liv is very good at reading lips, and while she may not hear, she'll know we're talking about her. "I'm going to put the phone down to sign," I tell Sara.

As I explain the situation to Asher, I make sure that Olivia can understand exactly what I'm telling her father. I watch as the sadness washes over her face, but then there's a sort of acceptance that shifts to a smile when I talk about the soup.

She pulls on her father's arm. *"With pickles! It's going to be gross."*

Asher scrunches his face. *"Pickles?"*

"Don't knock it till you try it," I tell them.

"Asher?" Sara's voice comes through the phone.

"Yes, pain in my ass?"

She huffs. "Phoebe said she got into Texas, and that's amazing —really, it is—but you still don't have a nanny, and I won't be home before she has to leave. So, I'm just wondering what your plan is."

Asher looks heavenward. "I have time."

"Yes, but it's been how many weeks? Are you even trying? Did you call another agency or talk to Brynlee?"

I fight back a smile as his face changes to sheer annoyance. He starts to walk around the room, a sly grin on those perfect lips. "Sara, you're breaking up. What was that? Huh? Oh, you think I'm doing a great job? I know." Then he presses the end button and turns to us. "So, should we order pizza in case dinner is a disaster?"

Olivia signs. *"Yes."*

"Oh, ye of little faith."

I get up and check on it. It looks just about ready for the sour cream and flour mix, so I start to prepare that. The two of them watch with different variations of horror on their faces.

"You want us to eat this?"

I glare at Asher. "Yes. I do."

"And what if we die?"

I roll my eyes. "Then I'll call Sara and let her know she doesn't have to finish the job because I did it for her."

He chuckles and then turns so his back is to me and signs to Liv without saying the words.

Olivia snorts and then rushes out of the room. I turn my head, curious to see where she's going, but before I can move, Asher is there. He pushes me against the counter, his lips move to my neck, and his hands slide across my stomach.

"I thought about you all day," he grumbles against my ear. "Wishing I could be home with you naked in my bed, my head between your legs as you whimper and call out my name."

I melt, having to brace myself on the counter to stay upright. "You can't say shit like that. I have to cook."

"Do you have an excuse to stay tonight? I want to watch you on your knees as you wrap those perfect lips around my cock."

I was planning on going home. I really need to go home and get stuff ready to tour University of Texas.

"I can't."

"Can't or won't?" Asher's teeth scrape across where my neck and shoulder meet.

"Both," I manage to get out, but the word has no conviction behind it. Asher is much more skilled at this game than I am. He has years more experience, and honestly, I am not sexy. I don't have this big plan to get him to want me. I am just fortunate he does.

However, I have to keep my mind right. I can't start feeling or wanting things I have no place desiring. That's what got me in this predicament to start with.

I turn to face him, and he grins. "I like this position too."

Oh, I do too, but that's not the point. Any second, Olivia will be back, so I need to make this quick. "I have to do this. You have three days off, and I need to get my life in order."

Asher takes a step back, the heat still simmering in his blue eyes. "Can't blame a guy for trying."

I laugh. "No, I can't, and if this weren't important . . ."

"Phoebe, no explanations needed, that's the perk of this arrangement."

In my head, I literally just said that, but hearing it out loud makes my stomach tighten. Why? Why did my stomach tighten? No. Not happening. I mentally slap myself and then jut my hip out with my idea of a seductive smile.

"Just think of how much fun it'll be when I get back."

Without feelings, Phoebe.

twenty-two

ASHER

"**I** *miss Phoebe*," Olivia signs as we walk down to the creek.

Me too, kid. *"She'll be back soon."*

"She is going to leave."

I nod. *"Yes, she has grad school."*

Which matters a lot to her. I remember her eyes and the way her face lit up when we walked into the audiology department. She was taking it in like a kid at Christmas. I saw the joy. I saw the desire. I saw it all. Some days, I wish I didn't see her as much as I do.

Olivia looks to the left, trying to hide the sadness all over her face. She loves Phoebe, which is definitely not how I foresaw this whole thing going. I hoped they'd get along, but the intention was never for Phoebe to seep into our lives, filling the cracks we didn't know existed.

But that's what she's doing.

Despite my resistance, she's finding her way into deeper crevices.

This morning, she left for Texas. Her father drove her to the airport, but she sent me a text before she took off as well as promised to send another when she landed.

Liv is silent as we walk, and once we reach our spot, she turns to me. *"I don't want her to go."*

I crouch down, giving her a lopsided smile. *"Would you want someone to stay and be unhappy?"*

This isn't a lesson I am prepared to give, but I think about how Sara did it when Denise told us she was getting married and leaving. She'd been with Olivia since she was a baby and had become more family than nanny.

Liv didn't handle her leaving well, and I'm sure she won't now either. Phoebe is younger, more fun, more friend than nanny, and she treats Liv like an equal instead of a child.

"No, but can't she be happy in Sugarloaf?"

"No."

No, she can't. She needs to leave and change the world.

Her chin falls, and she sighs. I gently lift her head to meet my gaze. *"She will come back. This is her home."*

"And we can be friends?"

I nod. *"I bet she'd like that. One day, you'll want to go away, and I'll miss you, but I'll need to let you go."*

"I'm going to be a doctor," Liv says. For as long as I can remember, that's what she's wanted to be.

"And so will Phoebe."

"She will be a good one."

I grin. *"So will you. Ready to fish?"*

Olivia shrugs and grabs her pole. *"I bet I'll catch one before you."*

I lift one eyebrow, not willing to let this challenge go unanswered. *"And if you don't?"*

She taps her finger on her chin. *"If you win, I do the dishes."*

She's doing them anyway, but the bet would make her doing them easier. *"What if you win?"*

"I get to sleep at Aunt Brynn's for the weekend."

"What? I have the whole weekend planned for us."

Liv lifts one shoulder. *"You're boring, Dad."*

I'm not boring. I'm the fun parent. I'm the one who does all the shit her mother doesn't allow. Now, I'm offended and plan to win and eat ice cream with my feet up as she does the dishes.

Not willing to waste a second, I grab my pole, toss hers like a javelin, bait mine, sink my line in, and prepare to win.

"I can't wait for our fun weekend," Brynn says as I walk Olivia into the cottage. Liv rushes to Brynn, wrapping her arms around her in a tight hug before stepping back.

Olivia signs. *"Can I go back to my room and unpack?"*

"Of course! And there is a special treat back there for our girls' weekend."

"Bye, Daddy!" Liv signs before giving me a hug and then running to the bedroom Brynn has set up for her.

"She's so excited. We're going to have a blast!"

"Glad the two of you will have fun," I grumble. "Not like I have anything to do."

No kid. No girlf—Phoebe, no friends, and I'm not hanging out with Rowan because every time I do, I get shitfaced and regret my choices.

Although maybe that's exactly what I need. To get drunk, forget everything, and make shit choices.

"Oh, stop, you can go back to your house to brood and be your grumpy self," Brynn says, brushing her shoulder against mine. "Besides, you've had a lot of Olivia time, consider this your off weekend. Go do something. Find a friend."

"I think I'll call Rowan."

She laughs. "Well, that's never a good idea. It seems my big brother is upset about something."

"I'm not upset about anything."

"No? You never go out with Rowan unless you want to drink your worries away."

I huff. "Not true."

It's actually true, but I'm not admitting it to her.

"Let's see, you did it when you found out Sara was pregnant, when you were upset about getting passed over for the assistant chief position." She keeps counting them off on her hand. "When you were angry because my dad showed up, and then . . . well, you know the other time."

Yes, the time I found out my sister had been taken advantage of. The time I found out a *friend* hurt her. Someone I trusted, someone who was supposed to help protect her did the opposite.

I lost my mind. I went absolutely insane when I found out that my supposed best friend touched my sister when she was only sixteen fucking years old and he was twenty-seven.

"There's nothing bothering me," I say again.

"Asher, you can talk to me."

No, I can't talk to her about this. I can't tell her that I'm a bear because I keep thinking about Phoebe and wondering if she's okay. It's bad enough that I've been texting her every hour because I can't see her, touch her, or smell her sweet perfume.

"Yes, but I won't."

She shakes her head. "Brothers. You're all the same—dumb."

"And you are the smart one?"

"Of course I am! By the way, have you spoken to Grady?"

"Not recently," I say.

Brynn jumps up, grabbing my arm. "Oh! I have an amazing idea!"

Never ever words I want to hear. "No."

"What?"

"Whatever it is, no. Your ideas are never good and always end up with me wanting to slam my head against the wall."

My sister huffs. "You should go away for the weekend."

I could go to Austin . . .

Although, I don't think that's what Brynlee means. "You want me to go away for the weekend? To where?"

"Go down to Florida! Help Grady pack or just take him out and get him to talk to you. He'll be up here in a few weeks, and I'm sure he needs help."

I sigh deeply. "I'm not going to show up at Grady's house and help him pack. Do you remember our brother at all? He hates surprises. He hates people touching his shit. He hates anyone giving him any kind of direction either."

Brynn flops back on the couch. "Ugh. True."

But . . . I could go to Texas. Spend a weekend with Phoebe without worrying about my daughter walking in or having to hide.

"I could go visit a friend."

"You have friends?" Brynn asks.

"Yes, I have friends. One of the guys I was in the academy with moved away, and he's been up my ass about coming to see him."

Brynn's smile widens. "You should go, Ash! You never do anything fun. You work or are with Liv. She and I can spend the weekend together, and you can go enjoy a few days by yourself."

Only I won't be by myself. Not if I can get this to work the way I want.

twenty-three

PHOEBE

"We only have one apartment on the property left, and if you wanted to put down a deposit today, it would be yours three weeks before the semester begins."

I love this apartment. It's seriously perfect. The property was renovated last year, it has a pool, gym, movies on Fridays, and they actually have Wi-Fi as an amenity. That would cut out a bill, but it wouldn't offset the difference between how much I want to pay for a place and how much this one costs. I'm so torn because it is worth the extra money, but it's going to mean I really don't have any extra money each month.

Still . . .

"I want the apartment," I tell Bianca, who I also happen to like. "I'm just worried if I end up going to a different school . . . just . . . it's a lot of money."

Her head tilts to the side. "It's on the high side for the area. Okay, here's what I can do. Since it's the last apartment, and you're not fully committed to Texas, I can do just a hundred dollar deposit and secure it. Once you know, you can pay the remaining balance, and then we'll do the paperwork."

My heart is near to bursting. "Oh my God! Are you serious? Wow. Thank you!"

Bianca smiles. "It's my pleasure."

I'm feeling really excited to have one big thing done. Tomorrow is my official college tour, and I'm meeting with one of the professors in the program and a student another day. All of this feels really good and exciting, but a part of me is nervous.

My hotel is just a few blocks away, so I start walking and pull out my phone to call Asher and check on Olivia, which is when I see two text alerts.

EMMELINE

Did you find a place?

> I did! I'm going to the campus in a bit to walk around on my own before my tour.

EMMELINE

Awesome. Is the apartment nice?

> A hundred times better than what we had. It's really great, Em. I'm excited about it.

EMMELINE

So, you're liking Texas?

Am I? I don't know. Maybe. I could be. A part of me says it's too soon to tell, but this city just feels so fun. Austin is brimming with life, and everything feels fresh and artsy.

> We'll see after the official tour and see if I get into Vanderbilt. That's the big question mark.

EMMELINE

Can't wait to hear more. Gotta run, my dad is glaring at me since I'm on my phone.

I laugh and then check the one from Olivia.

> **OLIVIA**
> Miss me yet?

I smile.

> I do! Do you miss me?

> **OLIVIA**
> Yes! I'm with Aunt Brynn for the next few days.
> We are having a spa weekend, and she's taking
> me to New Jersey to visit my friend.

Why is she with Brynlee? That doesn't make any sense because
Asher is off. It's why I picked this weekend to come to Texas.

> That sounds fun! Where is your dad?

Speak of the devil . . . his name pops on my phone.

> **ASHER**
> Where are you?

Uhhh, he knows where I am.

> ASHER
>
> In Austin, you know, touring the school . . . more important question is, where are you?
>
> Don't worry about me. Where exactly are you?

Why?

> ASHER
>
> Because I was thinking of you.

Marshmallow.

> ASHER
>
> Say that to my face and see what happens.

I have every intention of that.

> You don't scare me. I have a few days for you to forget it anyway.

He doesn't reply, and again, I'm curious where he is.

> OLIVIA
>
> Dad went to visit his friend because Aunt Brynn said he is grumpy.

A part of me hopes he's grumpy because he misses me. Stupid, I know, considering we are nothing, but I miss him. I called him last night, but he couldn't talk, and since then, I've been eager to hear his voice.

As I'm walking up to my hotel, someone grabs my arm. "Excuse me, miss?"

My heart rate picks up, and I spin, but when I see who is there, I can't breathe. Asher is here. Asher is standing in front of me . . . in Texas. How? This can't be real. "Asher?"

He grins as his hands move to my face, holding me tenderly. "I missed you. God, I missed you, and I needed to see you."

His admission makes me want to weep. "I can't believe you're here. I don't understand how?"

"Brynn took Olivia, and suddenly, I had a free weekend. I don't know . . . I just found myself on a plane." Asher rubs his thumb across my cheek. "To be with the only person I wanted to see."

I bite my lower lip, my heart doing flips as my brain tries to catch up. "Me?"

He lowers his face so we're a mere breath apart. "You. We don't have to pretend here, Phoebe. I get to do this." His lips touch mine, and I melt into his embrace. "I can kiss you on the street. I can pull you into my arms, and I get to pretend, for a few days, that you're mine."

Oh, Asher, I think I became yours weeks ago, but this just made you mine.

I lift up on my toes and kiss him this time. When I drop back down, I take his hand. "Then let's not waste time standing out here. Let's go upstairs, and you can seal it with a kiss."

He grins. "I'll seal it with more than that."

"Good."

We get up to the room, holding hands on our way there. It's so weird being with Asher in the open. All we've had is kisses when

Olivia leaves the room and earth-shattering sex when she's asleep. We've never so much as touched in public or without worrying someone might see.

I put the key in the lock, and as soon as I step across the threshold, he drops his bag and lifts me into his arms. My legs wrap around his waist, hands sink into his hair, and our mouths meld together.

"Jesus, it's been days, and I am starved for you, Phoebe. I need to be inside you."

"Yes," I moan as he drops me onto the bed.

I need the same. We can do slow and orgasmic later. I'm sliding my pants down as he's doing the same. The two of us are frantic, stripping as fast as we can. I tear my shirt off, throwing it somewhere, and when I look up, I could die. Asher is there, hand gripping his already hard cock, stroking it as he stares at me. "I shouldn't be here."

"I disagree."

He keeps pumping his cock, and I want it so badly. I want him. I want to be joined with him because I feel whole when I am.

"The whole time I was driving to the airport, I told myself to turn around, to go back to my room and lie in my bed that smells like you—the perfect mix of lemons and vanilla—and deal with denying myself."

I sit up on my elbows, wanting to know why this man, who I have no business being with, came for me. "But you didn't. Why?"

"Because I wanted you too much. It felt cloudy when you left, and I needed to see the sun."

"I thought of you too," I offer the confession, wanting him to know how I feel as well. "I wanted you to come here. I dreamed of it."

"I dreamed of you."

Then there are no more words, just touching. Asher climbs atop me, his warm body covering mine. Our mouths clash and tongues duel. He doesn't preamble . . . he just adjusts his hips and enters me quickly.

I gasp as he fills me so fully that I can't breathe.

His teeth nip at my neck and shoulder before he slides his tongue over the spots he bit.

"You're mine," he says against my skin. "Goddamn it, Phoebe."

His hips rear back, and he slams against me, angry and forceful, and I love it. "Yours."

"Fuck you for making me need you," he curses, and when he pumps his hips again, I rise to meet him. "Fuck you for making me come here."

Yes, fuck me indeed.

I grip his hair and pull his head back so his blue eyes meet mine. "Just fuck me, Asher. Fuck me."

He does. He pumps over and over until his relentless pace has us both out of breath and the smell of sweat and sex filling the air around us.

Asher pulls out. "Get on your hands and knees."

I obey, not even thinking twice. When I do, I feel his hand rub my ass, and I know what's coming. Every muscle in me clenches, and I feel myself grow even wetter. I want this. I want him to slap my ass and tell me how angry it makes him to want me. How it's me who he thinks of. Me who makes him weak.

Before I can say anything, his palm slaps on the globe of my ass hard enough to warm the skin. I groan, dropping my head, as both the pain and the pleasure war.

"Asher."

"Do you know how gorgeous you are like this, sweetheart? Do you know how fucking magnificent you look with your ass in the air, pussy dripping wet because you want me?"

I moan, his words sending another rush through me. "Tell me."

I swear I can feel his approval in the way his hands move to my hips right before he slides deep. "I'd rather show you."

He hits me again at the same time that he pulls back, almost leaving me empty. Then right after, he pushes deep, and I scream out his name. An orgasm rockets through me so fast I can't stay up. I begin to crumple, but he holds me where he wants me, driving at a pace that seems inhuman. Asher slams into me. Once. Twice. And then he groans, murmuring my name over and over.

The two of us are panting as we fall to the mattress, and he reaches for me, pulling me to his chest and kissing my forehead.

We clean up, he tosses the condom, and I wash up a little. Then we walk hand-in-hand back to bed. I curl up against his chest, listening to the steady thrum of his heart.

"I'm glad you came."

"Because of the sex?"

I should say yes. It would be the smart response, but I remember his confessions when we were overcome with desire. How he was almost angry at his feelings, and I don't want to lie to him. I've had enough of those with men.

Our situation is what it is, a short-term affair that we both know the ending of. It sucks because it can never be more while also having the potential to be everything. What it can be is honest and heartbreaking at the same time.

"No, not because of the sex." I trail my fingers over his chest, making patterns of nothing. "Because I missed you too."

"This is . . ."

I look up, his eyes finding mine, and he doesn't have to finish it. "I know."

He brushes my hair back and then rests his palm against my cheek. "I have never flown thousands of miles for anyone, Phoebe. I have never craved someone the way I do you. I know we only have a month, but fuck, I don't want to miss any time together."

"And what happens when I leave? Because I have to go, you understand that, right? No matter how I feel, I can't stay in Sugarloaf."

Asher gives me a lopsided grin. "I would never let you. You have a life to live and people to help. That means you going to finish your degree. I just want to have all the time I can."

"I want that too."

"Then, when you're home, stay with me every night. Stay and let me have what I can so, when you go, there are no regrets."

I lay my head back down on his chest and squeeze my arm tighter. When I go, I worry leaving will be my regret because in just a few weeks, I have fallen for Asher Whitlock.

Fuck me is right.

twenty-four

PHOEBE

"The campus was amazing," Asher says as we walk back toward our hotel, his hand in mine.

"It really was. I can see myself there, which I know seems funny because it's not like I'm swimming in options. I just . . . I liked it. I liked the professors a lot too. They seemed excited about me possibly attending."

"Your professor in Iowa really sang your praises." He smiles. "I didn't realize you had all those honors."

I shake my head. "I gave all that up by leaving, though."

Speaking of leaving, we leave soon, back to the world where I can't sit with him at the restaurant or touch him as we walk anywhere.

As much as I love every second of this, I hate it too.

It gave me a glimpse of a life we can never have.

"Has Olivia ever seen you with a woman?" I ask as he puts the key in the door. His hand freezes, and he looks to me with a panicked expression.

"Why?"

"I'm just curious."

Asher gets the door open after another attempt, and when we enter, his demeanor shifts a bit. "No."

Okay. "I wasn't . . ."

"No, she hasn't. I am very protective of her. When we had her, both Sara and I agreed that we wouldn't have random men or women through the door. I have never had a woman in the house when she's there. I never even considered it until . . ."

Me.

"I think that was the best thing you could've ever done," I say, wanting him to know I respect it. "Has she met the Ford guy?"

"Yes, once things got serious, Sara told me she was going to introduce them."

"And you've never had anyone?"

Asher's blue eyes are blank. "It'll never happen for me."

Never. Right. God, why am I so dumb? I know the answers to these questions just like I know that we will never be more than a summer affair.

I force a smile, pretending as if my heart didn't just break in my chest. "One day, you may meet a girl who steals your heart and makes you want to introduce her to Olivia." As soon as I say it, I hate myself. If I try to clarify that I wasn't talking about me, then I'll look ridiculous. Asher stands there, his gaze tracking mine, and I sigh. "I didn't mean me, sheesh. I'm saying never is a strong word. I know what we are. I'm not asking for anything."

He seems to relax and nods. "I didn't take it that way. Come here, Phoebs."

I do as he says, hating that I said any of this and ruined the small sliver of time we get to be more than just some clandestine relationship.

He pulls me into his arms, and I am too weak to resist him. "If I were younger, if you weren't Olivia's nanny, my boss's daughter, and preparing to leave, maybe . . . maybe we could've been more."

"Maybe a lot of things, but we're not. We have now, and we have to accept that. I don't want to think about the future, Asher. I just want to be here—with you."

He gently lifts my chin and gives me the sweetest kiss before we tumble back into bed where we have no problems.

"Tell me what you were like growing up," I ask, wearing nothing but his T-shirt, as we sit on the bed and eat dumplings.

Asher is in his boxers, and I admire his amazing body. Every muscle is on display, and I can't seem to stop staring.

He laughs, raising one brow. "I was an asshole."

"Was?"

He pinches my arm for that, and I pull away, tsking at him. "I thought I was a marshmallow."

"Oh, you are. It's just under all that assholeness."

"Well, back then, I was all asshole. Anger radiated from me, and my mother's inability to stay single and not date total losers only enraged me more."

I try to picture a younger Asher, and I can't do it. He came to Sugarloaf when I was fourteen, and I definitely never saw him as young. He was Brynlee's older brother who never smiled and then became a cop who my dad thought was great.

I thought he was a dick.

"And when did that stop because you're the calmest guy I think I've ever met. Nothing really rattles you."

Asher grins. "You have no idea, sweetheart."

"I don't, that's why I'm asking." He swipes the dumplings and pops one into his mouth with a wink. "See, the asshole is still in there. Now, tell me about when you got to Sugarloaf."

Once he's done chewing, he leans back against the headboard. "I don't know. I was coming back to take care of my mom and Brynn. God knows her biological father wasn't going to step up. My mother had the worst fucking taste in men. Four failed marriages and each one seemed to be trying to be worse than the last. Brynn's father takes the cake, though. I hate him."

"Because?"

"He treats my sister like shit and only shows up in her life when he wants something. Brynn has a bleeding heart and can never say no to him, which he knows. My father is no better, but at least none of us have heard from him in ten years. For all I know, he could be dead."

My throat tightens at that statement. "And that doesn't bother you?"

"Not in the least. He walked out when Rowan was two, and we've seen him maybe three times since then."

That makes me sad. "It's his loss. Not only because you, Grady, and Rowan have grown into being great men but also because he doesn't know the gift that is Olivia."

He leans forward, crooking his finger. When I shift toward him, he kisses me twice and then leans back. "What was that for?"

"I just needed to kiss you."

And I need to remember earlier when he reminded me exactly what we are.

Do not fall in love with Asher. Do not let yourself go there.

"Marshmallow is back."

He rolls his eyes. "Anyway, going back even further to when I was a kid, I was pissed off at the world, wanting to fight everyone and everything, and then Brynn was born. I don't know how to explain it, but all three of us changed after Mom brought her home. It was as if we couldn't be angry because we needed to protect her. Brynlee became the single most valuable thing we ever had. It's crazy, but it just felt like if we could be better, we could deserve her."

"Well," I say, clearing my throat, "if that isn't the single most beautiful thing I've ever heard . . ."

"Are you crying?" he asks as I wipe my cheek.

"No."

Asher doesn't say a word before he's shifting to pull me toward him. Then I'm back in my most favorite place in the world, in his arms.

"I think you are the one who's soft at heart, sweetheart."

I nod, not willing to talk and risk actually crying.

He chuckles and runs his fingertips up and down my arm.

"We've tried to always be there for her, and when I failed, I've never really forgiven myself for it."

I glance up at him. "She loves you. Anyone can see that."

"She does, and I am grateful for it. I've done everything I can to atone for the failure I've had with her."

I place my hand on his chest. "Asher, you haven't failed her."

His eyes move to the door. "I have. Once. I failed her, and by the grace of God, she's forgiven me."

"She has never said anything even close to that, and she adores you. You came and raised her, loved her, protected her, and have given her everything. I don't know what you think you failed her on, but I can promise you that, if you actually had, she wouldn't be able to move on from it. When someone truly fails you, it's . . . well, it's hard to forget."

He kisses the top of my head. "I want to ask you something," Asher says, his voice even.

I don't need to hear the words to know what information he is going to ask for. I sit up, pull my legs to my chest, and wrap my arms around them. "You want to know why I left Iowa."

"Only if you're able to trust me."

"I trust you. I trust you more than I ever thought I could, it's just . . . I'm ashamed."

He sits forward but allows me some space, which I appreciate. "Ashamed of what?"

"The whole thing. I was so stupid. I was trusting and blind." I pause, trying to put up defenses so that, when he hears it all, I'm okay with his reaction.

"I am not one to judge. I am sleeping with my boss's daughter, who is almost fifteen years younger than I am. Fuck, you're younger than my sister. I flew down here after telling everyone I was visiting a friend who I went through the academy with. I'm lying to everyone, and I can't find a single ounce of regret. I have made more mistakes than you can ever imagine."

"Did you ever sleep with a married woman?" I ask.

He jerks back. "No. Never."

I laugh once. "Well, I have. Not woman, but a married man."

Asher blinks a few times, clearly stunned at my admission. "In Iowa?"

"I want to preface this by admitting that I was really naïve going to school. I grew up in Sugarloaf with a father who was a cop. No one really dated me. Hell, even now, I've never really had a date. I got to school, kept my head down, and focused on school, and four years passed without ever having a boyfriend."

"For real?"

I glance at my clasped hands, hating that I am so inept in this way. "Yeah, and then I got into Iowa, and I was determined to have a relationship. I wanted to find love and friendship while I was in grad school. My friends were all dating, and I just thought, if I could find someone to love me, I'd be happy."

"So, you slept with a married man?" he asks without the judgment that I deserve.

I nod. "Yes, but it wasn't like that. I didn't know he was married. I didn't know any of it. But it's even worse than that, which is bad enough on its own. He was my professor. Seems I have a penchant for older guys who hold authority." Bile rises in my throat as I think about it all, but Asher asked, and I wanted to give him a reason to walk away, so here it is.

"Hey, I'm not married," he defends. "I want you to be happy."

I lean forward, taking his hand. "I know that, which is why we're here now. I know you're not lying or trying to hurt me. He was in his mid-thirties and attractive. I had no desire to have some secret relationship. I wanted love. At first, he would find ways to get me alone, but nothing ever happened. We'd just talk. He told me about his divorce and how he was struggling because she wanted to ruin his life. I felt so bad for him. I thought, what a bitch she was to hurt him when he was so nice. I guess that was part of his game," I say, feeling foolish.

Asher entwines my fingers with his. "Go on."

"I fell for it all. The lies, the secrets, the promises. I thought, God, this guy is perfect. He would take me to dinner a few towns

FORBIDDEN HEARTS

away because we couldn't admit to what we were doing, he could be fired. Then we'd sneak away in classrooms that were empty, like the thrill of it all was too much. Then I'd go back to my room, hiding what we were doing from everyone."

"Phoebe . . ." I can hear the change in his voice.

"Let me get it out, please."

He nods.

"He promised that as soon as the semester was over and he wasn't my professor, we would tell everyone. We'd be together, and he wanted the world to know he loved me. It was a . . . whirl-wind, and I believed I was in love with him. I told myself over and over that he was the one."

"Did you love him?" Asher asks, and my eyes lift to his. I was lost there for a moment.

"No. Not even a little. I was just caught up in the thrill of it. When I look back, every sign was there. He never took me to his place. If he was divorced, why would that matter? Why did we have to be at a hotel or in his car like fucking teenagers doing something wrong? Everything he did fed the lies. We got careless, and one day we were in his office and someone took a photo."

His fingers tighten. "A photo of you?"

"Yes, of me about to kiss him. They posted it with a photo of him, his wife, and his brand-new baby beside it. I . . . I tried to ignore it, but I couldn't escape the names they called me or the way they said I was coming onto him. I was called a whore, a slut, a homewrecker. The comments on the thread made me sick, and then his wife commented, and I couldn't take it. She said I'd hit on him over and over again, and when he kept telling me no, I assaulted him."

I look at him, feeling like every name I was called, and wait for the condemnation. "I know you don't believe this, but it wasn't your fault. He took advantage of you and manipulated the situation."

"I let him."

"And now I'm doing it to you."

239

I shake my head, moving to him quickly. "Are you insane? You're not lying about being married. You're not offering me fake promises. You freed me, Asher. You showed me I was beautiful. You came here for me, not because you didn't want me out in public but because you missed me." I straddle his hips, taking his face in my hands. "You've made me feel smart, wanted, and have never offered me false hope. What we're doing is between two consenting adults who really, really want each other. This isn't lies and deceit, this is honest."

"I will never lie to you," he promises.

"I know."

He rests his head against mine. "I want to kill him for hurting you. I would tear him apart and show the world what a coward he is. If anyone is the fool, Phoebe, it's him. You are a fucking gift, and he never deserved you."

I smile and kiss his nose. "Marshmallow."

"Only with you."

twenty-five
ASHER

Phoebe went to meet a grad student in the AuD program for lunch, and I've spent my time preparing for tonight. We fly home tomorrow and go back to the reality of what we are.

So, I am going to give us one night that we will be able to look back on, and hopefully, it will erase the pain of her past.

I hear the door lock click, and I stand here, waiting in my sport coat, jeans, and brown shoes I bought today, with a bouquet of roses in my hands. "Asher? Oh my God, I have to tell you about today and the—" She stops, her big brown eyes going wide, and she sucks in a breath. "What are you . . . you're all dressed up."

Moving toward her, I extend the flowers. "These are for you."

"Asher, what are you doing?"

"I would think it's obvious. We're going on a date."

"A date?" She tries to fight back a smile. "We can't though, I don't have anything to wear."

I step to the side. "There is a dress for you on the bed. The girl said you'd love it, and I have no idea if that's true, but I really hope it is. There are also shoes and everything else you might need for tonight."

Phoebe's eyes are like saucers. "You did all this for me?"

There's not much I wouldn't do for her at this point, which is a dangerous thought to have. "You deserve to have a man work for you, Phoebe. You deserve so much more than I can give you, but tonight, I am going to give you what I can."

She does smile now and rests her hands on my chest. "And what's that?"

"A date."

Phoebe lifts up onto her toes and gives me a soft kiss. "You are the sweetest man. You flew out here to spend the weekend with me and now this?"

And each time I tell myself not to do something, feel something, want something with her, I find myself unable to stop. All I want is to make her smile and look at me like that so she knows what she should have in her life.

"I may not be able to give you forever, but I can give you right now. I can show you what a real man does for a woman he wants, and it isn't keeping you locked up like a dirty secret. While we're here, I get to give you that, so go get dressed, sweetheart, we have a date."

An hour later, I'm sitting on the sofa, jacket off and shirt unbuttoned as I watch another show on ESPN. In my brilliant plan, I didn't account for the fact that she'd have to get ready and that she'd take freaking forever.

She popped her head out about fifteen minutes ago, saying she was almost done.

I'm not sure how much longer it'll be, but I am trying not to rush her.

I go on the app for the restaurant and push our reservation back another fifteen minutes, hoping we can make it. This is the last option they have for a slot.

"Phoebe?" I ask as I knock on the door.

"Yes?"

"We have to go in ten minutes. Are you close?"

"Umm . . . define close?"

She is killing me. "You can't possibly need this much work. You're fucking perfect without trying."

"Stop saying sweet things to me!"

"Then get your ass out here so we don't miss our dinner."

She sighs loudly. "This is my first date, and I want to look stunning."

I lean my head against the door. "You always do."

"Sweet things, damn you!"

My smile grows wider. "You have five minutes before I carry you out over my shoulder no matter what state you're in."

There, that wasn't sweet.

"Go away so I can finish."

I head back to the couch, fixing my buttons and pulling on my jacket. I have no idea what the dress looks like, and I'm anxious to see it. After I'd explained my plan to the store clerk, she was extremely excited and went to work finding everything Phoebe would need.

I check my watch, she has three minutes left.

Then the door opens, and I wait, but she doesn't exit.

"Phoebe?"

"One minute. I just need one minute. Don't come here, just . . . let me come out."

My heart is pounding as the anticipation mounts, and it's almost as if I'm a teenager again and this is my first date. It is for her, and I want to make it perfect, so I do as she asks.

The air tension is heavy, and when she steps out, it feels as if all the oxygen has been sucked out of the room. She's fucking stunning. Beyond stunning. Beyond anything I've ever seen before. Her dark brown hair is in waves down her back, and the strapless black dress fits her perfectly. It goes to about her mid-thigh and hugs every curve. Her makeup is more dramatic than I've ever seen, but it makes her beautiful eyes even more striking.

I should say something.

I should tell her all of this, but I can't breathe, let alone speak.

Phoebe looks down at herself and fidgets. "Do I look okay?"

"No," I say, going toward her. "No, you don't look okay. You look more than okay. You are radiant, stunning, gorgeous, and any other adjective that I can't think of. You take my breath away."

She bites on her lower lip, blush painting her cheeks. "You look very handsome." Her hands move to my jacket, and she brushes the shoulders. "Every woman in the room is going to wish they were me."

I laugh. "You have that wrong. Every woman in the world pales in comparison to you."

"You and that mouth."

"I think you like my mouth," I tease, wrapping my arm around her back.

"It makes me jealous of the woman who is going to one day steal your heart."

With all of my control, I force my thoughts not to go to her or what I feel now. Instead, I shake my head. "I have no heart."

"We know that's not true."

"Well, I have no patience for a relationship."

Phoebe leans in, her voice warm and velvety. "You are very patient in other places."

"Only with you, remember?"

She grins and then kisses my cheek. "Good. So, where are you taking me?"

"Dinner and then a surprise."

We walk along the street to the restaurant, holding hands and talking. Her day was really great, she loved the student who talked more about the program and really feels like Texas might be the place for her. As happy as I should be for her, I can't seem to honestly feel it. I want her to find her place, follow her dreams, and live her life, but I suddenly just wish she were doing it closer.

"The restaurant is in a house?" she asks.

"It's converted, and I was told it's the best."

I step back, opening the door for her and extending my hand

for her to go in front. Chivalry is a dying practice, and while I didn't have the model of it growing up, I have always tried to be the man I wished my mother would've found.

"Thank you."

Her soft scent fills my nose as she walks past, and I can't wait until tonight when I can appreciate it closer.

I give my name to the hostess, and she's able to seat us right away at a great table by a window that looks out onto the street. This bungalow was converted into one of the best restaurants in Austin, and it's far nicer than anything we have in Sugarloaf.

"This place looks amazing," she says, taking in the white walls with contrasts of black.

"So do you."

"You've said that already." Phoebe blushes, looking down.

"Because it warrants saying again."

She smiles. "I'm glad you think so. Texas has been a pleasant surprise all the way around."

The waiter explains the menu is seasonal and that one of the selections isn't available due to the meat not being up to the chef's standards. Then he takes our drink orders before giving us a moment to look over the options.

"Do you know what you'd like?" I ask.

"Everything looks so fancy," Phoebe notes. "What about you?"

I show her what I'm going to try, and she places her menu down. "I'll have the same."

"You can get anything you want, sweetheart."

"I appreciate that, but I can't decide, so I'll just get what you're having."

We place our order and then have one of the best dates I've ever had. At one point, our conversation turns to sports, and I decide she's clearly been dropped on her head since she's a Giants fan.

"You can't like them, you're from Pennsylvania," I argue.

I shake my head, reaching my hand out to her. Phoebe places

her palm in mine, and I gently brush her knuckles. "So, you think University of Texas is the place for you?"

My question seems to catch her off guard as she looks down at our hands. "I don't know where the place for me is."

With me.

I banish that thought. Fucking hell, if this is my gut reaction, I'm in deep shit and better find a way out of it right now.

"Where do you feel comfortable?"

"Right now? Sugarloaf—with you, but that's not an option."

"You have plans, Phoebe," I remind her as much as myself. "You have dreams that are bigger than Sugarloaf and any of the people in it. Wherever you decide to go, it's going to open doors that never could be at home, no matter what you're leaving behind."

"I know. I just—" She sighs heavily. "I never seem to have my timing right, you know? I always meet a great guy after he's met someone else, or I would work up the nerve to try out for a sport, only to realize everyone else has been training for years already and way above my level. I don't know how I was ever a cheerleader since I had no skill. Now it feels the same, I am on this amazing date with this amazing guy, and the timing isn't right. No matter how much we want things to be different, they are what they are."

"When you leave, life will go back to how it was meant to."

I'll be alone, grumpy, and focused on my job.

Phoebe squeezes my hand. "I wasn't supposed to like you."

"I definitely wasn't supposed to like you."

She laughs. "And, yet, I do."

"More than I should," I admit.

"I'm glad you came here," Phoebe says softly, rubbing her lip between her teeth. "I will never forget this weekend, Asher. I'll never forget how you made me feel, and I am so grateful my first date was with you."

"If any date doesn't compare to this one, Phoebe, walk away. No man should ever make you feel small or irrelevant. He should want you to feel exactly like you do now. If he doesn't achieve it, he's not worth your time."

No man will ever be.

Her eyes fill with an emotion I can't name before she looks away, a smile on her lips when her attention returns to me. "I'll make sure the next man does better."

twenty-six

PHOEBE

Returning back to life in Sugarloaf has been strange. Asher and I settled back in our routine after Texas, no one ever thinking we were together, which is exactly as we hoped.

Olivia has had a bunch of appointments with different specialists, and I have been soaking up anything I can while we're there. The speech pathologist has been the most interesting to learn from. She's been working with Olivia on attempting to make noises.

"I hate it."

"Hate what?" I ask her.

"I don't want to make noise."

"Why?"

"Because they make fun of me."

Oh, my heart.

"Who does?"

She rolls her eyes like I'm an idiot. *"Kids at school."*

The speech pathologist, Kelly, waves her hand to get Olivia's attention. *"No one will make fun of you here."*

"Why should I talk if I can't hear?"

I don't really have a good answer for her, so I let Kelly take this one. *"It's not about talking. It's about using your voice if you need to."*

Okay, I can understand that. "When did she stop using her voice?" I ask Kelly.

"She's been coming here at least five years, and it was before that. We worked her up a bit, but it's sporadic at best."

I turn to Olivia. *"If you don't use your voice, it can weaken. If that happens and you ever need to use it, you could hurt yourself."* She turns away. Well, that went well.

Kelly laughs once. "She's stubborn, but I get it. Sara explained she tried to speak in kindergarten and everyone laughed at her. She couldn't hear them, obviously, but some of the boys were pointing, and after that, she really won't make any noise."

"She laughed a few weeks ago, and a woman was a total bitch about it. Thankfully, I shut it down before Olivia could catch on to what she said."

"People are cruel," Kelly says.

"I agree."

We finish up the appointment without Olivia doing much other than ignoring our attempts to get her to cooperate. When we get back to the house, Asher is already there, waiting to take her out on the ATVs.

"You ready?" he asks her as she comes in the door.

"Finally something fun."

And then she runs upstairs to get changed.

"What's wrong with her?" he asks.

I fill him in on our session and her attitude during it.

He glances up toward her room and sighs deeply. "I wanted to destroy every kid in that classroom who hurt her. Sara and I have tried everything, but Olivia just . . . she can't control the ability to hear, but she can control the ability to speak."

"Asher, how did Olivia lose her hearing?"

I have always wondered this because it's kind of key in knowing what can be done. Not that I don't think her current team is brilliant and able to fix it if they could, but the curiosity in me can't be helped.

"She was born that way. Sara had horrible preeclampsia. She

did everything she was told, spent the last three months of her pregnancy bedridden or in the hospital, but even still, it was difficult to manage. Olivia was born in duress at thirty-three weeks."

"Oh God," I say, imagining what Asher must've been feeling.

"It was horrible. Sara was so sick, and Olivia had a lot of issues breathing. She spent almost two months in the NICU, and it was then we realized she was Deaf."

"I didn't know . . ."

"Phoebe, you would've been, what? Fifteen? Of course, you didn't know."

When he says it like that, I realize just how much of an age difference we have. "Still, I feel bad. Dad never mentioned anything. Just that you had a baby."

"It was hard, but Sara and I were determined to give Olivia every opportunity she could have. We may joke a lot about not liking each other, but we've been a team that fights for our daughter whenever needed."

That is why I am so freaking smitten with him. How many parents put their own shit aside for the better of their children? Not as many as there should be. Three of my friends in high school had divorced parents, and all of them were terrible to each other. These two were never even a real couple, and they put Liv first.

"I'm going to think of a way to encourage her to speak."

He pulls me closer before kissing my forehead. "I know you will."

I gasp, looking up because that was the most natural and innocent gesture that never should have happened. Not here. Not with Olivia home.

"You can't. I can't."

Because I'll want it. I need for us to keep our already blurred lines at least somewhat intact when we're here.

"I know. I . . . the weekend we had, and I shouldn't have."

Olivia comes barreling down the stairs, and the two of us step apart.

253

My chest is aching with the desire to have this be our lives, the two of us hugging, kissing, and being affectionate like we were in Austin, but we aren't in Texas anymore. We're home where the agreement is sex until I leave.

With the strength of Midas, I keep myself calm and easygoing. *"Are you excited?"* I ask Liv.

"Yes. Don't tell my mom."

I laugh. *"I won't."*

Although, I am pretty sure she knows and just allows Asher and Liv their secrets.

Then she rushes toward me and wraps her arms around me in a tight hug before she steps back. *"You're the best."*

"Don't tell your dad."

She shakes her head, looking over at him. *"I won't."*

When she leaves the room, Asher comes up behind me, his lips at my ear. "Her dad already knows and plans to show you tonight."

My muscles lock, and I don't move for a solid five minutes, not until after I hear the ATVs ride away, taking my heart with them.

"I'm sorry, Phoebe, really I am," Joey says as I'm standing on the dance floor at the firehouse.

"You promised!" I look and sound ridiculous, but I can't do this without a partner. The rules are very clear, and Lord knows Mayor Sutton will not bend them.

"I know, and I would've done it, but I'm dating Melinda now, and since she's my girlfriend, I should dance with her."

I groan. Freaking Melinda. "You've been dating for, like, two minutes." Not to mention, she's over there, running her finger down Asher's chest.

Ugh, I hate her.

However, Asher removes her hand, gives her a quick bow of his head, and then walks away. Ha. Take that.

Not like she can't be all over him in a few weeks. Whatever, not going there. No, right now, I am partnerless and this dance-a-thon is about to start.

"You know how she is."

"No, Joey, I really don't. What I do know is that you totally screwed me. My father demands that I dance in this thing because I win every year and Run to Me needs this. I have to have a partner."

Austin walks by, and I grab his arms. "You, you have to save me."

"Save you?"

"Yes, I saved you at the bar, and now you have to be my partner."

Austin looks to Joey. "Officer McNair is your partner."

"No, apparently not."

"Sorry, Phoebs, I can't. I'm already partnered up. My publicist says this is good for my image, so I signed up weeks ago and made a hefty donation."

I groan. "I'm so screwed."

"Are you registering, dear?" Mrs. Cooke asks.

"I don't know."

"Time is almost up to do it."

I'm aware.

Olivia waves at me. *"Are you ready?"*

I shake my head. *"No, Joey bailed on me. I don't have a partner."*

She pouts her lips. *"You have to dance. You always win."*

"I know, but there's no one left."

Everyone else paired off weeks ago. Stupid me for not having a backup. I search around the room for someone, anyone, who doesn't have a partner. My dad is here, and while it's meant to be for fun and charity, if I get stuck with him, we'll be out by hour three. Stamina is not really his forte.

I keep going, too young, too old, doesn't wear deodorant . . .

I turn to ask Liv if she has any ideas, but she's gone. Great.

"Phoebe, dear, are you registering?" Mrs. Cooke asks again.

255

"One minute, Mrs. C."

"Are you okay?" Ellie asks as she puts her hand on my shoulder.

"I'm fine. Just looking for a partner."

She turns to Connor, who gives me a wide grin. "You don't have a partner."

"No."

"So, then we might actually win." He looks far too happy about this.

"I meant, no, my partner isn't here. Not that I don't have one."

Ellie looks to me. "I thought Joey was your partner."

"Nope, I changed last minute." I try to look happy about this instead of murderous.

Connor laughs, clearly reading through my bullshit. "Come on, Ellie, let's stretch now that the contest isn't rigged."

I roll my eyes. It was never rigged. I am just better than all of them.

"Phoebe, you have two minutes!" Mrs. Cooke says.

I fight back the urge to scream. As I keep looking around, desperation creeping in, Asher rushes toward me with Olivia trailing behind.

"What's wrong?" He looks me over.

"I have no partner."

"What?"

"My partner . . . for the dance. That's what's wrong."

He turns to Liv. *"You said it was an emergency."*

"It is, Daddy. She needs a partner."

Sweet God above, no way. I can't dance with him for twenty-four hours in front of the entire town. *"Thank you, Liv, but your dad is working."*

Yes, he's in charge of the refreshment table.

"I can take over for him," Mrs. Cooke unhelpfully offers.

"I couldn't ask you to do that."

She takes a pen, stands, and then hands us both the papers with the numbers. "Here you two go. Break a leg."

Those moments when people say it's like time stopped? I'm experiencing one now. I'm standing next to Asher and Olivia, holding the number seventeen, unsure of what the hell just happened.

Of all the people in the town, I never would've chosen him as my dance partner. Not because I don't want to spend a full twenty-four hours in Asher's arms but because that's exactly what I want.

Now, I either forfeit or suck it up.

He looks to Olivia, signing as he says, *"I guess I have no choice."*

The smile on Olivia's face says it all. She is excited that her father has to do the one thing in this town he's never participated in. He may work it every year, but he has never danced.

He squats down, and Olivia tapes the number on his back. Then I do the same, still sort of in a trance.

"Ready?"

"Are you? I mean, this is a big deal. I have a reputation of being ruthless when it comes to winning."

"You realize the money has already been raised, right?"

I jerk my head back. "But the bragging rights and the medals are still up for grabs. Listen, I need a serious partner here."

Asher shakes his head. "You need a partner, and you got me." He extends his hand. "Dance with me, Phoebe. I won't let you down."

I don't think he's even capable of letting me down.

"You're going down, Bettencourt," Connor says as he points his two fingers toward his eyes and then at me.

"Focus on the dancing, Arrowood. You've yet to win."

Asher turns us so we're away from them. "You all need help, you know this?"

I shrug. "Connor has come in second for the last three years, so he's bitter. Okay, so we have four more hours, and this is when it becomes do or die." I yawn and rest my head on his chest. "So tired."

His hand moves up my back, resting in the middle. "I like that we can touch right now and no one cares."

I snuggle deeper. "We can be like we were in Texas."

He chuckles. "I wouldn't go that far. But I can hold you in my arms, rub your back, or whisper in your ear, and they have no idea that, for weeks, you've been mine."

His. Only his. His words wrap around me like a blanket, warming me everywhere. I want to stay here, in a place where he is mine and I'm his, but the truth lingers that in a few weeks, all of it will be over.

I need to leave and let this be a memory I hold close. I push myself up. "Our time is dwindling."

"I know." Asher's blue eyes fill with disappointment. "Have you made a decision on Texas?"

I shake my head. "I will in the next week or so. I was hoping I'd hear from Vanderbilt, but I don't want to talk about it."

"No?"

I shake my head again. "Right now, I want you to hold me tight, keep me on my feet, and let me pretend again."

Asher sways us, making sure we keep moving. This is the point in which I always regret my choice to do this. I'm exhausted, and most of the other dancers have already quit. It's down to us, Ellie and Connor, and the Settimo twins, who came in third last year. They're a sleeper team and are worthy opponents.

"What would you pretend was real right now?" His deep voice causes me to shiver.

I lean back so I can look at him, wanting to tell him that my dream would be to have it all. "I don't think I should say it."

"Tell me or I'll sit."

"Well, that was unfair." I sigh deeply and then bring my hands back to his chest. "I'm not sure what you want to know." That's a lie. I know exactly what he wants to hear, but I'm afraid to admit it.

"If you could have this be our reality, what would you want, Phoebe?"

"You. Us," I blurt it out, too tired to be more eloquent. "I would want to be a couple, to date, to fall in love, to dance at these stupid contests every year." My fingers inch up, resting above his heart. "I would want my days to be spent helping people in this area with quality care. My nights would be spent in your arms, making love to you. That's what I would want, but no one ever said we could have what we want, did they?"

I phrase it that way because, whatever he's going to say now, I really don't want to know. If the fantasy he paints doesn't include me, I'd rather never hear it. If it does, then again, I can't handle it. The truth is, we are perfect for each other in so many ways, but this isn't our time.

"No, we definitely don't get what we want. Except we are going to win this year."

"You sound confident."

"I am, if I can't give you everything else you want, I can at least give you this."

I smile. "It'll be enough to have that."

It has to be.

twenty-seven

ASHER

I hear a loud scream from the living room and drop my towel, not caring that I have just my underwear on. I swipe my gun out of the safe, ready to kill anything in this house. However, I don't find an intruder, I find Olivia and Phoebe jumping up and down, that stupid dance medal still around Phoebe's neck.

Olivia catches sight of me first, and her eyes widen.

Then I hear Phoebe try to stifle a giggle.

"What the fuck was that?" I ask, still looking around.

"What?"

"You screamed!"

She pulls her lips between her teeth. "I got into Vanderbilt."

I start to walk forward, but then Liv points to where my pants should be. Shit. I raise my hand and go back to my room to get dressed.

As I pull my clothes on, I have a million things in my head. She seemed excited, but she fell in love with Texas when we were there. She keeps saying how she isn't sure, but I could see how her eyes lit up when she walked around.

However, Vanderbilt is closer than Texas. If she goes there, we could ...

What the fuck am I thinking? We? There is no we. I will do nothing but support her decisions.

We're not a couple, and I won't be anything like the piece of shit who used her and manipulated her to get what he wanted.

I exit my room, wanting to hear everything I can about what she's going to do, and she's on the phone with someone.

"No, it's all good. I mean, Vanderbilt was my top choice when I was applying to Iowa." She pauses. "Yeah, I know, and they offered me a really nice scholarship, Em! This is amazing. I have options, and . . ." I turn the corner and find her on the couch, legs tucked under her. "It's also closer to Sugarloaf." She's quiet, probably listening to her friend. "He's different. It's different. I . . . can't talk about it now, but it's a factor in this decision. I just need another week before I decide."

What is? God, the asshole in me wants it to be me. For her to factor me in because if it's her choice, then it can't be manipulation.

How this girl has my head spinning, I don't know, but she does. I want her to be with me, to kiss me in the ice cream store or hold my hand as we walk into Sugarlips for lunch. I want her in my bed every night and to wake up beside her.

The thing of it is that I will never ask it of her. After she told me about her fantasy with us, I was ready to kiss her there on the dance floor, but then she ended it by saying she can't have what she wants.

So, for me to have kissed her, it would have been selfish. She's had enough men hurt her, and I will never be another in that category. She wanted to spend her life helping people, and that would disappear if I asked her to stay.

I take two steps back into the hallway, resting my head on the wall. "Phoebe?" I call out before walking back into the living room.

She gets to her feet, a smile on her beautiful face and her hand up, silencing me. "Em, I gotta go. Thank you, and I'll let you know what I decide." She hangs up and walks to me. "Sorry. That was Emmeline. I was so excited I had to tell her."

I go to brush her hair back behind her ear, but I stop myself. "I'm happy for you."

Her long lashes flutter. "I wish I could kiss you."

"I wish the same."

She glances up the stairs to where Liv's room is. I shake my head. "We can't."

"No," she says quickly. "No, I know. I would never risk Liv. I just . . . I thought maybe I could just hug you?"

"Friends hug," I say, more to myself than anything. "I see nothing inappropriate with hugging. Plus, we danced, and that wasn't scandalous."

Phoebe laughs and takes one step. "Good. I mean, employers can hug employees, right?"

I step to her this time. "I've never hugged your dad, but I mean, I'm sure it happens right before sexual harassment suits are filed."

Her voice drops low and sultry. "I promise not to tell anyone, Mr. Whitlock."

Fuck my life. I want to push her down and ravage her. "A hug," I remind her.

"For now."

I embrace her, hugging her like I would anyone I didn't want to screw six ways till Sunday. She makes another squeal of joy and then pulls back. "I can't believe this. After everything bad that has happened, things are finally going right." Phoebe starts to pace around the room. "I have so much to think about and consider. God, it's overwhelming."

"Take it one step at a time. Are you going to visit that school?"

She turns to me and exhales. "Yes, that has to be the first step. I've at least been there before and already know I love it. The program there is also amazing. On paper, Vanderbilt is the more ideal school. It's rated so high, and . . . I'd be kind of stupid not to go there."

"Because of the program?"

She takes a step back toward me. "Yes, but there are other factors. Nashville isn't . . . far. I could come home more frequently."

I could tell her that I want her to pick that school, to come home all the time, and when she can't, I would go to her. The words are there, but then Olivia comes down the stairs and rushes to Phoebe.

"Can you stay tonight, and we can have pizza and ice cream?"

Phoebe has already promised to stay, even on my days off. Her warm brown eyes look to me, and she nods. *"Of course."*

We spend the next few hours eating and playing board games. Phoebe is on her laptop, searching for housing options while Olivia sleeps on the couch next to her, and I'm reading a report.

The two of them have become so close, I worry about how Olivia will handle it when Phoebe does leave. More than that, I worry about how I'll handle it. Right now, all I want is to walk over to her, close the computer, and tuck her against my side. Every time this girl is near, I'm unable to resist her pull.

"Ugh, there's nothing," she says, closing the laptop.

"You'll find the right place."

Her eyes meet mine. "Maybe I shouldn't go back."

"What?"

"I just mean that I'm doing all of this very last minute. Most students are already in internships and planning their thesis, and I'm going to transfer only a year in? I'm already at a disadvantage and . . ."

"You have to finish school," I say, sounding more like a father than a friend with benefits.

"I thought I did too, but . . . I can take a mid-grad school gap year."

"And do what?"

"Apparently, I can nanny. Sara already mentioned that, if I didn't get into another program, I could stay on and help with Liv."

Anger flows through my veins at that comment. "When?"

"What?"

"When did she say that?" I clarify.

"Before my trip, I guess. I don't know. I was telling her how I was going to check out Texas, and she mentioned if it wasn't the right fit, she would like to discuss my staying on with Olivia since we get along so well."

"No."

That word echoes through the room. "What? Why?"

I shift forward, keeping my voice even. "Because if you're staying in this town and not going to college, you're not nanny-ing. I can't handle it. Do you understand?"

Her lips part. "No, I don't."

She does. She just wants me to say it. Fine. I'm not sure I could hold the words in even if I wanted to. "If you're here, you're not her nanny. You won't be working for us—you'll just be mine."

"And what will you do with me?" Phoebe asks, leaning back in the couch, her legs parting.

I glance at Olivia, who is fast asleep. "Don't play this game," I warn. "You won't like the consequences."

She smiles softly. "Put Olivia to bed so you can take me to yours."

I stand, cage Phoebe in, my lips at her ear. "Be naked and on all fours when I get there. I want to see how wet you are as you wait for me to fuck you until you're breathless."

Somehow, I manage to keep my composure, scoop Olivia up, and bring her up to her room.

I flop back onto the bed, struggling to catch my breath after another very fast and frantic fuck.

Phoebe lets out a soft laugh and then tries to sit up, but she falls back. "That was . . ."

"Yeah." Is all I can get out. It was.

Intense. Amazing. Fucking perfect.

Every time I touch her, I find myself even more crazed for her. As soon as I got into the room, my view was better than I imagined. Phoebe was there, exactly like I told her. Her long, dark hair flowing down her back and over her shoulder, perfect tits hanging like fruit, waiting to be plucked. I used every ounce of self-control I had just to get undressed slowly because her anticipation was my only goal.

And good God, did it pay off.

I wrap a fistful of her hair in my hand, gently tugging her head back. She moves to me and presses her lips to mine.

"You are trying to kill me," I say as it becomes easier to breathe.

"Death by orgasms?"

I laugh. "It would be one of those uncomfortable conversations. I've never had to give a notification like, 'Yes, ma'am, I'm sorry to inform you that your brother died while having an orgasm.'"

Phoebe laughs softly. "Can you imagine the eulogy? Dear friends, Asher was a good man, loving father, brother, and friend. He served his town with respect and dignity. He was a freak in the bed, and his heart just couldn't take it when he was banging the nanny."

I pinch her ass, and she laughs. "I'd come back from the dead to kill you for that."

"If it meant another night like this, I might let you in your undead state."

"You'd become a zombie for me?"

She shrugs. "If your mouth still worked like it does now . . . I could be persuaded."

I shake my head, laughing as I get up. I extend my hand and walk her to the bathroom with me.

"What are we doing?"

"Cuddling a different way."

I head to the tub, which I really saw no point in but now

266

seems like a great idea that Brynn talked me into. I turn the knobs on, letting the water warm and fill. I am not a bath guy, but I am a hold Phoebe as she's wet and naked guy.

I climb in, and she shakes her head. "Not like that."

"What?" I ask as I settle back against the cool porcelain. "Get in, sweetheart."

"Scoot forward."

"I'm sorry, what?"

"Please." Her soft plea is the only reason I slide forward, and then she slips in behind me. She wraps her arms and legs around me, and I suddenly see the appeal. "Lie back, Asher."

I do, feeling her breasts against my back as my head settles right at the base of her neck. "Not what my plan was."

"I want to hold you tonight," she says while her hand cups water and pours it on my chest. "I want to just sit like this with you."

"I like holding you."

She kisses the side of my head. "And I like being held, but this is really nice too."

It is. I sink into the embrace, trying to remember the last time anyone held me. I don't think it's ever happened. Phoebe's legs tighten around my middle, and her head rests against my neck.

I close my eyes, loving how she clamps onto me like she never wants to let go, and God knows I never want her to.

I hear a soft hiccup, and I feel her chest shake. "Phoebe?"

"I'm sorry," she says, and I try to sit up, but she keeps her grip.

"Are you crying, sweetheart?"

"No." She tries to cover it, but I hear the ache in that word.

Forcing her arms to release their death grip, I get free enough to turn. There isn't much room, so I am basically now on top of her, but I see the tears going down her face. "No tears, Phoebe. Talk to me. Why are you crying?"

"I can't tell you."

"You can."

She shakes her head. "I can't. Don't you get it? I can't. I can't admit the words. I can't tell you because I can't take them back if I do."

She doesn't have to give voice to them because I know. I feel it between us, and I am grappling with the same thing. She's right, if we say them out loud, then there's no denying the truth between us any longer.

"I don't like seeing you cry."

"I don't want to cry. I'm stronger than this, but when I got in here and put my arms and legs around you . . . I just felt . . ."

I put my finger to her lips and then wipe away the tear that is moving down her cheek. "You don't have to say it, sweetheart. I feel what you can't say."

"Leaving is going to hurt."

Her leaving is going to kill me. Watching her drive off, wanting her to turn around and turn to me but knowing that's not fair to ask and selfish to desire. So I will have to take the pain because it's what's best for her.

"I won't let anyone hurt you. I will destroy anyone who hurts you."

Even if that person is me.

twenty-eight

PHOEBE

"Hello, Phoebe, it's great to see you again," Dr. Schwartz says as she enters.

She's one of my favorite doctors ever. She's warm, friendly, and she radiates the kind of energy you want to be around. I've spent so much of my life with her around thanks to my parents' friendship with her and her husband. Plus, our town only has one doctor, and Dr. Schwartz does pretty much everything. The office treats infants to elderly to everything in between. I've been a patient here since I was in my mother's womb.

"It's so good to see you, Miss Lucy! How are you? How are the boys? And Jerome?" I ask, missing Jerome terribly.

He and my dad taught me to play Blackjack when I was little. They had a standing card game every Sunday, and while they played, Lucy and my mother would drink wine on the porch as her boys ran around. I was much older, so I hung with the men.

"He's good. A little irritated you haven't found your way to see us since you've been back."

Yeah, I should've expected that.

"To be fair, my father did strongarm me into working as a nanny the minute I got in town. I haven't had loads of free time."

Mostly because, when I do, I'm on my back. Not going to tell her that, though.

"You're forgiven—this time." She winks. "Now, the nurse said you're here for a physical for grad school admissions? Didn't we do one last year?"

I launch into telling her about my changes and how Iowa wasn't a good fit.

"Honey, I have known you since you were four days old, and there is not a lie in this world you can tell without my knowing it. Out with the truth."

I should've gone to an urgent care. "You're bound by confidentiality, right?"

Her lips purse, and she puts a hand on her hip. "You did not just ask me that."

I laugh. "All right, I could use some advice from someone who isn't crazy."

After fifteen minutes of me basically blurting out the mess that is my life, I have a box of tissues on my lap and tears streaming down my face. I am so emotional over all of this. It's been too much. I told her about Jonathan, Asher, my feelings about college, how much I don't want to go, but how I know it's what I need to do. I am pretty sure I talked about the orgasms, which—I regret that one, but there is no judgment in Lucy's eyes, only love.

Her dark brown hand rests on mine. "You've had a pretty eventful few months."

"I have." I sniff.

"And you've been holding all this in?"

I nod. "I can't tell anyone."

"Oh, honey, even if I weren't your doctor, you could've told me. I love you like I love my own kids, maybe even more since you don't talk back near as much as they do. You never have to be afraid to talk to me. This is a lot of feelings to unpack. Also, you're lying to yourself about whatever is going on with Asher."

"I'm afraid I could be in love with him."

Her hand tightens. "I think you know the truth on that one."

I do. The fact that I even considered not going to college or that Vanderbilt is now clearly my top school because I can get home a little faster says it all.

"Are you practicing safe sex?" Lucy asks.

"Yes, we are. I take my birth control every night before bed, and we use condoms."

She lets out a deep sigh. "Well, that's good. I'm not going to say this as your doctor, but as your other mother. You should talk to Asher. Tell him how you feel, and if it's going to hurt your future, baby girl, walk away."

My chest tightens, and I move my hand there. It hurts to think about walking away from him and knowing that's exactly what will happen. "How did this happen to me?"

"What?"

"Falling in love with the guy I hated! He's Asher Whitlock, the world's biggest jerk to me. He just . . . God, he isn't a jerk. That's the issue. He's so sweet, so thoughtful, and I swore this would be easy and fun. Now, I'm here crying about it. I can't fall in love with him this fast."

Lucy raises both brows at that. "Do you not remember the story of your parents? Your mother spoke three words to that man, and the next ones out of her mouth were, 'I'm going to marry him.' Three weeks later, they tied the knot. She loved him the moment she met him, and she loved him until the day she died. Love doesn't work on a time schedule."

"I wish it did."

She smiles. "We all wish a lot of things, but we have choices. You can be honest with him and decide to walk away now before you're in too deep. I just"—Lucy clasps both hands and places them on her lap, and I know the mother part of her talk is coming —"I want you to remember your why. How you called me when you finally decided what you wanted to do. How you were over-joyed by the prospect of becoming an audiologist. You learned ASL, studied hard, and worked through undergrad to make sure

273

you could go where you wanted. You told me how there was no time for love and relationships until you established yourself. Remember your why, Phoebe, and maybe the how will become clearer."

It feels as though she just hit me with a bat, and the air in the room is harder to find. School has been my goal, and helping children just like Olivia is my dream. I didn't date in college, mostly because I had no time for horny boys who had no desire to be serious. And I am serious.

I like serious.

Because I wasn't for so long, and I was lost.

"It's not easy."

"Oh, honey, nothing is." She gets up, puts her coat on, and washes her hands. "All right, for these schools, we need a full physical. I'd also like to do some bloodwork since it's been a while and you had those issues with your iron and thyroid the last time."

"Okay. I saw the OB in Iowa, she said she sent the results."

Lucy scrolls through her tablet. "She did. I have them here. So, we'll get things started and then you'll be all set."

The rest of the appointment goes great, I pee in the cup, get my blood drawn, have a full exam, and then I get dressed. While we wait for the lab to finish with the sugar test and the other quick ones, Lucy and I chat about Jerome and how he's coaching the basketball team full of kids who can't play. She tells me about her youngest, who is getting ready to graduate high school this year.

"I can't believe TJ is going to college."

She huffs. "Tell me about it. I feel old."

"You don't look a day over twenty."

At that, she rolls her eyes. "All right. You're all done here. I am going to check your urine tests, and I'll come back in with your signed forms for the schools."

"Thanks, Dr. Schwartz."

She smirks. "You always were my favorite."

Once she leaves, I grab my phone.

ASHER

I'm taking Olivia fishing for a while.

I'm sure she'll love that.

ASHER

Tonight, we're going to Rowan's, I'd like it if you came and hung out.

I don't know if that's a good idea.

We're already in murky waters, and I don't need to make this harder than it is. If we start going to functions together, I'll yearn for more. For us.

ASHER

I want to see you, sweetheart. I want to kiss you behind the barn and see you in the firelight, smiling and laughing. Then we'll go back to the house, and I'll kiss you exactly where you like it most.

You don't fight fair.

ASHER

I never said I would.

I think it's better if we don't. Maybe another time. Besides, I'm sure your siblings don't want me hanging around on family bonfire night.

CORINNE MICHAELS

About a minute later, my phone pings, and I am prepared for his next angle at trying to convince me.

Only it's not him.

> **BRYNLEE**
> Hey! I'm having a shindig at Rowan's tonight. Dinner and drinks, nothing fancy, but please come. I am always the only girl, and my brothers are annoying when they drink.

I sigh. High-handed asshole.

> So, you had your sister text me?

> **ASHER**
> I want you there, Phoebe. There are no lengths I won't go to monopolize your time.

I really wish that didn't turn me on.

I text Brynn back.

> I just have a few things to do first, but I should be able to stop by.

I slip my phone back in my purse and there's a knock on the door. "Hey, everything good?"

Lucy smiles and nods. "Everything looks good, but . . ."

The pause has me concerned. "Is it my thyroid again?"

276

She shakes her head. "No, it was something else. Phoebe, you're pregnant."

My entire world fades away, and I think I might be dying. The lights are dimming, and the world is shrinking in around me, cutting off my air. I don't know what is happening because I swear she just told me I'm pregnant.

I can't be pregnant.

I'm on the pill and take it daily. I've missed a few here and there, but I double up, just like you're supposed to do. Except for that one time, Asher and I have never not used a condom.

My words won't come out, I just keep shaking my head. "No."

"I checked the urine, which came back as positive, and then I looked at your HCG bloodwork, and your levels are extremely high."

The fog just keeps rolling in. "No. I had my period! I had a period, like, three weeks ago."

It was lighter than normal, but my stress has been insane.

"And you're having sex regularly."

Oh God, Asher. He already has one surprise kid, and now I'm pregnant. This can't be happening to me. He's never going to be okay with this. What about school? What about this life I am working so hard to have? I can't have a baby now.

I'll never finish grad school before the baby comes, and . . . I can't be pregnant.

"It was one time without a condom—one time, and I had just had my period. There's no way I'm pregnant. We use condoms every time. I'm on the pill. Asher and I don't have unprotected sex like that."

Lucy moves in front of me, clasping both of my hands. "Listen, your levels are well above trace amounts. We're running another test on the blood to be sure, but I'd like to do an ultrasound as well. It would allow us to measure the baby and see what's going on. I could be wrong, but I don't think I am."

"It would only be like two or three weeks."

"We can see that in an ultrasound. If you want definitive answers, we should do it now, that way you know."

My limbs start to tremble.

"So, you can see that you're wrong."

She nods. "We can see what's going on. If you're pregnant, we can measure the size of the baby, or if it's nothing, we can see."

My breath comes out in puffs. "Okay . . ."

I say a prayer that this is nothing.

twenty-nine

PHOEBE

"T his is the fetus." Lucy points to the screen. "I'm doing
some measuring now."

Tears continue to streak down my face. I'm pregnant.

This just . . . can't be real.

The little heartbeat on the screen and a very strange looking
alien tells me it is, though. I can't speak or even comprehend
what's happening. However, I do know the baby on the screen
looks like a baby, and there's no way this baby is only two or three
weeks old. There are arms, legs, and a little head.

Lucy finishes, places the wand back on the machine, and
helps me sit up. I have to ask, even though I really don't want to
know. I would rather pretend that the truth didn't just appear on
the screen.

"How far along am I?"

"You're about eleven weeks," she says, and the ache in my
chest is too much. I struggle to catch my breath, and then Lucy's
hand is on my back, her face is close to mine, and she's urging me
to breathe.

If I'm eleven weeks, then this is so much worse than I
thought. This baby isn't Asher's. This baby belongs to another
man, a man who ruined my life and has a family of his own.

All of this . . . I just can't take it.

Lucy keeps talking, trying to get me to calm down, but everything is spiraling so fast. Eventually, I'm able to focus on her voice, and I do as she says, inhaling through my nose and exhaling through my mouth. I repeat it, over and over, until I finally stop gasping.

"Okay?" Lucy asks, hand still resting on my back.

I nod. "As much as I can be."

"You were in Iowa eleven weeks ago."

"Yes."

"You have options, Phoebe. You're still within your first trimester. You just . . . need to make a decision."

"How? How did I not know? I'm not stupid. I'm in the medical field. I understand how all this works, and yet, I'm eleven weeks pregnant."

"You bled, that is how. You're on the pill, you had what you assumed was a period, and you were also under extreme stress, which would've affected your cycle. I know you're not stupid, Phoebe, you're human."

"I don't even know where I go from here," I confess.

"You go home, cry it out, and then make a choice. You're not alone, and you have the support of friends and family, no matter what you decide."

"I have to tell him," I say, not even sure which him I'm referring to. Both, I guess. I don't know that I have to tell Asher, but a part of me doesn't think I could keep it from him. He's my safe place, and I'm going to lose that. "I have to tell both of them, don't I?"

Why would Asher ever want to be with me now? I'm pregnant with another man's baby.

"You don't have to tell anyone anything until you're ready. As for Asher, I don't know what to say. It's not his baby, so there's no reason to disclose this information unless you want to."

I drop my face in my hands, feeling worse than I did when that photo was posted. At least I knew I would come out of that at the end of the day without any scars. This time, I can't run away, avoid the issue, or pretend it never happened. I will forever be altered.

"How do you tell the man you love, who you've been sleeping with for a month, that you're pregnant with another man's baby?"

"I really don't know."

No, because most people don't end up in a mess like this. "Right."

"Would you like to talk to someone beforehand?"

"Talk to someone?"

"Brenna Arrowood is on staff for any patient of mine. I could—"

"No. No, I want to limit the number of people I tell until I know what I'm going to do. How I'm going to handle this."

Lucy gives me a soft smile. "I understand. I'm always here for you, as a friend as well as your doctor. I know this feels insurmountable, but I promise, it'll work out."

"I'm not so sure about that."

I leave the office, driving the fifteen minutes to Asher's house. I don't know why I came here because I know he's at Brynn's. I just couldn't go to my father's. He can't see me this way. My nose is bright red from crying, my makeup is running down my face, and I'm a wreck. I need to be alone.

The house is silent, which I'm grateful for because the noise in my head is so loud. A million things are hitting me all at once. I'm pregnant. With Jonathan's baby. His wife, who believed it was just that kiss and I'd initiated it, is going to be devastated, but the joke's on me.

My hand moves to my belly, heart so heavy it could sink through the floor.

I grab my phone out of my purse and see there are two missed calls. One from Emmeline, and one from Asher.

Then I look at the texts.

> **ASHER**
> Where are you?
>
> Please come tonight, sweetheart, I want to see you.

I shake my head, knowing I can't face him. Not now. Not until I am prepared to lose him completely.

> I'm not feeling well. I'm going to lie down. Have fun.
>
> **ASHER**
> Are you okay?
>
> I'm fine, I'll probably stop by later.

Lie. I am going to cry myself to sleep after I make this phone call. I pull up Jonathan's number, knowing that, no matter what, I have to get this part over with. I could keep it from him, but that's not who I am. I would never want someone to do that to me, therefore, I'll tell him. Ultimately, it's my decision what I do, but he has a right to know and at least give me his thoughts.

He is probably still on campus, so hopefully this goes well.

The phone rings three times, and then his deep voice is in my ear. "Phoebe?"

"Hi, Jonathan."

"Phoebe, God, I miss you. I miss you so fucking much. I'm miserable—"

"I only called to let you know that I'm pregnant." I blurt the words out, not wanting to hear his stream of bullshit.

He's silent.

"Hello?" I say after almost a full minute.

"You're pregnant?"

"Yes."

He clears his throat. "Wow, that's terrible. I'm sorry to hear that."

My eyes blink as the seconds tick by. He's sorry? That is how he reacts to this? I literally need at least ten seconds to force the next words out of my mouth. "You're sorry to hear that?"

"I know you weren't very careful when we were together. It's a shame you're in this situation. Who else have you been with, any chance it's not mine?"

I rear back because, as far as he knows, I am alone. "I'm eleven weeks pregnant. You are the father."

"Not possible."

"It very much is possible since I left the doctor not even twenty minutes ago. I'm pregnant, Johnathan, and it's your baby."

He laughs once. "Did you lie about being on the pill? What? Couldn't keep me some other way so you did this to trap me into whatever life you wanted? Did you think I'd leave my wife if you were pregnant?"

My chest feels as though someone is squeezing it, and I want to throw up. "You didn't even tell me you had a wife! How exactly would I be trapping you into what you promised? *You* are the one who said you were single. *You* are the one who convinced me that we didn't need condoms, saying how it felt too good being inside me raw. So, maybe it's *you* who wanted *me* to get pregnant."

"You're delusional. You knew everything, you just wanted it to be different."

My God, he's such a piece of shit. Gone is the sadness and feelings of helplessness. I could spit fire right now. "I know now. I'm pregnant, and it's yours."

"Get rid of it."

No hesitation. No concern. Not even a glimmer of the man he pretended to be. "What?"

"Either you get rid of it, or you keep it and I never want to know. I'll send you a couple hundred bucks so you can do what you want, but that . . . *child* . . . isn't mine. I have my family, and I will not let you destroy it. You were a good lay, Phoebe, but not the mother of my children. I will never claim that baby as mine, so you're on your own."

With that, he disconnects the phone, and I empty the contents of my stomach.

thirty

ASHER

"**I**s Phoebe coming?" Olivia asks for the tenth time.

I give her my best attempt at a smile. *"I don't know."*

Brynn taps Olivia's arm. *"Tell him to go check on her."*

My sister has said *that* ten times, but optics matter. I can't go running after my daughter's nanny, not when I'm clearly fucking desperate for her.

I've tried to keep my phone out of my hand, but I've failed miserably. She hasn't responded to my last two texts, and I don't know what is going on, but I'm worried she's sick and alone.

"She doesn't want me to check on her. She's probably asleep."

> Are you at my house or yours?

Rowan hands me a beer. "She's probably banging some guy. It's not like you give her any time off."

I could break his nose for that. "She's not banging some guy."

How do I know? Because she's banging me too often to fit another man in.

"Well, she's not banging me." He practically falls into the chair beside me. "If she were, she'd be right here." Rowan pats the chair beside him.

Jackass.

"You know that not all women are impressed by you, Rowan," Brynn notes.

"It's all a façade. The ladies love a bad boy."

He's not wrong about the façade, but it's not them—it's him. Rowan likes to play the part of being the eternal bad boy, always out for fun, nothing in life is serious, but those who actually know him are aware that he's a liar. Rowan wants a family more than anything. He wants love, but he isn't willing to sacrifice for it.

Like it seems that I am by sitting here, pretending that I don't care about Phoebe when nothing can be further from the truth.

PHOEBE

Yours, but I just got sick. I'm going to stay here. Have fun.

Fuck it. She's sick and alone. I'm not staying here to drink beer, knowing that she doesn't feel good.

"I'm going to the house, can Liv stay here?"

Brynlee smiles. "Of course! Please make sure she's okay. She isn't answering my texts."

So, it's not just me.

"I'll be back," I tell Liv.

My legs yearn to break into a run, wanting to get to her in case she needs me, but I force myself to walk away at a reasonable speed. Then I get on the quad and drive to my house a bit faster than normal.

I go in through the back door, trying to keep quiet in case

she's resting. Only, when I reach the hallway that leads to both our bedrooms, I hear her crying.

She's not quiet, and the agony in her cries are enough to break my own heart. I don't knock before I push her door open, but then I freeze in the threshold. Her head jerks up, tears are flowing down her face, her nose is bright red, and the pain in her gaze is bone deep.

"What's wrong?" I ask, my voice hoarse.

Phoebe wipes at her face. "No."

"No what?"

"I'm not ready."

"Phoebe, ready for what?"

"You shouldn't be here. You should be with your family at the bonfire, having fun."

I move to her side, taking her face in my hands. "Clearly not. I should be here—with you. I was worried about you, and right-fully so."

Another tear falls, and her lip quivers. "Please, just go back to Brynn's and pretend you never saw this."

"That's not going to happen." Like I could leave her now? Not a chance in hell. I pull her into my arms, holding her to my chest. "What is wrong? Who or what is making you cry?"

"Please don't ask that." She shifts off my lap. "Please don't touch me. I don't deserve it."

"Why? What is going on, Phoebe?"

She looks so broken, so sad, and I will do anything to take that from her. Instead of telling me, she gets to her feet and starts to pace. "I need time, Asher. I need to figure things out . . . please. Don't ask me what's wrong. Don't look at me like you want to make it better. Don't make me want you more than I already do! This is all hard enough."

Fuck, it's me that's hurting her, although I don't know what I've done. "Phoebe."

She spins to face me. "Don't say my name like that."

"Like what?" I ask, confused because I hadn't said her name any specific way.

"Like you care about me. Like you would protect me."

"I do care about you! Fuck, I would do anything for you!" I take her hands in mine. If I'm holding a small part of her then she can't walk away from me. "I would do anything," I say softly this time, gentle. "I care about you too much. I want you. I fucking need you, and I will protect you with everything I am. Talk to me."

"No. We have an agreement."

"Fuck the agreement. It doesn't matter."

That agreement went to shit the minute I got on a plane, and that weekend with Phoebe changed everything. I was enough for her, and she was everything for me. We have a million obstacles, all of them complicated and messy, but she's worth it.

"You say that now, but you don't mean it. You have Olivia, and I'm a mess. I'm a mess who will just screw up your life."

I shake my head. "What the hell is going on? When you left this morning, you were perfectly happy, and we had plans for tonight. I don't understand what changed. Did they find out about us? Did someone say something?"

She pulls her hands out of my grasp, stepping back, but there's nowhere to go. Her back is against the wall. "Yes."

"Yes to what?"

"Yes to it all. Everything has changed."

I'm not a guy who likes riddles and games. It's why these arrangements—as she called it—worked for me. There are rules, and we don't cross the lines. No one gets hurt, and at the end of the day, we part as friends. Sara and I messed up, but we've found new rules, and they work. With Phoebe, she made every rule irrelevant and basically erased any chance at an arrangement.

I have never felt like this, and I'm not about to let her walk away without even telling me what the fuck is going on.

I take a deep breath and step back because crowding her isn't helping. "Let me fix it."

"You can't fix this."

"What is *this*?"

"This is the end, Asher."

Anger and frustration course through me. Doesn't she see it? Doesn't she know how much I care about her? How I left my family to come to her? How I broke every damn rule because I need her more than air?

No. It's not the end.

"The fuck it is."

Her back slides down the wall, and she curls protectively around herself. In an instant, I'm there, but she puts her hands up, stopping me from coming close.

She looks up, her eyes filled with so much sadness it could fill the room. "It will be."

"Why?"

"Because I'm pregnant."

I struggle to suck in a breath because suddenly it's hard to breathe. She's . . . no. This can't be. Not again. Not that I don't love my daughter, but I had no plans of having another child, if I did— not like this.

"You're pregnant?" I choke on the words.

"It's not yours," she says quickly. "I'm eleven weeks, and we both know, I wasn't here . . . eleven weeks ago."

Phoebe's eyes glimmer again, the tears flooding those brown eyes I love looking into.

And while I felt dread a few seconds ago, now it's even worse. "The father . . . isn't me?"

"Not unless you were in Iowa and we have no memory of it, no. It's not yours."

I'm not relieved. I'm not happy. I'm not really sure what the hell I am. Those words terrified me as much now as they did ten years ago, only for a far different reason.

Phoebe is pregnant, and it's not my child, which means it's another man's baby growing inside the woman I'm falling in love with. If I'm not already there, which I'm pretty sure I am.

I feel a million chaotic emotions, but the most important

thing I can do is keep calm and take things one step at a time. The first priority is making sure she's okay.

I move to her slowly, squatting in front of her. "Are you healthy?"

She blinks, the tears falling. "What?"

"You and the baby, are you both okay?"

"Am I okay? I don't know. No. I'm not okay. I'm pregnant with a married man's baby, and he told me to get rid of it. So, yeah, not okay."

What a piece of shit he is. I would love nothing more than to beat the fuck out of him for treating her this way. He doesn't deserve to have ever touched her, to have known her or looked at her or breathed the same air as her because she's too good for this world.

"You told him." I'm not sure why I'm stating the obvious other than the less I say, the better chance I have of not screwing up.

She wipes under her eyes, and I sit on the floor beside her, back against the wall. "I don't know why I thought he'd be any different reacting to this. I just wanted to believe maybe there'd be a sliver of compassion. I debated not even telling him but," Phoebe admits, pausing and letting out a laugh. "I couldn't. I wouldn't because that's just not who I am. He had a right to know, and I have a right to protect myself and whatever . . . God, what am I going to do?"

She's going to have me, and we'll figure this out. I don't know how or where I go with this, but one step at a time. I entwine our fingers together. "You don't have to do anything right now."

"I don't have a lot of time to make a decision."

"Well, you don't have to do it today."

Not when she's this upset.

She rests her head on my shoulder. "How do I do this? How do I raise a baby and try to have the life I've worked so hard for? Why was I so stupid? Why? I'm so dumb, and I'm so sad because I believed him. I fell for all his fucking bullshit like a fool. And now what? Now I lose it all? My career is gone, my father is going to freak out, and worst of all is that I lose you as well. I'm alone and pregnant and in love with a man who isn't the father of the baby."

My hand stills at her confession, which I don't even know she meant to say. She loves me? I thought she might, but hearing it causes my heart to swell, and all I want is to make this better for her.

"You're not alone." I barely get the words out, and I hate that they don't hold the conviction I want them to because I'm still reeling from my own realizations. I know I'll never want to walk away from her. No matter what she decides, I can't imagine my life without her and nor do I want to.

"But I am. I'm alone, and I'm going to lose you."

Not a fucking chance. Even though this entire situation is a hundred degrees of fucked up, her fears aren't valid here.

"You won't lose me, Phoebe." I shift, needing her to hear me, to see the truth in that. "You won't lose me. You have me. I'm not walking away from you." I take her beautiful face in my hands and bring my lips to hers. "You won't lose me."

She throws herself into my arms, and I adjust her on my lap. Her tears soak my shirt, and I do nothing but hold her together even when everything around us is falling apart.

thirty-one
PHOEBE

The tears eventually stop, but the confusion and uncertainty still weigh heavily. I move out of Asher's lap, hating myself for telling him I love him in the worst way possible. You know, every man wants to hear that after you tell them you're pregnant with another man's baby.

Way to go, Phoebe.

He gets to his feet and then helps me up, but when I go to move away from him, he doesn't relinquish his hold on my hands. "I meant what I said."

My gaze is blurry from unshed tears. "About what?"

"You won't lose me. You're not alone. I'll be here for you in whatever way you want or need."

"I don't deserve you."

"No, sweetheart, you don't deserve what was done to you, but you're more than deserving of how I feel about you." His lips turn up slightly as he tucks my hair behind my ear before resting his palm against my cheek. "I don't know much about relationships. I've spent most of my life avoiding them, but I have never felt this way before, Phoebe. You consume my thoughts, dreams, wants, and desires. You make me want to fight every man who looks at you, touches you, or even breathes your air. I want to protect you with every bone in my body, but more than that, I want to be the man who makes you happy. I don't know if it's love. I don't know if it's more than that, if such a thing exists, but I know that I don't care if you're pregnant or not pregnant any more than I care if it's his baby or mine. None of that matters because all I want is you. However I can have you. However you want me, I'm yours."

I shake my head, refusing to accept it. "No."

"Yes."

He doesn't mean that, or maybe he thinks he does, but that will change once he has time to think about it. Tomorrow, when the world is bright again and his brain cells return, he'll see that this is insane.

I walk back and out of his reach. "I appreciate that you said any of that, Asher. I really do. You have no idea how much I wish it could be the truth. I am in love with you." I laugh because it's just . . . one more thing. "I am. I didn't want to be. I promised myself it wasn't even possible. You're you, and I don't mean that in a bad way. It's just that you're Asher Whitlock, and I am definitely not in your league. While you will never be able to understand that what you said is the single most incredible thing anyone has ever said to me, you also don't know what you're saying."

Asher steps closer. "I am not some kid off the street who doesn't know what he wants. I'm a grown man with a child, a life, a good job, and a home." His hand moves to cup my cheek again, and I don't move away. "I've waited my entire life to feel this way, and while we have every reason to stay apart, I can't come up with a single one that's good enough to make me walk away. I know what I want, Phoebe, and I'm looking at her."

He leans in, bringing his lips to mine in a soft, gentle kiss. I suck in a gasp of air and then fall into his arms. Asher catches me, holding me up while I struggle not to fall apart again.

The kiss slows and then stops before he pulls back and rests his forehead against mine. "We'll figure this out."

Guilt for putting him in this situation assaults me. "You're willing to stand by me? Why?"

"Because I love you, Phoebe."

I want to argue that it's not possible, but I'm no different. I am so in love with him that it physically aches. He is everything I want, and while this already messy situation just got worse, I think what hurt me the most was the idea that we were going to be over before our time was up. I didn't want it to be over. I never want it to be over.

"You're going to be okay with this? With me being pregnant and . . . the baby isn't yours?"

"Love doesn't come with conditions." Tears fill my eyes, but this time, they aren't from sadness. They are because I feel so incredibly lucky to have found this man. "Don't cry." Asher half smiles and touches the tip of my nose. "I may be a marshmallow, but you're Rudolph."

I laugh for the first time in hours and drop my head to his chest. "It's so bad. I really wish I could cry without the whole world knowing."

He lifts my chin to look at him. "I think you're beautiful."

"I think you're crazy."

"I am. Come on, let's get you cleaned up and go to my sister's house."

I change my clothes into something more comfortable and that doesn't remind me of this horribly manic day, wash my face, and we head out to the ATV. Asher drives to Brynn's driveway, but then he pulls to a stop and turns to face me. "I don't want us to keep lying to everyone, but when it comes to Olivia . . ."

"No, we don't tell anyone until we know what we're telling people." My palm rests on his cheek. "For now, we keep everything as it has been, and we'll figure out the best way to tell others."

He leans in, kissing me softly. "I want to tell Sara about us first, but then I think we should tell your father."

"Oh, that'll be super fun."

"I know, but the sooner we're honest, the better. I want the whole town to know you're mine and I love you."

"Yes, nothing says love and luck like falling for a knocked-up hot mess."

He laughs once. "I happen to like hot messes."

"Good thing, otherwise, we'd be in trouble."

Asher's lips find mine again for a brief kiss, and then he turns back around. I wrap my arms around his middle, and we head up the driveway, leaving the day behind us.

As soon as the ATV stops, Olivia is rushing toward us.

She's signing so fast that I can't catch half the words. *"Wait."* I smile as I try to stop her.

Her huff is loud as Asher helps me off the quad. She taps her wrists, and I tilt my head. *"Can I talk now?"*

"Yes."

"Are you okay? Dad said you were sick."

Before I answer, Asher's already answering. *"She's okay. She just ate something bad."*

"I'm glad you're here. We are going to play cornhole. Will you be on my team?"

"Of course."

Brynn waves as she approaches. "Glad you made it. We were worried about you, Phoebe."

"I'm good, thank you."

She gives me a hug and then playfully slaps her brother's chest. "You're on my team."

"Great, now I'm going to lose," Asher says jokingly.

"Whatever, you're the one who can't play."

Olivia taps my arm. *"I'm the best."*

"You are?"

"I win every time. It's why Dad always wants me on his team."

I grin. *"Is Aunt Brynn good?"*

She shakes her head. *"No."*

Brynn laughs and signs as she says, *"I'm not bad!"*

"She's not good either," Asher informs the group. *"But I am."*

He's good at everything, dancing, sex, being sweet and kind, and fixing broken hearts, so why wouldn't he also be good at yard games.

However, I'm actually really good at cornhole. I spent a lot of time in college playing at parties. I turn to Liv, deciding that I may not be winning at the game of life, but I can kick some ass at the Whitlock cornhole competition.

"I'll do my best."

Olivia smiles. *"We will have fun."*

Yes, we will have a ton of fun gloating after we win.

Olivia still has a smile at breakfast because we didn't just win, we annihilated them. Brynn really does suck, and Asher tried to carry her, but he was no match for Olivia and me. As our celebration, I decided we needed to have pancakes. So, we're here at Sugarlips, where I feel like everyone is staring at me. Like there's a sign on my head that reads: pregnant and a mess.

"What do you want to do today?" I ask Olivia.

Her speech therapist canceled today for a family emergency, so we are free to do whatever we want. *"Can we go shopping?"*

She doesn't have to ask me twice. *"I love shopping, but what do you need?"*

She glances down at what remains of her pancakes. *"A bra."*

Oh. Shit. I'm not sure what the protocol is on this, but if she's asking me, I don't want to say no. I wonder if Sara put this in the binder. Doubtful.

I smile. *"I would love to take you shopping, but I just want to ask your mom."*

She shakes her head. *"No, she will be weird. Please. I don't want to tell anyone."*

As her nanny, I am sure this is not a good idea, but as her friend, I don't want to say no. Considering I am not really a nanny and sleeping with my boss, I should definitely handle this right.

Olivia is nine, and she is definitely a bit more developed. If she's uncomfortable, then I can help her handle it.

"I don't want to keep things from your mom or dad. I think we should at least ask your mom."

Normally I run on the whole ask for forgiveness rather than permission, but not this time.

"Please, Phoebe. She's even worse than my dad."

I shake my head. *"Not this time. I will ask her, and then we'll go. We'll let her tell your dad."*

"Hello, my daughter," Dad says from the edge of the table.

I leap up, wrapping my arms around him. "Daddy!"

He chuckles and squeezes me tighter. "Can I join you?"

I turn to Olivia. *"Is it okay if my dad sits with us?"*

Olivia nods with a smile.

A few days ago, the speech therapist recommended an app for Olivia that is sort of like Google translate. It takes audio and translates it to sign language and vice versa. I tried it a few times, and while it's severely lacking, we agreed to keep trying.

I open the app and set the phone on the table so the screen is facing Olivia. "Let's try."

"Okay."

I explain the app to my father and let him know that he needs to speak very slowly and clearly. I get one raised brow, but no other protest.

"How are you?" he asks.

Olivia smiles. *"Good."*

There is about a ten-second delay before the app replies with what she signed.

My dad looks at me. "This isn't exactly great."

"No, but it's something."

This could help so many if it were better developed. Not all the signs are correct, and it feels almost as if the creator took online ASL lessons and didn't actually speak to people who are fluent. I called my friend at Gallaudet University, and she said they aren't working on this particular one, but she loves the idea.

There is a more complex software available, but that doesn't help the immediate needs when someone is out or is in an emergency situation.

I turn to Liv. *"Ask him a question."*

She presses the button on her phone. *"Can Phoebe live with me forever?"*

I laugh and shake my head. *"You're silly."*

She shrugs.

My dad is grinning. "She's pretty great, but she needs to go back to grad school." My stomach plummets, and I work hard to stay calm.

The app translates that, and Olivia's face puckers. I grab the phone and play back the last sign. "She's pretty grape, but she heeds to go back to dad's cool."

Oh Lord. I translate what it should've said, and she nods.

"Have you made a decision?" Daddy asks.

"I haven't."

Because now, I don't know what to do. I would have the baby in December or January, which is right when finals are. I can't imagine being in a class nine months pregnant while constantly worrying about going into labor.

I just don't see a way around having to take a year off without it also meaning my possibly not being accepted into either schools' program.

The idea of staying here and being Asher's unemployed girlfriend seems equally bad because gossip in a small town can be just as bad as a viral post of you kissing your married professor. When we tell people that we're together, it'll be all anyone talks about, and when they all find out I'm having a baby?

A shudder runs down my spine.

"Time is running out, Birdie."

"I know. Trust me, I know."

I have to make a decision in the next day or so, and I really don't know what to do.

"I think you should stay," Olivia tells me.

"And why is that?"

"Because you're my best friend."

"You're mine too."

And I hope she'll still feel that way when she finds out about me and her dad.

thirty-two

ASHER

It's late, I'm exhausted, and all I want is to be with Phoebe. It's been two days since I told her I love her, and other than the first night, I haven't really seen her much. Yesterday, I ended up on a call that went well past my shift, I slept at the station because I had to be back at work in six hours, and today has been nonstop.

> How is Liv?

PHOEBE
She's good. Misses you. As do I.

> What did you guys do today?

The bubbles pop up. Stop. Start. Stop again. And then start before the text comes through.

PHOEBE:

> We went shopping. I spoke with Sara because Olivia asked me to take her to buy some . . . girl things. She was okay with it, so Brynn and I took her.

Girl things? What the hell could my nine-year-old daughter need that . . . no, she's so young. She can't have started already.

> Not possible.

PHOEBE

> Yes, it is. She needed a bra, Asher. Sara, Brynn, and I all agreed.

I stare at the words on the screen. A bra? I'm so not ready for this stage. To me, Olivia is still three, happy to sit on my shoulders and jump in rain puddles.

> Can we pretend she's still a baby?

PHOEBE

> My dad is a pro at it, ask him for pointers.

I laugh because it's true. It's also why he's probably going to shoot me when we tell him that we're together and she's pregnant.

> Maybe we can lead with that when we tell him about us.

PHOEBE

> You should be more concerned with making it out alive.

> True.

PHOEBE

> Olivia is asleep, it was an exhausting day. Are you coming home tonight?

Home. That's where she is. In my home, in my head, in my every thought.

> Yes, I'll be home in a few hours.

PHOEBE

> I'll wait up.

> Be sure you do.

I put my phone away and get to work on the report from today's call. It takes about an hour before I'm happy with the details and sure I haven't missed anything, and then I'm headed home. When I get there, the lights are off, and I go through my normal routine. I check on Liv, who is snoring in her room, and then head to Phoebe's room, but she's not there.

"Phoebe?" I call out, wondering where she is, and when I hear nothing, I start to panic.

Where is she?

I check her bathroom, but she's not there.

Then I go to the kitchen, living room—double-checking the

couch to see if she fell asleep there—and the laundry room, but . . . nothing.

I head into my room, and that's when I hear the . . . singing . . . if we can call it that, coming from my shower.

Well, this works out well.

I strip out of my uniform, already growing hard at the idea of her naked and wet.

Her eyes are closed, wet silky brown hair down her back as she sings another note—not the right one—and sways her perfect ass. I grip my cock, stroking as I watch her. God, she's fucking perfect.

I wait for her to notice me, but she doesn't. I pull the glass door open, which startles her into glancing over her shoulder to me, and slip in behind her. "When I said to wait up for me, I didn't specify naked. Good job on the improv."

"You should really not sneak up on people."

"I was standing there for a solid minute," I say, sliding my hands around her from behind.

She smirks, looking at me through her thick lashes. "Watching?"

"Yes."

"Pervert."

I squeeze her breasts and then pinch her nipple. "You like it."

"I do."

I do it again, her moan echoing in the shower. "I think you'll like this more." My hand moves down her stomach, and she parts her legs. I grin against her neck. "Already wanting me there."

Her arm comes up around my neck, giving me a perfect view of the water running down her slick body. "Always wanting you," she rasps.

"That's right, you want me, only me." The possessiveness flares, wanting to own her, claim her, be everything she needs.

I press against where she wants me most, letting the tension between us build. Her body arches, and her other hand grips my thigh, nails biting into the skin. "Asher."

"What, baby?" I ask as I lighten the pressure.

"Please."

"Please what?"

"I want to . . . I want you."

I kiss down the slope of her neck. "Turn around." She does, and I back her against the tile before pressing both her arms above her head. "I'm going to make you come once here, and then I'm going to carry you to bed and make love to you for hours."

When I'm inside her this time, it won't be like before when we pretended it didn't matter.

She moans as I kiss down her body, but then I hover over her stomach where she's carrying a child, and she sucks in a breath. There is worry swirling in her eyes, and I keep our gazes locked as I place a kiss there.

Her fingers tangle in my hair, and I move lower. "Open your legs for me, beautiful."

She does, and I slide my tongue against her core. Her taste fills my mouth, and I could drown in her pleasure. Each stroke has her panting louder, her head is tilted toward the ceiling as I work her faster. I want this to be fast. I don't want to wait to be inside her.

I move my hand to her ass, pulling her forward so she can't move away from me.

"Oh, God. Oh, Asher. I can't stop it."

I flick harder, using my finger to just graze her entrance, and then she's there. She lets out a soundless scream, hands slapping against the tile as her legs start to tremble. I bring her down slowly, drawing out her orgasm. She sags against the wall, and I stand and wrap my arms around her to keep her upright. Her smile is lazy as she flutters her eyelashes.

"You are really, really good at this."

I laugh. "So are you. Put your arms around my neck."

She does, and I scoop her up. We exit the shower, and then I wrap her in a towel before grabbing one for myself. Once we're dry, I lift her back up and carry her to bed.

We lie next to each other, her hand resting on my heart. "I missed you."

"I'm right here."

"Yes, and I am so lucky you are."

This is the only place I want to be. "And I'm the lucky one, sweetheart. When I'm with you, I'm winning everything."

"How so?"

"Because you're my prize, and trust me, there's nothing else in the world that can compare."

Her smile is wide as her finger traces my lip. "I think you might be the sweetest, most perfect man I've ever met. I never had a chance of resisting you, did I?"

"Like I said, only with you."

I pull her closer, pressing my lips to hers. She reacts instantly, her hands cup my face, holding me to her as she deepens the kiss. I moan into her mouth, feeling it reverberate in the room.

I want to make her feel good, make her feel loved and cherished.

"Tell me what you want, Phoebe, and I'll give it to you," I say before shifting so I'm above her, pressing her to the mattress.

She's breathtaking lying beneath me. Her fingers slide through my wet hair. "Make love to me, Asher."

Her legs part, and I align myself with her entrance. "Keep your eyes on me as I take you. I want you to look at me, see how much I love you as I enter your body."

She moves her hands slowly down my spine as I start to push into her. Her heat surrounds me, and I force myself to do as I requested of her. The pleasure is so much that I want to close my eyes and sink into it, but I keep my gaze locked. I want her to see it all, feel how much I fucking love her.

"Oh, God." She moans, her fingers tightening against my skin.

"You're mine, Phoebe. All of you. I want you to give me every part of you."

"Yes." She pants, her body trembling as we keep the connection. "I love you."

When I'm fully inside her, I pause, my heart pounding against my ribs as I drop my forehead to hers. "I knew you'd destroy me. I just didn't know it would feel so good."

And then I take my time, making sure she has no doubt that I want all of her.

thirty-three

PHOEBE

"So, what are we going to tell people and when?" I ask as I lie on his chest, his fingertips stroking my spine.

"First, I think we tell Sara and your father tomorrow. Then Olivia has to be next, the same day."

I let out a breath through my nose, suddenly nervous. I love Olivia, but being the cool, fun nanny and being your father's new girlfriend are two very different things. "I worry she's going to be upset."

Asher pushes my hair back. "Liv is a good kid, and even if she's upset at first, she'll come around."

"Not if she thinks there's a baby to compete with. I don't know how we do this," I confess. "It's all so complicated. I don't want to lie to anyone or have people assume this baby is yours."

"Who the fuck cares what they assume?"

I shift to fall back against the pillow and stare at the ceiling. "You didn't knock me up."

"No, but no one in this town is owed an explanation about our lives."

I laugh once, turning to look at him. "You and I both know that's not how this works."

"We make it work that way," Asher says, rolling onto his side. "I don't care if they think it's my baby or not."

"And what do we say if they ask?"

"That we're together and figuring things out."

I don't like any of this. I wish I could go back in time and fix my life so none of this was his problem. "I'm not going to be able to go to grad school this year."

"Why not?"

My eyes widen. "Why do you think? I'd be dealing with finals while also being ready to give birth. I can't. I have to defer and see where I am in a year."

"Can you do that?"

"I think so. I can ask them for a gap year due to a medical condition. Then I could go back after the baby is born and hopefully things are more stable."

Asher runs his finger down my nose. "You know I'm here. I want to help and be here for you, to love you and the baby."

It all feels so fast, as if we skipped the dating portion and went right to marriage. Which, we're not married, but it feels as though it's all so permanent.

"Why didn't you marry Sara or move in with her when she was pregnant?" I ask, feeling stupid as soon as I ask it.

"I didn't want to marry Sara, and I sure as fuck wasn't going to live with her."

"You didn't love her?"

He shakes his head. "No. Not at all. We were fun and we were careless, but even after we found out she was pregnant with Olivia, we never considered getting married or living together."

I sit up, pulling the sheet with me. "And what do you want with me?"

Asher adjusts himself so his back is against the headboard. "I want to be with you."

"I know that, but what does that look like to you? Do I live with my dad? Do I try to get a job somewhere close and an apartment? I'm sure I could rent the apartment in the barn at Declan and Sydney's." Which actually might be perfect.

"You'll live here."

I'm sorry, did he just say that? "What?"

"You can stay as long as you want."

"As what? Your nanny?"

"I don't mind you tucking me in if you're naked."

I roll my eyes. He can't be serious. "Asher—" I nearly choke on his name. "You can't ask me to move in. This is too much too fast. We can't go from zero to a thousand overnight."

"Why? I'm almost forty years old, and I have never once asked a woman to live with me. The fact that I didn't hesitate to ask you, says something. I want you here, in my home, in my bed, and in my life every day."

I shake my head, trying to wrap my brain around it. "I think we have to go slow—for Olivia."

He sighs heavily, running his hands through his dark brown hair. "I don't think Olivia will care. She loves you."

"Yes, she does, but . . . she needs time to absorb that we're dating before she finds out I'm pregnant and moving in with you. No, it's a lot for her to take in."

"If you really think she needs that, then fine, but it doesn't change my answer to your question. I want you here."

"I do think she needs time, and honestly, I need it."

This relationship was never supposed to be. We were meant to be fun, and somewhere along the way, I fell in love.

"Why do you need it?"

"Because we've been doing this relationship behind closed doors. Sure, we've spent months together." I move, taking his beautiful face in my hands. "We've touched, kissed, loved, and no one knew. To us, it makes sense for me to move in with you. But, to the rest of the world, you're the grumpy jerk who thinks I'm a mess." He grins, and I rub his lips before dropping my hands. "Which I am proving to be quite an accurate description of myself. Plus, I have to deal with Jonathan. I need to get him to sign his rights away or . . . I don't even know. But he's married and has a kid already, I can't imagine he'll fight me since he wants me to get rid of the baby anyway."

"Jonathan?" he asks.

"The father—or sperm donor if we call him that. My professor's name was Jonathan and . . ." I stop talking when I see Asher's face.

"What does Jonathan teach?" he asks with his jaw clenched.

"Philosophy."

"Is he old?"

I shake my head. "No, he was almost forty. Apparently, I have a type."

"What's his last name?" His voice is like ice cracking underfoot. My stomach drops, and I don't know why.

"Loa." As soon as I say the name, he tosses the sheets off and climbs out of bed. I swear I can see the anger rolling off him in waves. "Asher? What's wrong?"

He doesn't answer. He just starts putting his clothes on. I scramble off the bed, wrapping myself in the sheet.

"Where are you going?" I ask him, but again, he ignores me. He's now fully dressed, and reaching into his side drawer, he pops open his safe. "Asher! What the hell are you doing?"

His eyes finally find mine, and the look on his face causes me to freeze. I've seen rage before, and this exceeds that. "Stay here with Olivia."

No, no way. I move to him, grabbing his arm. "Stop! Why are you so mad?"

"I'm doing what I should've done years ago. I'm going to kill him."

My heart is pounding as I try to understand what's going on. "What are you talking about?"

Asher pulls his arm from my grasp and slams his hand on the wall. "Fuck!" He doesn't look at me as he repeats the gesture. "I'm going. Stay here."

"Please don't leave like this. Please talk to me." He practically tears the door open, and I chase after him, still wearing only a bed sheet. "Asher!"

When he gets to the end of the hallway, he pauses. "Call Brynn. Tell her everything, and you'll understand."

Then he leaves me, and I feel sick.

I called, texted, and waited for him to return for the last hour. When it was clear he wouldn't, I called his sister, asking her to come over right away.

Not five minutes after I ended that call, a knock on the door snaps me out of this wave of confusion, and I drop my phone, praying it's Asher but knowing it's Brynn.

"What's wrong? Are you okay? Is it Olivia or . . .?" she asks as I pull the door open to let her in. Her strawberry blonde hair is up in a ponytail, and she's in her pajamas, but at least she put shoes on before rushing over.

"It's Asher. He left, and . . . I'm going to have to tell you everything, and it's going to be a lot."

She nods, and we walk into the kitchen where I put the tea kettle on before joining her at the table.

"What happened?" Brynn finally asks, completely calm.

I start at the beginning, telling her about why I came home from school, how hard things were, and then how it all started with Asher.

"So, you and Asher?"

"Yeah, it was never our intention for it to be more than scratching an itch."

She laughs. "Oh, my brothers are all ridiculous. I'm not going to lie and say I'm surprised. You guys were always looking at each other and trying not to look at each other at the same time."

"I'm sorry we lied."

319

Brynn shrugs. "We all have secrets. I'm not one to judge. However, I don't understand what happened to lead us to now."

I continue on, giving her the backstory, the length of time we've been together, before telling her about my appointment the other day. "I'm pregnant with the professor's kid."

Brynn's eyes widen. "Oh."

"Yeah."

The surprise leaves her face and is replaced with disappointment. "And Asher left you when you told him?"

"No, not at all. He's actually been incredible about the whole thing."

Brynn sits back. "That sounds more like him. Asher isn't the fly-off-the-handle brother. He's so much more . . . I don't know, calm? When things happen, I always tell him stuff first because usually he doesn't react irrationally. It's what makes him a really good SWAT commander."

"I know, and that's why I am so confused. He wouldn't talk to me. He wouldn't even look at me." I stumble over the last word as my heart aches. "It was like I was disgusting or . . . I don't know. It just was so unlike him, and it contradicts everything he said."

Brynn takes a sip of her tea. "I feel like I'm missing something."

I let out a heavy breath. "Right before he left, we were talking about where we go from here. I'm pregnant, it isn't his child, and we love each other. He asked me to move in, and I explained why I didn't think it would be a good idea."

"Jesus, Asher's foot is on the gas. Okay. Phoebe, he must really love you." She rests her hand on mine. "Asher is not the kind of man to ever bring a woman around, let alone ask someone to move in with him. If he's asking you? That tells me he's really, really serious."

"I know, but I told him I didn't think we should. That we should allow Olivia some time to get used to him dating me, and that I needed to handle getting any parental rights away from the father. He lost it."

"I don't know why he'd be so upset about that."

"He said to call you and that you'd know. I don't think it was about the moving in together thing so much as the baby's father."

Brynlee schools her face and breathes in deeply. "And he said to call me?"

"Yes."

"Is the guy's name Jonathan Loa?"

My chest is so tight I worry it'll crack. "Yes."

"We're going to need more tea."

Brynn and I move into the living room, my mind spinning in a million directions as I try to figure out why and how Asher and Brynn know Jonathan.

We sit on the couch and Brynn's face is ashen. It's clear this is not a good story. "We moved to Sugarloaf when I was in elementary school, and I remember how much I hated it because I missed Michigan and my dad, even though he was a horrible father." She laughs to herself. "I missed my friends too, it was lonely here, being the new girl in a town where everyone was basically born here. My grandparents did their best to help, but I was alone. My brothers were all in school, and I was here with my mom. Asher was always good about coming here on breaks to visit. The summer before my mom died, Asher brought his friend home from college, his name was Jonathan Loa."

I suck in a breath because this has to be the world's worst joke. "He knows him."

"More than that, Jonathan was his best friend."

"Was. Past tense?"

She nods. "Jonathan was . . . well, he was incredibly hand-some, even to my almost fifteen-year-old self, I just thought he was beyond dreamy, and he was so nice to me. I remember he was always willing to do whatever I asked. If I wanted to go to the store, he would convince Asher we should. He started coming home with Asher every break and every summer since his parents were never around. It was just . . . normal. He'd help with the

321

farm, go fishing, camping, and we'd all hang out. Rowan thought he was great, and even Grady loved him."

"I feel like this story takes a very bad turn."

Her eyes fill with unshed tears as she forces a smile. "It does. It was the summer my mom died. I was . . . you understand. My mom was my rock. She was the only thing that ever was consistent."

I know that all too well. "I understand what you mean."

"It's a sad club we belong to. Grady had just joined the Navy. Rowan was in college, and . . . well, I wasn't about to be his responsibility." Brynn laughs and then sighs. "So, Asher quit the academy in Michigan where he was going to school, came home, and became my guardian. That was Asher. See a problem and fix it. My brother is my hero, and I love him with my whole heart. There's not much I won't do for those stupid boys."

I reach my hand out, squeezing hers because while I may not know exactly what's coming, I have a pretty strong feeling I know.

Brynn pats my hand with her other one and continues on. "I never told anyone about what happened until six years ago."

"Jonathan?"

She nods. "He was here visiting Asher. I was sixteen and thought I knew everything. I thought I was a grown woman and that I loved him. I know that's stupid, but . . . I was so young and naïve. I begged him to just let it be him who I gave myself to." Brynn wipes a tear. "Looking back, I can see how he manipulated me into feeling that way, but back then, all I saw was him. It started so innocent. Just a hand hold, and I was all for it. Then it was riding on the quad with him behind me, holding my stomach and just brushing his thumb under my breast. I wanted it, Phoebe. I was desperate for it. When I literally begged for it to happen, I was so ashamed and so . . . mad at myself."

"Brynn . . . none of that was your fault."

Her jaw shakes, and she soldiers on. "I got pregnant, and when I told him, he said it wasn't his because we'd never been together. He just . . . pretended it didn't happen." She scoffs. "It happened, Phoebe. It may have only been the one time, but it happened. He didn't use a condom, and I was too stupid to make him. He was twenty-seven and I was sixteen. It was so wrong in so many ways, but I was so desperate to be loved by a man who wasn't my brothers."

Tears stream down my face as I listen to her. "And what about the baby?"

She shakes her head and then wipes her cheek. "I ended up losing the baby a week later. I went to a clinic three towns over, bleeding and alone. I used a fake ID that said I was eighteen. It was years before I told anyone, and really, it was my therapist who recommended we bring each of my brothers in for a session."

I can only imagine how that went. "I'm going to assume this is when Asher didn't handle things well."

"No. He didn't. He was the one I thought would be the calmest, but he went insane. He was . . . I'd never seen him that way. He was . . . beside himself. He kept saying it was his fault. He should've known. He should've stopped it. He left me with Jonathan, thinking I was safe. Asher carries the weight of the world for those he loves. There's nothing he won't do to protect the people he cares about, and to find out someone had hurt me? Someone he trusted? I'd never seen him so devastated.

"Asher urged me to press charges, but I refused. It had happened years prior, and I didn't want people to know. I told Asher that if he filed the charges anyway, I would refuse to testify on anything. I couldn't do it. I couldn't bear that. I wasn't strong enough, and I didn't want to face it. I think that upset Asher even more because he couldn't find another way to fix it either."

And, now, another who Asher loves has been hurt by this man. "Brynn, we have to stop him from whatever he's going to do."

"I don't know if that's possible. He threatened Jonathan that if he ever came near me or anyone he loved, he'd kill him."

Asher has his gun. Asher is clearly not thinking. I can't let him ruin his life or Olivia's life because of me. This is insane. I'm on my feet before I can draw another breath. "I have to go after him. I have to stop him."

"I'll stay with Olivia. If there's anyone who can stop him, it's you."

I grab my purse and my keys, running to the door, hoping I can get to him before he does something stupid.

thirty-four
ASHER

The memory I've long buried flashes through me as I continue the drive to Iowa.

"You touched my sister?" I screamed in Jonathan's face, anger unlike I'd ever known pumped through my veins. "She was a fucking child! You son of a bitch!" I reared my arm back, but someone grabbed me from behind.

"I don't know what she told you, Asher. I never was with your sister."

Liar. Fucking liar.

"You don't deserve to breathe the same air! I would ruin you if I could!"

Our other friend, Chris, was holding both my arms behind my back as he tried to pull me away. I attempted to fight him off, but he had a good fifty pounds on me and was a black belt. "Asher, relax."

I twisted again, wanting to rip my so-called best friend's head off. "He raped Brynlee!"

Chris pulled me farther out of the room and pushed me against the wall. "Stop. What the fuck are you talking about?"

I told him everything Brynn said in therapy. How he touched her and made her keep secrets about it. Then about how, when she got pregnant, he told her it couldn't be his because they were never together.

My sister. My fucking sister, who I'd do anything to protect, was touched by that piece of shit.

"You're sure?" Chris asked, looking into the room where Jonathan was pacing.

"She wouldn't lie about this."

He stepped back, running his hand through his hair. "So, what? You're going to kill him? You have a baby, Asher. You have a daughter, and you're going to miss her life for him?"

"So, he gets away with it?"

Chris shook his head. "No. I don't know. Is Brynn willing to press charges?"

I released a heavy breath. "No."

That was the kicker. I'd begged her every day since she told me, and she refused. She thought it wouldn't matter because there was no proof, and she wasn't about to get into a court battle that she probably wouldn't win. The only reason she said anything was because her therapist encouraged her to so she could heal and because of Olivia. She wanted to make sure that Olivia was never around him.

My sister was brave and strong, and I was proud of her for telling us, but I felt weak and stupid for not protecting her from it. It was my fault he was in her life. My fault he was ever around her. He touched my sister, and when she needed him, he walked away. There should be consequences for what he'd done.

This, at least, explained why our friendship had changed. I'd always thought it was just how life went sometimes. He'd moved to Iowa to start his career as a professor, and I was in Sugarloaf.

The reason was not the distance. It was because he was a piece of shit.

I looked to Chris. "If this were your sister or daughter, what would you do?"

"They'd never find his body, but I would also hope that I had a friend to stop me from ruining my life."

I pushed off the wall, feeling cagey and broken. "He's dead to me."

"As he should be."

"If he ever hurts someone again . . ."

"I won't stand in your way. I want to be clear that what he did isn't okay with me. I don't want anything to do with him after this, but you're my friend, and doing something you can't come back from solves nothing."

"I know."

"Okay."

When we walked back into the room, Jonathan stopped pacing and stared at me. "Asher, I don't know what she told you, but it's not true."

"Shut the fuck up and listen. You took advantage of my sister. You got her pregnant and then slithered away like a coward. This . . . friendship . . . is done. If you ever come near me, my family, or anyone I love, I'll ruin you. There is no rock you'll be able to hide under that I won't unearth. I will *never* forgive you for what you did to Brynn, and if Chris weren't here, you'd be dead."

I walked out, vowing if this man ever hurt someone I love again, I'd kill him.

Again, he'd done exactly that. Again, he'd taken advantage of a young girl. I should've . . . done so many things differently years ago. Phoebe never would've met him or been taken advantage of by a fucking predator.

Now she's going to have his baby, and I am going to make sure he never comes near her or that baby. I will never let him hurt either of them.

My phone rings again, and I decline the call without looking to see who it is. I don't want to hear all the reasons I should stop. I will never back down from this. It starts again. I can imagine that

Phoebe has gotten ahold of Brynlee by now and knows everything.

I've been driving for almost ten hours, and the rain is starting to fall more steadily, but I don't let up the gas. I'm too close to.

Another memory flashes.

"What the fuck are you doing?" Rowan asked, sitting in the chair next to mine by the fire.

I lifted the beer in my hand. "Having a drink."

"Or six," he said, glancing to the empty bottles on the ground by my feet.

"Seven."

He grabbed the bottle from my hand and drained it. "You can't beat yourself up, Ash."

"Pretty sure I'm already doing that."

Rowan was just as angry as I was when Brynn told us, but he wasn't at fault. I was. He had been my friend, and it wasn't enough that I threatened him. The past would remain, and my sister will never forget it.

That was on me.

"She turned out all right, despite it all," Rowan said as he stared at the flames.

"Doesn't matter."

"Doesn't it?"

I shook my head. "Nope. It never should've happened."

"It still doesn't make it your fault. You didn't know, and if you did, you sure as fuck wouldn't have let it happen."

"Doesn't change the fact it did. She was alone and pregnant at fucking sixteen. He was eleven years older than her! I can't, Row. I can't sit here and not want to wrap my fingers around his neck."

Rowan placed his hand on my shoulder. "Brynn knows that. We all do, but this"—he pointed to the bottles of beer—"ain't you. This isn't going to fix the past, and it sure as hell isn't going to help Brynn."

I turned to the house, and there stood my sister at the door, watching. After she told us what happened, she spent a few days at her friend's house, which was probably for the better. My emotions haven't exactly been calm. I got home yesterday from my trip out to Iowa, told Brynn what happened, and let her know she'd never have to worry about him again. Then I came out to this old barn and started setting shit on fire.

"I failed her, Rowan. I failed her, and what the hell does that say about my ability to protect Olivia?"

"You didn't fail Brynlee, and you're not going to fail your daughter. You're a good man who trusted a piece of shit. We all did. Grady and I thought he was a great guy too. We had no idea about him and Brynn, and while I'd love to go off the handle, I know that she really can't take it. So, pull yourself together and be the man she needs."

Rowan slapped me on the back of the head before walking away.

I sat there, staring at the orange and red before soft footsteps sounded behind me.

"Asher?" Brynlee hesitated.

Immediately, I sprang to my feet. She took four steps before she wrapped her arms around me. "I'm so sorry, Brynn. I'm so fucking sorry I didn't protect you."

I held her tightly, and the two of us cried. I don't remember how long we stayed out there, but it was long enough that the fire died down and nothing was left but ash.

I pull into a gas station and fill up before going in to get some food and drinks. I take a leak, toss the junk food I got in the passenger side, and get back on the road.

The next hour and a half passes in a blur. I've been driving all night, and the rain hasn't relented once. I pull into the University of Iowa parking lot and find a spot. I have no plan past this.

No idea what exactly will happen, but I can't stand by and do nothing, not again. I love Phoebe, and how any man can look at her, touch her, and walk away is beyond me. She's the most beautiful woman I've ever seen, and she's been hurt by this piece of shit.

I'm fucking done.

I'm tired of Jonathan hurting God only knows how many women and getting away with it.

I walk through campus, not caring about the rain or how it's already soaking through my clothing. Some kid walks by, and I stop him. "Hey, do you know where Jonathan Loa's office is?"

"He's on the other side of campus, look for the arts building."

I nod and then walk the way he pointed. I have no idea where I'm going, but after about twenty minutes, I find the arts building, and sure enough, the motherfucker's office is listed as 210.

I take the stairs two at a time, running on caffeine and adrenaline. I have no idea if he's here or what he's doing, but I give zero fucks.

His office door is closed, so I knock a few times. After about a minute, it opens, and he's there, staring at me with wide eyes and shock on his face.

"Asher?"

I don't think.

I don't even know if I breathe. I rear my arm back and punch him in the nose.

"What the fuck?" He grips his nose with one hand while holding his other one up as if it could possibly keep me back.

"You piece of shit. You did it again."

He steps back. "You broke my goddamn nose."

"I'd like to break your dick off and shove it down your throat, but it's so small I'd probably never find it."

"If this is about your sister . . ." My hand clenches, and I raise it again, but he moves back even farther. "I haven't spoken to her. I did as you asked!"

"And what about Phoebe?" I say, inching closer. "What about

332

the girl who is pregnant now because you are a manipulative piece of shit who preys on young girls?"

"Phoebe? Why the hell do you know or care about her?"

I shake my head. "Don't pretend you didn't put two and two together. She lives in Sugarloaf."

"And that's why you drove out here to punch me in the face?" He laughs. "I see. You aren't here because she's from your town, you're here because you're with her. Wow, isn't that the pot calling the kettle black?"

"You know why we're nothing alike, Jonathan?" I ask, taking one step closer. "Because when she told me she was pregnant, do you know how I reacted? I held her while she cried." Another step. "I told her I loved her and promised I'd be at her side. When I found out that you, the biggest piece of shit I know, were the father? All I wanted to do was protect her. And what did you do? You told her to get rid of it."

"Of course, I told her that!" he yells. "I'm not going to lose my job and my wife over some"—my eyes narrow, and he lifts both hands—"student."

"Good because you will never, *ever* come near her or that child. You are going to get papers about giving up all rights, and you won't hesitate to sign them. If you think my threats about Brynlee were bad, they aren't even close to what I'll do to you if you hurt Phoebe."

When I open the door to walk out, my entire body locks when I see her there, hand up as though she was going to knock. Her hair is dripping wet, her makeup is running down her face, and she's wearing my work raincoat.

Phoebe's lips part when she sees me there. "You're alive."

"Yes, of course I am."

"I might still kill you, so don't be too secure in that statement." She takes a step back as Jonathan comes up behind me. "I would let him kill you, but I love him and would rather not worry about conjugal visits, so . . . you live for now."

"What are you doing here? How?" I ask her.

She turns to Jonathan. "You and I will deal with our situation later, however, I'm keeping this child, and I want *nothing* from you. I'll have paperwork sent to you so you can walk away without any worries. That way, your poor wife can continue to think she's married to someone who isn't a cheating asshole who doesn't know what to do with his mouth other than lie." Then Phoebe turns to me. "You. You can take us home now."

I look at him with a smirk on my face. That's right, I forgot that little tidbit. "By the way, it's a you problem, in case you were wondering."

"What is?"

I pat his chest. "I have no problem making Phoebe scream my name when I'm between her legs. Seems she just needed a man who knew his way around a pussy instead of just being one."

And with that, we walk away, and I hope to never see his sorry ass again.

thirty-five

PHOEBE

A sher and I walk down the hall, his hand is in mine, and I'm trembling. It could be the cold, the fact that I'm dripping wet, the nerves, the terror, the anger, or the lack of sleep, but I'm at the very edge of my breaking point.

The only thing keeping me moving forward is that I will not let Jonathan see me fall apart. I would rather die.

Last night was hell. I am not entirely sure how I didn't have a nervous breakdown, but I'm pretty sure it was mostly because Emmeline was my voice of reason and kept me calm and planning possible scenarios for when I got here.

As we get to the stairs, I hear my name. "Phoebe? Is that you?"

I know that voice. It's the sweet, caring, mothering voice of Professor Calloway.

Asher releases my hand, and I spin around to see her. "Hey."

She walks over to me, looking slightly concerned. "Oh, it's so good to see you. Are you okay?"

No. Not even a little. "I'm great, thank you. This is Asher Whitlock, my . . ."

"Boyfriend," he finishes. "It's nice to meet you."

"You as well, I'm Debbie. Phoebe, here, was my best ASL student."

Asher places his hand on the small of my back. "My daughter is Deaf. It's actually partly the reason Phoebe and I found each other. I'm sorry to ask this, but would you happen to have a towel or something Phoebe can dry off with?"

He's just as soaked through as I am, if not worse, but he doesn't ask for one for himself. He can pretend all he wants, but I heard his teeth rattle as well.

"Yes! Let me run into my office."

She heads off, Asher leads us to a bench where we sit, and she returns with two towels. Asher immediately starts to dry me with his towel instead of himself. His blue eyes are filled with concern. "Are you okay?"

I nod. "Dry yourself."

"That rain came out of nowhere," Debbie notes.

"It did. Thank you for the towels. It seems like I'm always in your debt."

She shakes her head. "You're not. So, you are back home and still working on your ASL?"

"Yes, Asher's daughter is amazing, and I've spent the last few months with her. Taking her to appointments and working with the speech pathologist have been great opportunities to see the things I've been learning about in practice."

She smiles brightly. "That's wonderful. So, did you decide on which school you're going to attend?"

It's really the last thing I want to discuss, but at the same time, I owe her the truth. Professor Calloway has been kind, and I want to thank her and explain why I won't be attending Texas after all the trouble she went through.

"I wish I had a delicate way to say all this, but I have to defer for a year. I've put in requests with both Vanderbilt and Texas," I explain.

"I'm so sorry to hear that. Why would you defer?"

"I'm pregnant, so I can't exactly do it all."

"Oh. Wow. Congratulations," Professor Calloway says cautiously.

I smile because, what else can I do at this point? There is no reason for anyone who isn't in my close circle to know that the baby is Jonathan's, and there is no need for me to explain anything beyond my being pregnant.

"Thank you, but it means a change. I'm going to find something to do for the year, and then I plan to finish grad school."

She nods once. "That's a good idea. Life often goes in another direction when we least expect it. Phoebe, you're on the East Coast, correct?"

"Yes, I'm in Pennsylvania."

"I thought that was the case. Listen, maybe this is fate stepping in, but there's a startup company that is looking for someone who is fluent in ASL to work on a project. I was offered the position, but I don't have the ability to commit to being in New York City once a month for round-table meetings. However, you might be perfect for it."

"Really?" I ask, feeling a little hopeful. "I don't even know what to say."

"Let me reach out to them, pass on your info, and see what they think. They're hoping to have the program up and running in the next year, which might work with your pregnancy?"

She is like my fairy godmother. "You have no idea how much your kindness means to me. Seriously."

"You were an excellent student who cared about the people you worked with more than yourself. While I try very hard not to get involved in what goes on, you're not the first girl who has gotten mixed up with a professor and paid the consequences."

Asher's hand rubs my back. "Hopefully, she's the last."

Professor Calloway nods. "I hope so too." She looks down at her watch. "I have to run. I'll send that email today, and good luck, Phoebe."

"Thank you."

We sit here for a few minutes, and the weight of the last twenty-four hours is enough to crush me.

I turn to Asher, needing to say everything I need to before I have to endure a twelve-hour car ride. "You left me. You left all of us and didn't give us any way to reach you."

"I know, and I was wrong."

"Yes, you were. You were wrong to do that. Wrong to make me out of my goddamn mind with fear. I was so angry with you. I'm *still* angry."

"I deserve it. I'm sorry."

Yes, he does. I pull the towel tighter around me. "I'll forgive you before we hit Sugarloaf, which I think is generous."

He laughs once. "It is. I'd like to know exactly how you got here so fast?"

I release a breath through my nose. "I asked Jacob Arrowood to let me use his private plane."

"You flew on a private plane to get here?" Asher asks as though it's impossible.

"You drove twelve hours to punch a man in the face?"

He leans back, looking up at the ceiling. "Touché. I was beyond angry and frustrated. I couldn't believe I let this happen to someone else."

"*Let* this happen? You didn't even know—"

"I knew him, what he was, who he is. If I hadn't let him get away with it years ago, maybe he wouldn't still be doing it again now."

I get to my feet, my frustration mounting. "While I understand and appreciate your need to protect me and all the people you love, you can't. You're a cop, so you know as well as anyone that sometimes people do horrible things, and sometimes they get away with it. Your sister made peace with it, she doesn't blame you, and I sure as hell don't either. However, you had me terrified. I was so worried about you, and the only thing I cared about was getting to you before you did something stupid, which you did by even coming here. You stupid, caring, dumb, wonderful, overprotective ass of a man, if you ever leave me like that again, I will rip your arms off and beat you with them. Understand?"

He smiles and dips his head to kiss me. "I'll never leave you like that again."

"How about you just never leave me period."

"I can handle that."

"Good, now let's go. I am exhausted, and we need to get back home and deal with this situation because I have no doubt the entire town knows we're together now."

We're just getting back on the road now. We stayed the night somewhere in Ohio after driving as much as we could. Brynn was adamant she was fine and Olivia was more than taken care of. I'm grateful for that because even with the two of us napping as the other drove, we were worn out.

"I say we go home and tell Olivia," Asher suggests as we stop at a rest area near Sugarloaf. We called Sara this morning and broke the news to her. She took it much better than I thought. I could tell that, at first, she wasn't all that happy about it. By the time Asher was done explaining everything, she wished us the best and also informed us she'd be home early.

They wrapped up filming two days ago, and she's just waiting for the rest of the crew to get home, and then she'll be back.

"I'm more concerned about telling your dad," Asher admits.

Asher opens my car door, helping me in like the perfect gentleman, even though last night he was anything but. The two of us were like caged animals, working off the last of our anger and frustration in the hotel. Then he held me all night, and I don't know that I've ever slept so soundly.

"He'll be upset because that's what all you overprotective fathers do, but he'll accept it."

He leans in and kisses me. "Let's hope so."

On the ride back, we agree to just head to my father first so we can get that out of the way before heading to tell Olivia. Then I don't know what we will do.

"I want you to live with me," Asher says as we pass the Welcome to Luzerne County sign.

"And I think we should go slow."

"Sunshine, we're past that. We love each other, I know what I want, and it's you with me every night. You're having a baby, and we're going to do this together. How does slow tie into that?"

"How about we figure it out after we tell everyone?"

He reaches for my hand, entwining our fingers. "It's not about anyone else but us. It's what we want, and if you think your father isn't going to ask, you're nuts."

"Maybe I am, but he's going to be more upset about school."

"You're not giving up on that," he says firmly.

"I know. As soon as the baby is born, we'll figure out a way to make it work."

He nods, and then we're in Sugarloaf, making the drive to my father's house.

As soon as we pull up, the door opens, he's in his uniform as he steps out. Oh, this is going to be fun. Asher gives me a tight smile and nods. "Let's go."

We exit the car, and when I reach the front of the car, I put my hands around his arm as we walk toward the man who has been my rock.

"So, it's true?" Dad asks.

"Yes, we're together, sir," Asher answers.

His hand rests on the top of his gun, and I swear it twitches. "For how long?"

"About a month now."

Dad looks at me. "And you kept this from me?"

"I know you don't want the details, but we didn't think we were going to fall in love. It happened very much without either of us realizing it. But we're here now, and I love him and he loves me."

"What about school?" The question I knew was going to be his concern.

"I'm pregnant, Dad. I'm going to take a year off, and then I'm going to finish my graduate program."

Tears well in his eyes, and he steps back. "You're pregnant?"

I nod.

"Can we go inside? I'd like to explain why I came home in the first place."

Dad takes a seat in his trusted recliner, and Asher and I sit on the couch. He lends me his strength the entire time I recount the events that led to my coming home. He holds my hand or rests his palm on my back. My father sits still, and when I get to the point of the story where I found out I was pregnant, he leans forward.

"Whose baby is it?" he asks.

Asher answers before I can. "It's our baby. No matter what, this is our child, so the biological father doesn't really matter."

Tears form in my eyes, and I reach up to touch his face. "You're going to make me cry."

"Only good tears." His voice is quiet so only I can hear.

My father clears his throat. "So, in two months you both fell in love, are having a baby, and you asked her to move in?"

"Yes," Asher answers without hesitation.

"And you support her finishing her degree?"

Asher looks my father straight in the eyes. "Phoebe's future, her happiness, her wants and desires are what I support. I don't want her to give up her dreams for a life in this town as my partner, just as I do whatever is needed to support Sara. I don't ever want to hold her back, and we'd always planned for her to go back to school, which was why the two of us didn't reveal our relationship until now."

"Which was wrong," I finish.

My father lets out a long sigh. "I always knew she'd fall for a cop."

I laugh and shake my head. "I just fell for the right man."

thirty-six

ASHER

As soon as the door opens, Olivia is running to me. I crouch down and wrap her in my arms. She pulls back and starts right in. *"Where were you?"*

"I had to deal with something."

"You didn't say goodbye."

"I'm sorry."

I have a lot of people pissed at me, and if they really knew how disappointed I was with myself, they probably wouldn't say a word.

I lift my hand and sign. *"I love you."*

Olivia lifts hers and does the same. Then our fingers touch in our version of a handshake.

Then she turns to Phoebe. *"You left too."*

"I had to go get your dad before he did something stupid."

"I was worried you weren't coming back," Olivia explains.

Phoebe gives her a soft smile and shakes her head. *"I'm here."*

"But you leave soon."

I glance at Phoebe, and she gives the tiniest nod. I wasn't nervous about telling Olivia when it seemed to be an abstract thing, but now, it's a little different. She loves Phoebe and Sara was concerned she'd feel like their friendship was fake.

"Olivia," I sign her name sign and brace myself. *"Phoebe is going to stay a while, but not as your nanny."*

I can see the confusion as she battles with being happy about part one of that but worried about what part two means.

"What do you mean?"

"I am in love with Phoebe, and she's my girlfriend now."

Can't really argue with just being direct. So, I'm going with that.

"Asher!" Phoebe gasps. "Jesus. You could ease into this." Then she turns to Olivia. *"I really like your dad, and I love you. Being your friend is the best thing in the world. I meant what I said . . . you're my best friend."*

"And you're with my dad?"

"Yes, but that doesn't change anything with us."

Olivia looks to me. *"Are you getting married?"*

"Maybe someday, but would you be upset if we did?"

"No. I love Phoebe."

Phoebe smiles. *"I love you."*

"And Daddy?"

"Yes?"

I'm not sure how much more we should tell her, but Brynn cuts in. "My turn to tell you that you're an idiot?"

Phoebe laughs and then lifts one shoulder. *"Come on, Olivia, let's finish our painting."* The two of them head upstairs, leaving me with my very disappointed sister.

"I get that you're pissed, but I did what I felt I needed to."

Brynn rolls her eyes. "You *needed* to be here and talk like a grown-up, but you men never seem to do the right thing unless a woman tells you what it is first. So, here it is. Next time you want to drive twelve hours in the middle of the night to confront someone from your past—don't. Wait until your girlfriend or I can guide you the right way."

"And what was that?"

"Talking to me first. I've spent a lot of time and money on

therapy to deal with my past, but you heard the man's name and went batshit crazy. Not Rowan or Grady . . . you." Brynn shakes her head as she sighs. "I have never been so worried about you, Asher. I worry about everyone else being stupid, but not you. Why would you leave like that?"

"He hurt another person I love."

"You love her."

"Yes, more than I ever thought possible."

Brynn purses her lips. "I thought so."

"And how do you feel about that?" I ask.

"If she makes you happy, then I'm okay with it. I think Phoebe is incredibly kind and caring. She also adores Olivia. She's younger than me, which was sort of weird at first, but we're all adults. However," Brynn's voice shifts. "I am curious to know how Sara and her father are going to take the news."

I laugh and follow my sister into the kitchen. When she was little, this was our thing. We'd come in here, talk, and most of the time, we'd eat cookies and laugh for hours. Life was easier to some extent when Brynn was a kid. Clearly, I missed some big things, but she and I were very close.

After giving her the abbreviated version of things, she blinks a few times and laughs. "You know, you don't do anything half-assed, do you?"

"Not really."

"Can I ask what your plan is?"

"I'm going to marry her. I'm going to somehow convince her to move in with me now, marry me eventually, and that child will be mine."

"Asher." Her voice is cautious. "You're going to be okay raising Jonathan Loa's child?"

I thought about that a lot on my ride out there. The idea of holding this baby in my arms, knowing it came from the person I hate most in this world, was hard to wrap my mind around. Then I thought about Brynlee's father. Howie was a horrific stepfather to me and my brothers. He was borderline abusive most days, drank nonstop, and was always yelling at my mother. I never thought I could hate a human more and hated the idea that my sister would be half his genetics. Only, when Mom brought home Brynn, I didn't see Howie.

I saw her.

This child didn't have a hand in her parentage but was part of my mother, who I loved.

Just as this baby will be part of Phoebe, and I can love this child because it'll come from her.

"It won't be Jonathan's baby. It will be mine and hers. I'm not saying there won't be times I'll struggle knowing that they have a kid together, but Phoebe and I will share the best parts of that child's life."

Brynlee pats the top of my hand. "And this is why I love you with my whole heart. You're a good man, a dumb one, but you're the best."

"Right back at you."

She removes her hand, looking at the purple stains on my knuckles, and grins. "Now, tell me about what happened when you saw him. I hope you broke his nose."

"You know, it's very cliché of you to fall in love with the nanny." Sara nudges my shoulder as we watch Phoebe help Olivia pack.

"Shut up."

"I'm serious. I thought you'd find a biker chick or someone like a former prison guard. You could do with a tough girl who can kick your ass."

This is why I never wanted to date her, she's annoying as fuck. "As opposed to your car salesman?"

"Hey, don't mock Finnegan. He's a sweet man who happens to adore me."

"So, he's unstable? Got it."

Sara scoffs. "Please, there's clearly something wrong with Phoebe if she finds you charming."

"I am charming, I just wasn't with you," I toss back.

We both laugh. "Good because if that was your version of charming, I would have felt bad for you."

"And, yet, here we are, tied together forever."

"Just until she's eighteen," Sara clarifies.

"You know, I actually missed this."

She smiles. "I did too, Ash. It's good to be home. I really hated being away from Liv, but I also missed you."

I know what she means by that. Sara and I have an odd friendship that is built off trusting someone who society says you shouldn't get along with. She and I promised to always put Olivia first and never play games when it came to her, and we've both held true to it.

Liv throws her shirt down on the bed and starts signing to Phoebe, who laughs and responds.

"Hey, let's go out in the hall and talk," Sara says before walking out. "What does Olivia know?"

I fill her in on what we told her, which is that Phoebe and I are together and Phoebe is going to be moving in with me. She doesn't know about the baby—yet—or that I'm planning to propose. Both of those things are happening soon, but I am in the early planning phases.

"So, you're really going to propose?"

"I know she's what I want, and I never want the baby to know otherwise."

"It's fast, Ash."

I shrug. "Again, why wait? We have a baby coming, and I want to spend the rest of my life with her."

Sara nods slowly. "Makes sense, I mean you're going to need someone to change your diapers in a few years. Best to secure her before you need the Viagra."

"You're not too far behind me."

"I'm joking." Sara rests her hand on my forearm. "Honestly, I am really happy for you. I know I just technically met Phoebe, but I see it. She is the exact opposite of you, which is what you need. You and I are too much piss and vinegar, and she's the honey that makes you less bitter."

"It's really hard not to fall in love with her," I say wistfully.

"Oh God." Sara chokes on a laugh. "You really are that far gone? Wow. Good for her."

"I am. I'm going to propose in two weeks. I'm taking her out to visit her best friend in Michigan, and I'll do it there."

Sara blinks a few times, clearly stunned. "Okay then. Well, I am looking forward to taking our daughter out of this sickly sweet lovefest."

"I've loved having her, Sara. I really want Liv to get to spend more time with us. She adores Phoebe, and I think Phoebe may love Olivia more than she loves me. They became really close, and having her home every day was something I never realized I was missing."

I wanted to have this conversation differently, but the opportunity presented itself and Sara should know how I feel. We've done the co-parenting thing really well, but on my other days off, I want Olivia here. Currently, I've had my daughter every other week when I have my three days off. It's not enough.

"That's going to be hard on her."

"I don't think it'll be that hard. Right now, I get her every weekend, so it isn't a huge change for me to have her the extra day and the two days in the middle of the week. It's basically giving me time every week instead of every other."

She leans against the wall and moves her jaw back and forth. "Can we get her settled back in with me first? Then we can talk to her and see how she feels? She's nine, and I don't want to say yes or no for her. She should get to decide this and feel a bit more involved in her living situation."

"I agree, I just wanted to let you know, and we decide from there."

"Also, I think we talk to her about this after she finds out about your impending marriage and child."

I nod. "Probably the best move."

We walk to the door to her room, and I look at the two girls I love the most in my life, hugging each other tightly.

thirty-seven

PHOEBE

"No, I completely understand," I tell Bobby, the owner of the tech startup. "Once a month into New York City won't be an issue until around November."

"Okay. Hours will be flexible as we're working with programmers who have other projects as well. That's not going to be an issue?"

"Nope," I say, feeling hopeful. I had my first interview two days ago, and they emailed this morning to ask if I was available for our second call today.

Asher is at work, and I went to Sydney's office today to start the parental rights termination process. She was really helpful and kind as I sat there crying. It makes no sense why I'm so emotional. I don't want Jonathan in the baby's life and have an amazing boyfriend who already loves me and the baby, but there was something so hard about the whole situation in that moment.

A failure that I had to accept.

But, that's over, the paperwork has been mailed, and I'm moving forward.

"Great. Well, I'd like to formally offer you the job if you'd like to come work with us?"

"I'd love to! I'm honestly so excited about this. I think there are so many in the deaf community who could benefit from this."

"Then let me be the first to welcome you to Talking Hands."

I want to squeal, but that would be incredibly unprofessional, so I just smile. "I look forward to working with you, Bobby."

"You as well. I'll send all the paperwork over tonight or tomorrow. I'd like to hit the ground running in the next few weeks."

"I am going away in two weeks, but after that, I'm free."

Asher is taking me to Cloverleigh to see Emmeline and spend a weekend away. I'm excited and also terrified for her to meet him, but I think they'll get along great.

"Not a problem, it'll take that long just to get the developers to email me back." Bobby chuckles. "We'll be in touch. Thanks, Phoebe."

"Thank you, I can't wait to get started."

We hang up, and then I do squeal because I am so damn excited. I send a text to Emmeline first.

> I got the job!

EMMELINE
> I knew you would! That's amazing! I can't wait to hear all about it when you come in two weeks.

> You're sure it's okay if we stay at the inn? I know it's wedding season.

EMMELINE
> I do get some perks being the owner's granddaughter.

> Okay. I need to tell Asher. I'll see you soon!

I get in the car and head to the station because I'd like to see my father as well. When I walk in, Joey is at the front desk.

"What did you do to get this job?" I ask.

"I've been on the shit list since the dance."

I grin. "Really?"

"Yeah, Asher stuck me here until he doesn't want to throat punch me, however long that is."

"Ha! That's what you get for ditching me and making him dance for twenty-four hours."

He shakes his head, and I head back to where Dad and Asher sit. Asher has his head down, seemingly invested in whatever he's reading, and it takes him a second to notice me.

"Sweetheart, are you okay?" He stands, coming to me, hands on both my elbows.

"I'm great. Is my dad here?"

"Sure am," my father says as he comes around the corner. "Hi, Birdie."

I kiss his cheek. "Daddy, I wanted to tell you both that I am proud to announce I am the project manager for Talking Hands. I will be in charge of coordinating all the ASL recordings from the content creators who are Deaf and then working to make sure the app can translate appropriately!"

"I'm so proud of you," Asher says, pulling me into his arms and kissing my forehead.

"Thank you."

My dad grumbles. "Enough of that. Good job, honey. I knew you'd find something."

I did. I found everything when it felt like I had nothing. While this wasn't my plan, it's working out in a way I never dreamed of, and I couldn't be happier.

We head over on the quad to the Whitlock family fire night, and I'm a little nervous this time. I'm going officially as his girlfriend, which I'm still getting used to.

Also, Grady is back home, and it's been forever since I've seen him. "Stop fidgeting," Asher says against my ear as he helps me off the ATV.

"I'm trying."

He chuckles softly, leading me toward the back of the house. We turn the corner and spot Brynn walking toward the fire with a tray of food for the barbeque, and Rowan is digging in the cooler.

Grady notices us first. "Asher!"

The two men embrace, and Asher places his hand on my back. "This is Phoebe."

"Welcome to the family, Phoebe."

I smile and immediately like this man. He is two years younger than Asher and looks nothing like him. He has much lighter hair and an almost studious look. He's tall, trim, and stands ramrod straight, and no one would have to tell me he was in the service for me to guess it.

"Thank you. Although, right now, I'm just an interloper."

"Are not! We'll keep you over that asshole," Rowan yells, and I laugh.

"How are you settling back home?"

"He loves it here!" Brynn answers from practically across the yard. "Don't let him fool you. He's being fed and getting a break from daddy duty."

Grady leans in. "She has freakishly good hearing. Watch what you say."

"I heard that!"

He raises his brows as he tilts his head as though to say . . . *see.* "It's weird being back, but I'm happy to be out of the navy and get the chance to raise Jett the way Lisa would've wanted it."

"I'm really sorry for your loss."

"Thank you." He turns to his brother. "So, another baby out of wedlock?"

Asher pulls me to his side, throwing his arm over my shoulder. "What can I say? The ladies love me."

"Oh Jesus."

Brynn waves her hand. "Hello! Anyone want to . . . you know . . . help?"

Asher and Grady head that way, but Rowan stays seated, grinning at his brothers as they pass. I stand beside him, and he hands me a soda. "Thanks. You're not helping?"

"I've learned the secret to life, young Phoebe. One must wait to see if you're needed."

"Oh, and are you not needed?"

Rowan jerks his head over to where Asher and Grady are fighting for the plate. "Do you want to go over there because I don't."

"Nope, I think you're the smarter Whitlock today."

"Stick with me, and I'll teach you my ways."

I laugh and sit in the rocking chair beside him. "How is the farming going?"

"Good. Cows moo, milk is made, all in a day's work. I love what I do, and I'll do it until I can't anymore."

"Why wouldn't you be able to do it?"

Rowan takes a long drain of his beer. "It's farming, which is hard and makes very little money. I do it because that's what my grandpa wanted. This farm, this land, was his dream. The only other sibling who loves this place like I do is Brynn, but we know she's not stomping through cowpies."

"No, definitely not," I say, not even able to imagine that.

"Asher loves the land, but he sure as hell isn't going near the animals. By the way, if he ever mentions any kind of animal, just say no. Trust me, the man shouldn't be allowed near them."

I have a feeling there's a story there, but I just nod. "Got it."

He sighs heavily. "I'm sorry for what you went through with Jonathan."

I stop rocking, knowing that this family has been deeply wounded by him. "I'll be okay."

357

"You will. Just like she is. Still, I know Asher taking off wasn't . . . smart, but it's what he should've done. Call me a pig or whatever, but no man has a right to hurt a woman without consequences. I would've lost all respect for Ash if he hadn't gone to set that record straight."

"I don't need Asher to fight my battles," I defend myself.

"No, but a man who loves his woman will fight the world for her."

I look over at Rowan, who everyone thinks is so impenetrable. "You speaking from experience?"

"No, I'm speaking from the lack of it. I've never cared enough to make a twelve-hour drive just to punch a guy in the face."

Asher heads back our way, and I glance behind him to see Grady holding the platter and tongs. "Did you lose, baby?" I ask.

"Fucker titty twisted me."

Rowan chuckles. "That's his signature move. You've lost your touch if you let him get that in on you."

"Awww, are you hurt?"

Asher squats next to my chair and puts both hands on the armrests. "Yes, maybe you should kiss me all better."

I grin. "Tonight."

Rowan gags. "And on that note, I'm going to help Grady."

Asher leans in, kissing me softly. "I told you not to worry about my family. They love you."

"They're great. I love that you have such a big family and that our nugget will get to have them."

"I'm going to marry you, Phoebe Bettencourt," Asher says with love soaking every word. "And then they'll be our family."

~Two weeks later~

"Emmeline!" I drop my bags on the ground as she rushes toward me.

"You look amazing. God, pregnancy and a hot cop look good on you!"

I shake my head, pulling back to look at her. She cut her hair to just brush her shoulders and is wearing it pin straight. "Wow, I love this look."

She turns her head side to side. "I needed a change." Then she looks to Asher. "And you must be Asher."

He extends his hand. "I am, nice to meet you."

Emmy laughs and pulls him in for a hug. "Come here, big guy. We hug, not shake."

When she releases him, I can't stop the laugh as I see the stunned and slightly terrified look on his face. "You get used to her," I tell him.

She grabs my bags, and we walk to the inn section of Cloverleigh Farms. It's exactly as she described it. When we came up the winding driveway, I was awestruck by the old farmhouse, which is where we will be staying. Beyond it, you can make out old barns and other buildings as well. Emmeline explains that there is the inn, which is a luxury five-star resort, a wedding venue, the winery, a tasting room, and a restaurant on location.

I don't know why the hell she'd ever want to leave here. It's freaking gorgeous. This is the exact place I would want us to get married.

Which is getting way ahead of myself. We've had a great two weeks, moving all of my stuff over to his room, learning how to sleep through his insane alarm that could wake the dead, and finding something to do now that Liv isn't at the house and I haven't started working yet.

Emmeline points out the areas on the property we should check out, and then we head inside. "Clearly, no wine tasting for you, but the food is great. Also, my sisters are really excited to meet you."

I grin. "I can't wait either. I need to hug them and give them my appreciation for dealing with a lunatic who I adore."

She laughs. "They would agree with you there. I think my

whole family would, and my dad can't wait for me to leave for school next week."

"I'm sure he loved having you here."

Emmeline raises one perfectly arched brow. "Not so sure about that, but honestly, I learned so many things they don't teach you in school. Dad and Aunt Chloe really worked together to fix issues that I would've just prayed for Google to give me the answers to. I think they actually created half of them to see what I would do."

Asher is quiet, walking along with us, and I grip his arm with both hands. "Hi."

He chuckles. "Hi."

Emmeline makes a gagging noise. "Anyway, here is your room, it's my favorite in the whole place. You have the best view of the property. The restaurant is downstairs, and there's a reservation in your name for seven."

"Umm, we came here to see you," I tell her.

"Yes, but I have to work because we have a wedding tomorrow. So, tonight you're on your own to explore and do whatever you want. The wedding is early afternoon, and I'll be done by dinner. Then we can have all the fun, and you can meet the family."

I've met her parents before, and it's really funny that, apparently, I am following in their footsteps. Her mother was the nanny for her three oldest sisters . . . and, the kicker is that her dad worked for her grandpa. The irony is not lost on me. However, you can't fight fate, no matter how forbidden your relationship is. The heart wants what it wants and often doesn't lose.

"I can't wait to meet your family."

"They're really excited to meet you as well." She gives me a big hug. "You have no idea how much I've missed you." Emmeline turns to Asher. "And thank you for loving her. There's no one else in the world that deserves it more."

thirty-eight

ASHER

Phoebe is standing at the window in her silky pajamas, staring out at the crystal-clear sky. We've had an amazing weekend here, and I can see why Emmeline and Phoebe are best friends. They're the opposite in almost everything and, yet, fit so perfectly.

Her family has been incredible as well. I had a good time talking to Emmeline's brothers-in-law. Dex is a fireman, Hutton is a tech billionaire, and Zach was a Navy SEAL, so we had a lot to talk about since Grady was navy as well.

I'm not ready to go home tomorrow evening.

I come up behind her, pulling her back to my chest. "You look deep in thought."

"I was just thinking about the sky."

"Oh?"

She rests her head on my shoulder. "It's vast and seemingly never-ending. There are billions of stars out there, and tonight, for whatever reason, I found that one first." She holds her finger up and circles around whatever star. There are so many, I couldn't pick out the one she chose, but she knows it.

"So, that has you mystified?" I ask.

Phoebe turns, looping her arms around my neck. "You have

me mystified. You had billions of stars to choose from, but you picked me out."

"I think you chose me, sweetheart. I haven't moved, but you, you're a comet in the night. You found me when you flew across my dark sky." I smile at her as she starts to look away. "Does that embarrass you?"

Her brown eyes find mine in the moonlight. "It makes me feel important."

She has no idea. "Sweetheart, you're my heart and soul, and I couldn't survive without you."

"You know, you should show this soft, squishy part to more people. They'd probably stop thinking you're unapproachable."

"What makes you think I want people to approach me?"

She shrugs. "You know what? You're right, keep up the grumpy façade, I like knowing the real man under all that crankiness."

I pull her closer, swaying a bit as the moonlight dances around her hair. "I want to lay you bare and kiss every inch of you."

"That sounds promising."

"It does?"

She nods. "Keep going."

"I want to spread your gorgeous legs and make you come on my tongue."

"Doable."

I fight back a laugh. "You're making dirty talk very hard."

"Hmm." She reaches between us and slides her hands into my boxers. Her delicate fingers wrap around my cock. "Yes, I can see how hard this is. But I was thinking"—she starts to stroke and my brain disconnects—"I don't want to talk tonight."

"No?" I manage to get the word out as she continues to jerk me off.

"No, I'd rather use my mouth for other things."

She sinks down on her knees and then slides my boxers off. I love that she's my fucking goddess with a naughty side. Her fingertips trace down my abs and then wrap back around my dick.

"Put your mouth on my cock, Phoebe," I tell her, knowing how she likes to be pushed. She draws out my dominant side and allows me to take control, which the two of us enjoy. She kisses the tip then runs her tongue along the rim. I lace my fingers in her hair. "Open." Phoebe does, and I slide inside. "That's it, suck."

Her head moves back and forth, and I stay still, watching her like this is fucking heaven. She takes me deeper, and the pleasure mounts. I think of anything to keep from coming in her mouth. "Touch yourself, Phoebe," I tell her through gritted teeth. "Take your other hand off my leg and touch your pussy." She moves it there, but I can't see. "Pull your pajamas up, I want to watch. Imagine it's my hand there, touching your clit, pressing right where you want it." She moans, and I swear, every muscle in me tenses. Then she takes her hand from where I wish mine was and lifts it toward my chest.

I force her to come up and off my cock so I can lick the sweetness off her fingers.

The taste of her is too much, I want more.

I lift her into my arms, carry her to the bed, and set her down. Then I get on my back. "Come here."

She crawls toward me, confusion in her eyes. "Grab the headboard and sit on my face." Phoebe gets in position, straddling my head, but she still isn't close enough. "That's it, good girl, now don't just sit, sweetheart, suffocate me."

I pull her hips down and lick. All I taste is her. All I feel is her heat. I move my face, forcing my tongue deep inside her, fucking her this way as I move my hand around to rub her clit. Phoebe is panting hard and rocking against my mouth.

I love it. I want to stay here and make her fall apart.

"Asher, I can't," she moans. "I can't hold back."

I push harder on her clit and shove my tongue as deep as I can. I feel her legs tense around my face and then she cries out, I lick and suck as she pulses around me. While she's still going, I slide her down my body until my cock hits her entrance, and then I push up and into her.

"Oh my God!" she cries at the same time I say her name.

I hold her hips, setting the pace as I make love to her from the bottom. My mind is worthless, and I start to say every thought that passes. "You are mine. Made for me. All mine. I love you."

"Yes." She pushes herself up, scoring her nails down my chest. "Yours."

"You are fucking hot. You are so gorgeous on top of me, beneath me, on your knees in front of me. God, you feel so good. Lean back."

She does, resting her hands on my thighs, her back bowing in the perfect arch. I move my thumb back to her clit. "Again, Phoebe. Come on my cock this time."

Her hair brushes my legs, and I watch as the pleasure pulses through her. Her mouth is open as she gasps, the angle hitting her just right. "You feel so good."

"You feel incredible," I tell her. "You're stunning, riding my cock, pulsing around me. Come on, sweetheart, don't hold back."

Phoebe moans and then sits upright, her eyes finding mine. "I love you," she says. "I love you. I love you. I love you."

Over and over, she says it until she can't talk anymore because her orgasms rob her of breath. She lies on my chest, gasping, and I follow her over, losing myself inside of her.

For long minutes, I keep my arms around her, and slowly, we each find our breath.

I flip her onto her back and kiss her nose, her lips, her neck, down her chest, each breast.

"Asher! What are you doing?" Phoebe laughs.

"I made a promise."

"What was that?"

I move lower, hovering over her stomach before pressing a kiss there. "That I was going to kiss every inch of you. But I wanted to kiss here"—I do it again—"where our child grows."

"Oh, Asher," Phoebe says as she lifts onto her elbows. "Just when I think I can't love you more than I do, you say something like that." Her hand moves to my cheek.

Tomorrow, I plan to say more, and I've never been more nervous in my life.

"Okay, so I'll tell her I need her help, and you can head down to the spot in the vineyard and get ready," Emmeline says as her sister keeps Phoebe busy with her daughters.

"She's going to suspect something."

She shakes her head. "I think she suspected it yesterday when we made her get dressed up."

"Okay, and you think she'll like the ring?" I ask her for the tenth time. Emmeline was very opinionated as I shopped.

"One hundred percent. Now, go. My brother-in-law hung lights around, so just plug them in when you see her coming."

I duck out of the room and go in the direction she told me to. There's a hill to the right that has a beautiful view of the entire vineyard, and Emmeline was emphatic it should be there.

I booked us on a nine PM flight so that Sara and Olivia had enough time to get here. It works out perfectly because the sunsets here are magic, and it's just starting to drop now, casting the sky in pinks and oranges.

"You look handsome," Sara says as I make it to the spot. "Your daughter and I turned on all these candles for you."

"Thanks. It looks great and would've taken me hours."

I turn to Liv, who is practically bouncing. *"I'm so excited!"*

"Me too."

"Do you think she knows?" Liv asks.

"No. Do you?"

She shakes her head.

I let out a deep sigh. *"Are you happy about Phoebe being my wife?"*

"I am. I love her too."

"And your new sibling?"

"Definitely."

It turned out that Phoebe had been worried for nothing because Olivia couldn't have been any happier when we told her about the baby. She jumped around and asked if the baby could take the upstairs room that Brynn used to sleep in. It was adorable, and she is going to be a great big sister.

Now I just need to worry about being a great husband. I don't know why I'm slightly concerned about that or even if she'll say yes. I know how we feel about each other—I love her, and she loves me. There's just something about getting on your knee and asking the girl you love to spend her life with you that is a little scary. Maybe it's because it feels like I'm stealing something from her.

She has plans, a whole life planned, and while I want to be a part of it, I don't want to take a single thing from her.

"Asher?" Phoebe's voice breaks my thoughts. "Are you okay? Asher!"

What the fuck? She sounds panicked. "I'm up here."

She turns to the sound of my voice and starts to run. "Asher! Keep talking, baby! I'll find you. Don't worry, I'm coming!"

I'm so confused. "What are you freaking out about?"

"You're hurt!"

I hear Emmeline in the background. "Sorry! You got it from here."

Phoebe starts to climb the hill, and I walk to meet her, extending my hand. "I'm not hurt," I tell her with a soft laugh.

"No? Then why the hell did I have to rush out of there?"

I pull her with me until we reach the top so we're standing under the string lights and in the center of hundreds of battery-operated candles on the ground. Olivia and Sara stand off to the side, and Sara moves in front of Liv so she can translate.

"What? Olivia?" Phoebe asks and then looks around more. "Oh. Oh you're . . ."

I get down on my knee and take her hand in mine. "When I

hired you, my plan was to get rid of you at the soonest available opportunity. You weren't right for Liv or me. I thought after you lied to me on that first day, I would fire you and that would be that, but I couldn't. I think, even then, I knew something about you was special. I think I knew the minute I saw you with Olivia that you were going to flip my world upside down. I had no idea that you'd capture my heart and soul. I didn't know that you'd be my starting point and finish line, the reason I breathe, why the sun rises and falls. You are the rays of sunlight in my ever-cloudy skies, as you said." Phoebe laughs as tears stream down her face. I release her hand and sign the rest. *"You are my sunshine, and I don't want to spend a single day without it. Marry me?"*

She gets down on her knees in front of me, takes my face in her hands, and brings our foreheads together. "Yes. Yes, I will marry you."

epilogue
PHOEBE

~Five Months Later~

"Y ou are stunning," Asher says, coming up behind me and resting his hand on my now incredibly swollen belly. I'm eight months, and I swear, I made Lucy retest me two months ago because I hadn't even been showing yet. She kept telling me it would happen, but because I'm small, it wouldn't be early.

Then, a week later, there was a bulge.

"I'm not sure stunning is the word I'd use, but . . ." I place my hand over his, the emerald cut diamond glimmering in the light. "Do we have to go to this event?"

It's the annual Christmas dinner and tree lighting ceremony. This year, Asher gets to flip the switch, much to my father's dismay. Aside from wanting to laugh as I watch my father snub Asher, I really have no desire to go.

"I begged you to run away with me and get married," he says against my ear.

"For the love of God," I grumble, letting my head rest on his chest. "We will get married, Ash. Just not now. Olivia has dealt with enough upheaval in her life, and there's no reason we need to marry before the baby comes. Which will be any damn day now if we go based on my expanding stomach."

He tried to convince me to elope when we got home from Cloverleigh Farms, but I wasn't having it. I want a real wedding, not some thrown-together mess because I'm pregnant. I want the white dress, my dad to walk me down the aisle, and food—lots and lots of different kinds of food. That isn't something I could have if we got married right now because I can barely eat without feeling nauseous.

Somehow, my pregnancy decided to be ass backwards, and I didn't have all this early on. No, I hit my third trimester and developed the most insane food aversions ever.

"All right, I'll stop pissing you off."

"Doubtful, but you could at least stop with the wedding. My father has made it perfectly clear that, if we run away, he'll shoot you."

Asher laughs and releases me before walking over to the bed where I laid out his suit. "I'm pretty sure he's itching for a reason anyway."

I turn to face him, leaning against the dresser. "Because you talked about moving again?"

He nods and then starts to undress. "He told me we were being selfish to think about taking his grandchild away, even if it was for you to finish school."

I haven't told anyone this, but I decided I won't be attending Vanderbilt or Texas next year. I applied to Penn State and have already pretty much been told that I'll get in. Bobby, the owner of Talking Hands, knows the dean and explained to him why I deferred and how I was working with him. So, now I'm just waiting for my acceptance letter.

It's two hours away, and I can take most of the classes online, and for the classes I have to be on campus for, I am sure I'll be able to find someone to watch the baby.

While it wasn't my dream school, I'm living my dream life, and that matters more than anything.

"Well, he'll get over it, no matter what we decide."

He drops his shirt, and I stand here gawking. Dear Lord, he's freaking perfect. No matter how many times I've seen him naked, he still makes my mouth water. All that yummy muscle under those clothes is just for my eyes, and I like it.

"Stop eye fucking me, or we're not going to make it to the tree lighting."

I wiggle both brows. "Don't tempt me with a good time."

He finishes buttoning his shirt and holds out his wrist so I can do those buttons for him. "I should spank you for that."

"I might like it." I lean in and kiss his cheek once I'm done.

"Oh, I know you would, but we need to make a detour before we head to the diner." He gives me a light smack on the ass before he grabs his jacket.

Now I'm intrigued. "Where is this detour?"

He holds out his arm and I hook mine in. "It's a surprise."

"I really don't like to be surprised."

"I know, it's why I like doing it so often."

I roll my eyes. "Ass."

"From what I remember, you like assholes."

He's not all that wrong. I recall the time I called him that when he walked in on me singing. I drop my voice the same way I had that night. "Oh my God, I have to tell you about this guy I'm engaged to. He keeps trying to get me to marry him, and he's such a dick."

Asher spins, putting my back to the wall, and then runs his nose down my throat. "I'd like to do something to you with my dick."

"Ohh, is it dirty?"

He pushes against me and nips my ear. "Very."

I use all my willpower, which really isn't all that much when it comes to him, and shove him back. "Too bad, no dirty dick time for you, it's time for the Holiday Extravaganza."

He groans, probably wishing he took my advice two days ago when I said we should feign sickness to get out of this stupid event. In two days, I have to head to New York City to work with Talking Hands, and I still have a lot of information to prepare. The program itself is incredibly complex. We started with a very simple group of signs like . . . hello, how are you? Where are you from? Where is the bathroom? And once that was perfected, we added more simple terms. The hope is that the system will continue to learn as we keep building the glossing index and translating it into spoken word. I told Bobby the other day that I felt he was extremely optimistic thinking this would be complete within a year. The amount of work we have to do means much more than that. Plus, I give birth in a month and I won't be able to do much in the first few weeks after she's born.

We get to the car, enjoying an extremely unseasonably warm day in the winter.

"I'm glad the weather is nice for this next part," Asher says.

"What part?"

"The surprise."

I huff, hating that he's teasing me about it. "It's bad enough you have this planned, but now you want to taunt me about it? Rude."

He chuckles, moving down the long, winding driveway. "Shit!"

"What?"

"I forgot something." He turns the car around once we get to the main road and then drives halfway up the driveway before stopping.

"Umm, did you forget where the house is?" I ask.

"Nope."

Asher exits the car, and I'm starting to wonder if I'm going to be the feature of a *True Crime* episode. Where my fiancé snaps and then chops me up before burying body parts all along the driveway.

I contemplate locking the door and calling my father so I have someone who knows my last location, but then Asher opens my door and extends his hand.

As though he can read my mind, he smirks. "I'm not going to kill you, and stop listening to that damn podcast before bed."

"It soothes me."

"Yes, nothing like a bedtime story about a gruesome murder."

I shrug. "Hey, no one will be able to murder me and get away with it. I have contingency plans and clues left all over, buddy. Go ahead and kill me, and we'll see how fast you land in a cell."

Asher shakes his head. "Yes, but you'll be dead, so you'll never know."

"My people will find me," I remind him.

"And yet, you'd still be dead. Come on, sweetheart, this doesn't include death. I promise. Besides, I wouldn't do it on my property, I'd definitely pick a hiking trail."

I nod in approval. "Good plan, lots of tracks and DNA to mess up the trail."

Asher pulls me to his side, guiding me around one of the rocks that I definitely would've tripped on.

Then we're in front of the entrance sign. Where many farms have it at the end of the drive, Asher's is about midway down. This is the original entrance of the property, and they kept it here as a reminder of how far the family has grown.

"Why are we here?"

"Because I wanted to show you something."

Confusion fills me as I look around, not really sure what the hell he could possibly want to show me in the middle of his driveway, but hey, what do I know?

"And what's that?"

He points up. "Look at it."

It looks like the same metal sign that has been there since his grandparents hung it, but it's not. His family had a vintage lock for the letter o, but this one is different. The new sign has a house sitting on the key with the sun behind it and underneath says Whitlock Farms with the o just having the keyhole.

"Asher . . ."

"Before I met you, Phoebe, I was locked. I was just like that old

375

sign with only the lock, stuck in the closed position. It turned out I just needed the key and the sunshine to show me what was there. You are both of those. You are what unlocked my heart, and then your light makes everything brighter. Each time you come home, I want you to see just how much you mean to me. I love you with every part of me, and this family wouldn't be the same without you."

Damn him and these hormones for making my eyes leak. "And I thought you were going to hack me up, I didn't know you were going to steal my heart from my chest."

He laughs, pulling me into his strong arms. "You stole mine, so it's only fair I take yours."

"It's only ever been yours," I tell him.

"And you'll always have mine."

From the very bottom of my heart, thank you for reading this story. I love it so much. I love every book, but there is something so special about this one. Next is Addison and Grady!

Preorder Broken Dreams

If you haven't met the Arrowood Brothers who reside in Sugarloaf, you can start those while we wait for Broken Dreams!

Read Come Back for Me Free in Kindle Unlimited!
***
I was so deeply in love with Asher and Phoebe, I wasn't ready to let them go. Swipe to the next page for access to an EXCLUSIVE Bonus Scene!

Dear Reader,

I hope you enjoyed Forbidden Hearts! I had a hard time saying goodbye to Asher & Phoebe. I wanted to give just a little more of a glimpse into their lives, so ... I wrote a super fun scene.

Since giving you a link would be a pain in the ... you know what ... I have an easy QR code you can scan, sign up, and you'll get and email giving you access! Or you can always type in the URL!

https://geni.us/FH_Bonus

If you'd like to just keep up with my sales and new releases, you can follow me on BookBub or sign up for text alerts!
BookBub: https://www.bookbub.com/authors/corinne-michaels

books by corinne michaels

Want a downloadable reading order?
https://geni.us/CM_ReadingGuide

The Salvation Series

Beloved

Beholden

Consolation

Conviction

Defenseless

Evermore: A 1001 Dark Night Novella

Indefinite

Infinite

The Hennington Brothers

Say You'll Stay

Say You Want Me

Say I'm Yours

Say You Won't Let Go: A Return to Me/Masters and Mercenaries Novella

Second Time Around Series

We Own Tonight

One Last Time

Not Until You

If I Only Knew

The Arrowood Brothers

Come Back for Me

Fight for Me

The One for Me

Stay for Me

Willow Creek Valley Series

Return to Us

Could Have Been Us

A Moment for Us

A Chance for Us

Rose Canyon Series

Help Me Remember

Give Me Love

Keep This Promise

Whitlock Family

Forbidden Hearts

Broken Dreams

Tempting Promises

Forgotten Desires

Co-Written with Melanie Harlow

Hold You Close

Imperfect Match

Standalone Novels

All I Ask

You Loved Me Once

acknowledgments

Writing a book is an incredible journey filled with ups and down and ... well, more downs than many of us like to admit. It is the people around us who lift us up. I am eternally grateful to each of them.

My husband and children. I love you all so much. Your love and support is why I get to even have an acknowledgment section.

My assistant, Christy Peckham, you always have my back and I can't imagine working with anyone else. I love you're face.

Melanie Harlow, you have no idea how much I cherish our friendship. You are truly one of my best friends in the world and I don't know what I would do without you. Thank you for lending me Emmeline in this book and I'm sorry if people want her book now.

My publicist, Nina Grinstead, you're stuck with me forever at this point. I love you. You are more than a publicist, you're a friend, a cheerleader, a shoulder to lean on, and more.

The entire team at Valentine PR who support me, rally behind me, and keep me smiling.

My betas and sensitivity readers for this book: Logan Chisholm, Kayla Compton, Madison Nankervis, and Lynette Mattiacci. Thank you for loving Asher and Phoebe and always helping me figure out what my brain couldn't untangle. Also to Kristie Carnevale for helping me with the beginning.

Thank you to my editor, Ashley Williams. My cover designer

who deals with my craziness, Sommer Stein. My proofreaders, Virginia, Julia, and ReGina.

Every influencer who picked this book up, made a post, video, phoned a friend … whatever it was. Thank you for making the book world a better place.

And, of course, to you for reading this story. Thank you for trusting me with your time and letting me into your heart.